In the Communist Mirror

In the Communist Mirror

Journeys in Eastern Europe

LESLEY CHAMBERLAIN

faber and faber

LONDON · BOSTON

First published in 1990
by Faber and Faber Limited
3 Queen Square London WC1N 3AU

Phototypeset by Input Typesetting Ltd, London
Printed in Great Britain by
Richard Clay Ltd, Bungay, Suffolk

© Lesley Chamberlain, 1990

Lesley Chamberlain is hereby identified as author
of this work in accordance with Section 77 of the
Copyright, Designs and Patents Act 1988.

All translations of extracts are by Lesley Chamberlain.

A CIP record for this book is available from the
British Library

ISBN 0–571–14165 X

. . . the *Zarathustra*, the *Phaedrus*, that *Brigge* book by Rilke . . . If Corde suffered, smarted in this Eastern Bloc capital, it was because that glorious stuff made him vulnerable still, because he had failed to put it aside at the proper time.

Saul Bellow *The Dean's December*

Contents

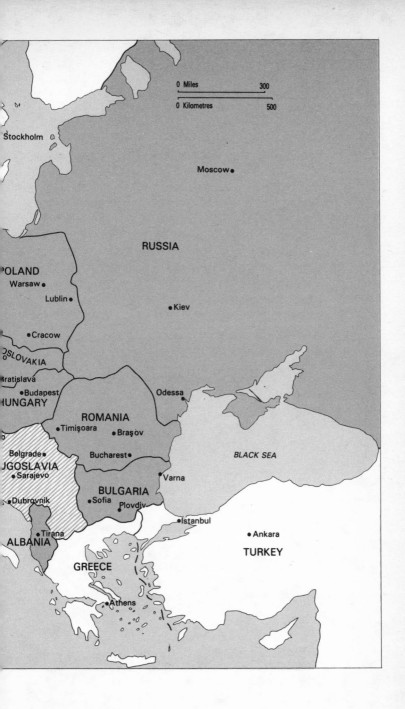

Preface

This book is dedicated to a pattern of daily life in the Soviet Union and Eastern Europe which has overnight passed into history. The speed of change has been extraordinary, and though when I sat down to write about my travels and reflections I considered the East Bloc a transient phenomenon unlikely to last even my lifetime, I couldn't have anticipated the instant readiness everywhere to dismantle the communist past. The loosening of the ideological stranglehold, inspired by cautious change in Moscow, precipitated even more radical upheaval in the former satellite countries, with free elections at the time of writing already held in Poland, about to take place in Hungary and promised in East Germany, Romania and Bulgaria. The Party in Russia is struggling for breath; elsewhere it is dying or already dead. Meanwhile the dissidents of the 1980s have become leaders of their countries into the last decade of the century. Vaclav Havel is President of Czechoslovakia by popular acclaim, the former Solidarity economist Tadeusz Mazowiecki is Prime Minister of Poland; the poet Mircea Dinescu is a leading member of Romania's National Salvation Front. In Bulgaria a public file on the murder of exiled writer Georgi Markov is likely to be opened.

It is true, there is still an enormous amount of ground to be covered before the citizens of East and West Europe may be said to enjoy similar freedoms and opportunities. Many differences will prevail as long as economic hardship in the East continues out of all proportion to what we know in the West; and with continuing economic disparity national differences will loom large. But with the pouring in of Western financial support and practical advice, and high level political contact, the prospect of a reintegrated, reunited Europe is now very real. By contrast, for forty years from the end of the Second World War, a war which did not truly end until the collapse of the division of the continent, one Europe was only a memory in the West and a dream of restoration in the East. The news bulletins which, over the past year, have day by day shown the barriers coming down have been perhaps the most positive and emotive political tidings my generation – just too young to experience the war – can remember. Many people have felt a surge of sympathy for those far-away countries, of whom we have for so long known so little.

My account of my travels in Eastern Europe, which comprises this book, is therefore now all the more a testament to the extraordinary human aberration and misery of those forty misguided years. The journeys were completed only a few years ago, but still when no hope of change was in sight. But even more perhaps this book is now a document marking the limits of one Western generation. Over those forty closed years the very existence of the East Bloc helped us define ourselves as 'the West' and see ourselves as free. Personally I felt oppressed and mystified by that distinction. My plan, albeit hazily conceived, for I did not set out to write a book, was simply to observe my responses as a Westerner at large in the East Bloc. On intermittent trips over three years I kept a record of how each communist country struck me, economically, politically, artistically and psychologically; and instinctively I compared their condition with my own as a person. In return, those journeys changed my life, giving me a feeling for freedom which was in fact more inward and personal and less easy to define than what I had set out to find.

We need opposites and extremes by which to define ourselves. Clearly the existence of an East Bloc made that act of definition possible for me. It also took me back in sympathy to a war I had not experienced, and gave me the link I sought with my parents' less privileged generation.

In the Communist Mirror was always intended as a personal account of differences between East and West, and conceived in an autobiographical framework. If it nevertheless now encourages interest in a neglected part of the world, but one which is rapidly becoming more accessible, I will be happy; as happy as I am to see my various friends and acquaintances in the other half of Europe free and to know my many exiled friends can at last return home.

Meanwhile what struck me even in the cold political age in which I travelled was the unreliability of politics as a means to knowledge. Despite the media one needs to touch and see for oneself. The countries of the former East Bloc were always individual and always had a fascinating if muted life of their own. I was oddly thrilled to encounter them in their darker years, and through them to become more aware of some of the deficiencies beneath the bright surface of our own society.

January 1990

Introduction
Russia 1978–9

In August 1978 I set off as a journalist for Russia, ripe for change and deeply unprepared. In one way I never arrived. I never became a journalist in the sense of having the optimum professional and personal virtues my best colleagues had: an ability to immerse themselves in any situation, to write about it dispassionately and move on. I was more inflexible, more inward-looking, with a hazy grasp of news and a feeling I wouldn't like it if I drew closer. The journey on which I was about to embark was disastrous for my editors though I have never regretted the pivotal effect it had on my life.

Hammond Innes once wrote of the sea that it was 'a catalyst, teaching self-reliance, the impersonal hostility of it enabling the young to find a new dimension within themselves'. For me Soviet Russia and later the East Bloc countries would play the same role.

From the start journalism was an ill-reflected compromise for a displaced soul who 'wanted to write and travel' and had run out of money. Before Fleet Street, where the half-hearted pursuit of a career directed me, I had spent seven years joyfully immersed in Russian and German literature. I have never found a greater source of excitement and pleasure than literature, but I believe now that that utter satisfaction and delight kept a more worldly, more comfortable personality in the shade. Outwardly my life had failed to flower. It was uneven, and seemed too unequivocally dedicated to literature in a world that had long ago moved on; to some eyes it looked unhappy. Moreover I was detached in spirit from my family and this only strengthened the air of solitude and self-sufficiency I had adopted. Literature had replaced anything else in which I might have invested my hopes: family, society, friendship, a political vision. If it hadn't replaced romantic love that was only because literature and love seemed inextricable.

I would describe myself then as a conservative romantic. It seemed like a peculiar thing to be and it is not a very accurate label. I loved literature and foreign languages for their own sake, I disliked 'progress' and my political awareness was virtually non-existent. My enthusiasm directed itself at 'philosophy', by which I vaguely meant poetry and intuition. This 'philosophy' was not logical positivism, nor a fashionable passion for the Orient. It had nothing of the scepticism of the academic philosophy faculty and its prevaricating concern with language. I simply believed in the self-sufficiency of days spent wondering whether beauty or goodness was the higher value. I spent my days inquiring what the relation of the one to the other was, and what beauty itself was. The closest I came to considering the outside world was to ask whether beauty could change it. My most realistic theme (which was to cause me a great deal of indignation, sadness and fascination when I became a journalist) was the tragic corruption of ideas in communication.

I loved intimately and unguardedly the German and Russian authors I read. I mocked Turgenev for his weakness (a judgement I now withdraw in middle age), I agonized with Gogol over the effort to sustain his fiction in *Dead Souls*, I listened intently to Tolstoy confessing how society seduced him from his ideals. 'You talk about them as if they were your friends,' said my one close friend, and that may have been so. Had those authors come back to life they would have been among the few people with whom I might have shared a joke. My commitment to 'philosophy' could seem by turns naive, eccentric, blind and gauche.

Yet I was not unworldly. I had been travelling alone in Europe since I was fourteen, and by the time I went up to university I knew French and German very well. From the age of seventeen I had lived alone and worked in every vacation. Moreover I had been in love, twice, always a qualification for thriving in the world if one can survive the torment of extreme happiness. I had spent time with men I did not love, and many lonely hours when I wondered painfully about the possibility of some less demanding, less urgent relationship I might call friendship.

2

Germany, where I often stayed as a teenager, escaping from my parents' unhappy marriage and forming consolatory attachments, was the great focus of my emotions and my energy in my teens and early twenties. It is fitting that 'the Russian experience', the formative influence on my later twenties, should have begun to creep up on me there. From the first Russian literature I read, at the age of twenty, Puskin's *Evegeny Onegin*, I sensed that Russia would mean something entirely different to me from Germany. Germany had brought out a passion for absolutes, whereas Pushkin's masterpiece exploring the limits of antisocial behaviour was punctuated with the word *dovol'no!* *(enough!)* I foresaw Russia might one day make demands on a social self I didn't yet possess.

In Munich as an undergraduate I had an introduction to a distinguished senior political commentator for Radio Liberty, the US anti-communist station which broadcasts to Soviet Russia. We never talked about politics. Viktor was an elderly émigré Russian from a philosophical family with whom I could share my love of German literature. What I learnt of present-day Russia was what I imbibed in the presence of his dignified, erudite, world-weary yet still fresh and approachable European personality. I don't thing we once spoke Russian, of which I then knew only a few words. We went to the opera and to restaurants, we talked about existentialism and German poetry. My evenings with Viktor were quiet, Platonic occasions, when we discussed ideas and poetry lightly, with only an occasional allusion to our personal lives, which did not touch. Then one evening we met Viktor's mother, who with the characteristic outspokeness of a Russian *babushka* – grandmother and matriarch – glanced at me and declared me 'a fallen woman'. Viktor shrugged it off, only told me to be careful. But the old woman's perception of my sensuality frightened me.

I use the word sensuality now to mean the entire unreflected life, and if I may interpret the old woman's verdict more generously than it was meant, she was clairvoyant, able to see what I was holding back. I could have learnt a lot, perversely, from that negative criticism, about how to understand my place in the world by accepting pragmatic concerns, like how to earn a living and make a satisfactory life, but difficulty and loneliness had a will to predominate a few years longer. They only strengthened my commitment to philosophy, to which I subordinated love and travel as handmaidens. I remained as long as I could at university, reading, writing and teaching, for seven years in all.

For the last of those years I taught Russian in the company of a number of Russian émigrés. As it transpired, this was a true foretaste of what I would experience in Russia. I had never before met people who considered their lives as dominated by politics. It seemed to me these men and women were forever marked by the highly political society in which they had grown up. For staff meetings we would sit in a tiny room under the roof, several floors up, as is the common fate of small departments, and I don't remember one occasion when these were not stormy, steamy, bickering encounters, when each Russian member of staff would in his native language lay his philosophy of life on the table. My closest friend would regularly punctuate our exchanges by crying out: 'But the students are politically illiterate!' I sat in near silence, knowing the description well applied to me. I dimly recognized I should move further away from the academic life to be happier.

Thus my departure for Russia came about. Reuters, the international news service, gave me a traineeship in 1977. But I was stubborn. I wasn't going to enter the world without a struggle. I spent an ambivalent preliminary year in the London office, secretly responding with fragments of school poetry to the more unusual datelines ('On a Peak in Darien, Mexico'). One editor lamented the 'literary' quality of my style, while another ordered me to stop disputing the meaning of words. I should have been scrutinizing the *International Herald Tribune* but I used to quote Hegel on the choice a man had to make, between God and newspapers, and I was quite confident of where I stood, with my feet on the magical ground of the Tübingen seminary of 1790. At Oxford all I had regretted during long hours spent squinting at Cyrillic microfiches in the Bodleian and trying to grasp Father Copleston's exegeses of German Idealism was the sunshine and blue sky in summer. From Fleet Street I often wished myself back in academe.

As the alert *babushka* had detected, only the life of the senses would have competed with the allure of metaphysics, but in my mid-twenties, apart from longing gazes at the sky, an inordinate delight at taking

4

my clothes off in the sunshine, and an instinctive expertise in food and wine which were surprising coming from one so absorbed in the ways of the mind, I had not become wholly conscious of sensual pleasure, despite being in love. I felt it unknowingly, like a child. That lack of awareness was probably rather frightening to others. But it was my permit for staying out of the world and I clung to it.

As I had much to learn about reporting the news, far beyond questions of written style, I tried to conform. But the quickest lesson I learnt from my colleagues was that there was no time for learning. I acquired some proficiency as a mimic. I hoped always to get stories that might be written to a formula, so that I wouldn't be caught out. As for going to Moscow, I was acutely aware that the only real qualification I had was to speak and read Russian.

But Reuters in those days was still a mild organization, more like a gentlemen's club, which provided a home for many eccentrics and lost persons on condition they could read and write and rise to an emergency when required. My posting was odd but not inexplicable. Only around 1973 had the management decided to recruit women graduate trainees as well as men and at first, not knowing what they were looking for, they were impressed with languages and degrees, a confusion which lasted into my year. For my part I was perversely impressed by the toughness affected by my soft-at-heart, ramshackle interviewers, and unqualifiedly admiring of that vast quantity of information they controlled. In the room where I waited with other nervous candidates, I stared at an open filing cabinet of 'Profiles' and made out the name of Indira Gandhi which excited me as the sound might have done a child, without any understanding being necessary. 'What would you like to do for us?' 'I'd like to write features,' I said. 'Bah, you're just saying that because we asked you to wait in "Features",' bawled the most senior member of the team. Yet there I was.

The morning of my departure for Moscow I caught a bus from Battersea to Victoria Station with the last of my belongings in plastic bags. This wasn't stylish or even efficient, and coincidentally catching sight of an established Reuter man I ducked behind a newsstand. I hadn't convinced myself of the role I was set to play. Above all, I felt the doubt I had inspired in my immediate future boss. He had viewed the ancient pale blue Austin which conveyed me about London, the single book-lined room and the 'record-player' surviving from my school days with visible concern and assured me that life in Moscow would be an improvement.

What a strange choice for Reuters nevertheless! It was not an institution where minor distinctions of the spirit carried much weight, unless by chance they helped make intelligible the Byzantine ways of communist regimes as they were practised in the first three decades after the war. In my head I can still hear our dour, perfectionist editor making two statements on the eve of my departure: 'We trust you, otherwise we wouldn't be sending you' and 'think three times before you do anything'. The first notion, 'bore no correspondence to reality', as the Russians used to say officially under Brezhnev when they did not wish to answer questions, while the second, a plea for sexual discretion, was irrelevantly addressed to someone torn between the extremes of romantic conservatism and energetic impulse. I was, as they say in German, already falling out of my role that morning on Victoria Station.

I travelled to Moscow by train to have some sense of the real distance I was moving away from familiar life and to prepare myself. A short trip when I was twenty had not greatly registered, except to familiarize me with certain aspects of Soviet behaviour and the smell of the disinfectant used by Soviet institutions. It was a pious hope that in two nights and three days of speeding across the monotonous flat landscape of Central Europe in a solitary compartment, in the Russian carriage which, from the first moment in Ostend smelt of that disinfectant, I would collect my wits. As we trundled across the Central European plain I tried to read Koestler's *Darkness at Noon* and failed. The language seemed flat. (This is another judgement I now retract, but in those days I was hardly capable of reading for a message.) The rest of the time I glanced at a pile of proscribed modern Russian titles I was taking to friends of one of my former teaching colleagues. These I spread out on the seat, oblivious to the fact they might be confiscated or at least create a bad impression among the Soviet personnel in the train. To these mysterious people with their familiar high, hectoring voices and to the few other Russians in the carriage, who wore the tight denim clothing, most unsuited to their bulky figures, which it was their privilege to buy in the West and advertise as a mark of superiority at home, I spoke a few nervous good mornings and good evenings, 'tea' and 'soap'.

Somewhere past Berlin a young man entered my compartment (I believe the carriage personnel had sent him, supposing that I was bored) but left when he elicited no response. I was very concentrated in my inwardness in that train, deliberately so, enjoying the space in my head and the silence. As I looked after my daily toilet and tiny meals as painstakingly as a lonely woman in extreme old age, it was as if I had put my whole life in slow motion under a magnifying glass. I had an acute sense of being free to control my fate and keep my balance, almost without reference to the world outside, but I had no idea where I was going. What had taken root through the years of poetry and philosophy was an awareness of inner government but none whatsoever of the way the world was run. Miraculously no one bothered about the proscribed books and all were delivered to their destinations over the next few months.

The sight of Moscow, an uneven city, with its mixture of mainly cold modern architectural styles, wide, third world boulevards and narrower, tree-lined avenues with nineteenth-century patrician houses, the pervasive stench of cheap petrol, the badly-dressed crowds, the propaganda banners, the cheap and childish sketches advertising films, filled me with instant shallow discomfort. I had mostly lived in places which were easy on the eye, a cathedral city, then Oxford, and here civic appearances seemed disconcertingly uncared for. Not that this response was exclusively directed towards Moscow. I had already felt it towards the only parts of London I could afford to live in. But my arrival in Russia disclosed to me my childish concern with pretty appearances, quite the opposite of what I believed I was pursuing.

I spent my first two or three months learning how the small, ill-lit Reuter office worked with its three male correspondents, myself as the junior, and two Soviet women translators. Every day the Soviet staff scanned the press of the sixteen republics for the often small items, which in the Brezhnev era might well have concealed a big story like an air crash or an important demotion. We watched the television and read the TASS printer, conferred with colleagues from other Western newspapers and press agencies, took it in turns to attend press conferences. Dissidents would ring up with stories, or what some hoped were stories. There was Sakharov, notoriously hard to decipher on the telephone with his lisp, some known Jewish refuseniks, and at the far opposite end of the scale a few oddballs. The year and a half before I arrived, 1976–8, dissident activity under the banner of monitoring Soviet infringements of the Helsinki Human Rights Accords had reached a peak, as had the rate of state prosecution of activists. The campaign was still being waged, and I attended dissident press briefings, though already the Helsinki monitoring had lost some of its intensity faced with such fierce retribution as the heavy sentences passed on Ginzburg and Shcharansky. Much of our attention now seemed to be focused on the plight of this or that family wishing to emigrate and whose cause had been taken up in the United States. The human rights card was frequently played by President Carter and visiting senators with sharp suits and blue-rinsed hair who came to peer at these strange Russians and deliver their lists of complaints. I rowed with my colleagues over which Russia we were telling the world about, the tiny vocal one of the protesters, or the great place with which we had little contact.

These were also the months in which the foundations of the never ratified strategic arms limitation agreement, SALT 2, were laid. The ethos of our work was never discussed. We were extremely busy with political news and rarely got out of the office except in our scant free time. The reason for non-discussion turned out to be the same as for not discussing the meaning of words in the London office: time too much present; also competition from other agencies and the need to give newspapers what they wanted to print. I earned the reputation amongst some of my colleagues of being pro-Soviet. I worried when I saw articles appearing in the Western press suggesting Soviet life was tougher, and more brutal, joyless and irreligious than I believed it to be. Small inaccuracies, like a report saying there were no tomatoes, when I had seen them with my own eyes, troubled me disproportionately, because here I was having my thesis about the impossibility of communication proved to me daily.

These were painful turning points. I discovered in myself a commitment I didn't know I had to passing on what I saw from *outside* any group. It seemed to me most valuable to be an outsider, even while I judged the Soviet outsiders on the other end of the telephone to be not at all representative of their country and some of them lunatics. Subconsciously their position reminded me of my own, which was for the first time being pressed into making itself felt as a force in the world. Yet unlike them I didn't have a cause, just a desire to speak plainly about what I saw. My professional unease was compounded by social unease at the difficulty of living in a bored expatriate community whose leading members, uninvited, immediately set to finding me a mate. About our own strained community there seemed as much to write as about Russia itself.

In the country at large, however, certain subjects fascinated me. One was the official attitude to culture, which came up on the occasion of Tolstoy's 150th birthday. Culture was not a commodity, as in the contemporary West, but a hallowed, invisible presence. There was hardly a volume of Tolstoy in the shops, even for foreign currency, but official critics were busy praising him for his sympathy for peasant life, his attacks on the established church and his pacifism. President Brezhnev wrote in the visitors' book at Yasnaya Polyana, the Tolstoy country estate, that the great novelist was linked with the Soviet people 'by sublime feelings of patriotism and heroism, by the same spirit of truth and decency, the same readiness to give their lives for the honour and independence of their motherland', which didn't sound at all like the devious, lusty, eccentric genius I loved, so aware of the consequences of inordinate human appetites, and whom, but for a sub-editor, I would have called the sanest non-conformist Russia had ever known. Shaky spots on television of the bearded old man stalking about his estate were accompanied by churchy choruses to ensure impressions were reverent at home and alien abroad. A burly, over-weight director in a hardly Soviet red shirt and sports jacket, looking like a charmless Bert Brecht, made a film called *Tolstoy – Our Contemporary* and to a press conference alternately bellowed and whispered his praise of the man in conventional, pompous rhetoric. Tolstoy was concerned with 'the flow of life', he eventually said. Now that at last was potentially valuable. The anniversary persuaded me I would have little time for 'official' culture.

Another fascination early in my stay was the Soviet attitude to history. It is a truism of Soviet ideology that Soviet reality springs from history. I accepted it as a professional tip and started frequenting museums to keep up with the constant reinterpretation of the past. I also joined the Lenin Library, a home away from home. In the library, in the Academicians' reading room where I sat as a foreign reader, the entry on Stalin had been excised with a razor blade from the English language encyclopaedia. It was an old story but it still made the authorities cross to be asked about it, twenty-five years on, and since even the angry reaction was conveyed in stereotyped words and gestures, by a middle-aged woman whose tone slowly approached the hysterical as her voice rose and her face reddened, I very much enjoyed provoking it in my newly assumed capacity as the shocking stranger. It seemed Soviet official culture had a self-deluding sense of the malleability of the past, coupled with the ardent desire to possess one.

It wasn't correct of my more distant colleagues to label me pro-Soviet. But it was true that at the same time as I condemned official dishonesty under Brezhnev I felt sympathy for the *official* Soviet plight. It showed in the way I pursued non-political stories and spent long hours in the Lenin Library reading books which instructed the new Soviet Man how to behave nicely in society, with such instructions as not arriving at other people's houses drunk, nor banging on their doors at all hours. These books were necessary because the upper classes who once provided the model had been abolished. Nor did I feel the West with its constant package of ready entertainments and comforts was a great loss. I tried to show some loyalty to the host country by refusing to import my food, preferring to trail round Russian markets and shops. I was happiest when I blended in with Moscovites going about their daily business of queueing and working and struggling against the weather. What I loathed were privileged shops for foreigners (where for dollars you could begin a collection of the most hideous Russian teapots or buy cheap Japanese stereo tackle). I much regretted the car number plates issued by the authorities and which made foreign correspondents stand out like Martians; nor did I want a maid, who was a spy one had to pay dearly for, though she made the beds and cooked a sort of lunch.

My disaffection wasn't pro- or anti-Soviet. It wasn't a political stance at all. I was the first to complain about the generally unhelpful, rude and obstreperous behaviour of Soviet officials and shop assistants. I felt nauseated by the fabric of half-lies out of which the newspapers composed their pages. I was wretched at the sight of so much time and energy being wasted by good people, simply to get through the day. My sympathy lay with what seemed to me the intellectual hopelessness of trying to reform with a *system* and slogans and a few hollow ideas a vast country which apart from its space drive and military technology still seemed to be living in an uncomfortable, prudish, non-egalitarian nineteenth century. The disaffected Soviet novelist Zinovy Zinik has described it in very aggressive fiction as the story of 'how metaphysics in one man's head can turn into shit on another's head, and much else besides', but for someone like myself who had spent years faithfully engrossed in the same metaphysics it was almost a tearful revelation to come and see great ideas gone awry.

Neither pro- nor anti-Soviet I was simply the product of my love of literature. Nourished by my readings of Gogol and Dostoevsky I intuited the Soviet plight as a psychological problem of how to combat inertia and formlessness. It wasn't too far removed from how I perceived my own problems, and I felt the desire for order not with the political fear of the post-war West but with the pathos of a writer trying to shape intractable material. The sight of a propaganda slogan like THE PARTY IS THE MIND, THE HONOUR AND THE CONSCIENCE OF OUR EPOCH infuriated me by its coercive simple-mindedness but also moved me to tears. I had spent years reading German metaphysics, the very 'philosophy' to which Russian intellectuals had turned in the early nineteenth century to try to bring Russian thinking into the modern world. In their hands German notions of beauty and disinterest had turned into political goals. Though it had done marvellous things for literature I decided metaphysics had made a terrible mess of this country, paralysed and obsessed as it was with abstract concepts which had long since ceased to mean anything. Slowly it would dawn on me that the same plight might be true of me.

My thesis had been on how beauty might change the world. I walked into a Moscow bookshop and immediately found on display, in a popular format, *Astonishing Aesthetics!*, as if this subject really were a matter of general concern and might be read on trains and trams to real effect. I cut out editorials from *Pravda* couched in terms of the eighteenth-century Enlightenment married to the nineteenth-century enthusiasm for industrial production. These were my ideals, my vocabulary, and look what had become of them 200 years on! Quite by accident I discovered the greatest living outlet for conservative romantics of my generation: Soviet Russia.

Yet nothing was straightforward. And just as I could see how the huge gap between aspiration and reality had enriched Russian literature, so I felt in a minor degree in myself that to come to Russia bogged down in metaphysics boosted my imagination and fantasy. A few years later I managed to pull together some of my responses into my first attempt at a novel. I will describe one of the many unpredictable moments in Soviet life I didn't include there, which seemed to me so resonant. Trying to find out more about the Soviet attitude to the past I toured an art restoration workshop. I talked to the men and women restoring some recently recovered paintings. One of them was working on a portrait of an unknown young hussar, who reminded me of the dashing romantic poet Lermontov. The point was that the Revolution nationalized the heirlooms of wealthy families, which meant stacking a good part of the country's Tsarist heritage in a cupboard. Some of that heritage was destroyed, with mistaken official encouragement at the time, by looting peasants. But the men and women in the workshop gave me the impression that the rest of the Russian past was still sitting in the damp and dusty basement of some provincial museum, waiting to be recognized by a visiting expert from Moscow. It sounded like a sketch for yet another Russian play about the futility of life.

I had never paid so much attention to the culture of my own country, nor found it so stimulating. Suddenly I was greatly excited by the prospect of a new life. I felt I lived at the heart of the world. Also that I had exchanged the contemplative life for the active one. For the first time I had gone beyond the bounds of literature. I had discovered a new fulfilment in travelling 'on assignment', and found a new role for travel which was not only to amplify 'philosophy'. By Christmas I had been to Soviet Karelia, to Siberia, to Armenia, and to Finland, and I had met a wide range of people of many nationalities;

though on those assignments whenever it was dark or we passed through a tunnel I stared at my face in the railway carriage window in disbelief.

Returning to England for a brief holiday I was full of my job but unable to talk about it. It was as if I had embarked on a course of treatment which would have been jeopardized had I disclosed what was happening.

After Christmas a setback in my personal life took my interest away from my job. A love affair I had been trying to continue long-distance collapsed after eight years and left me feeling strained and withdrawn. It was winter, a season of immobility and darkness I had never before experienced in such a degree of intensity, and office life was only so much routine. Like a child I pulled my fur hat down over my eyes (the office was also very cold) and hoped the world would go away. In the evenings I listened to Beethoven's late quartets and read Freud, or I worked in the Lenin Library. After a few quiet hours, coming out with a crowd of anonymous readers into the night, down the broad lamp-lit steps into the snowy street, I could feel my spirits lift. I still needed a great deal of solitude.

In February there was a reporting trip to Lithuania, and in March another to the Black Sea, which brought a few new insights and some interesting material. But in truth my attention was consumed now by Freud. In the library I researched his absence from Soviet culture. I plotted a curve of changing attitudes from a first enthusiastic welcome after the Revolution (on the basis that psychoanalysis was anti-bourgeois) to Freud's wholesale condemnation under Stalin as an apologist for bourgeois corruption. I tried to see how Freud's absence affected official literature and culture and even the way people viewed themselves. My subject was the banning of Freud in the Soviet Union, and the official cultural poverty ensuing, and it coincided with a sudden strong personal desire for psychoanalysis. It is striking to me now that some years later analysis would eventually make possible the completion of this book.

In Soviet Russia therefore, I was able to a small extent to look at my frustration with life as the frustration of a whole culture, barred from a certain understanding of itself. This was another turning point and perhaps a more joyful one. For from reading Freud and looking at Russia and my own loneliness I acquired a new respect for inward-ness. I awarded it a new legitimacy, for it seemed to me the only way to combat this dreadful, shallow official mass culture enveloping us. A similar official culture threatened us in the West, from commercial-ism and the mass media (for which, I had to remind myself, I was still nominally working). But here, with the force of government behind it, the threat seemed more potent.

At this point I began to understand the dissidents, at the same time as I realized literature could make its force felt in the world and that philosophy could have an active, public meaning. In the context of Soviet Russia, a tense and dissatisfied country, poetry and philosophy as I understood them were not just quirky personal values which belonged to a past culture, but custodians of the artistic and scientific integrity without which any society is worthless. They kept the spirit alive under political repression and provided the only way for men and women to preserve their sanity under that repression and to hope to undo it.

Thus Russia drew me out of the intellectual shell in which I had buried myself successfully for most of my teens and twenties, by not only legitimizing inwardness but by demanding that its weaknesses in the world be overcome. In this I felt I had suddenly grasped something important to me, that nub of energy Freud calls the libido, the life force.

I took to skiing and horse-riding and felt very passionate about the spring when it came. With a new friend I set off for splendid explora-tory weekends which took us to Pskov, to Turgenev's home in exile at Orel, Tolstoy's Yasnaya Polyana near Tula, and Pushkin's estate at Mikhailovskoe. Our relationship was Platonic (much to the surprise of the Russian hotel staff and the gossips back in Moscow) and perhaps that is why I remember those country visits in voluptuous detail and colour: the understated countryside with its wide vistas, birch trees and wild ponds, the aristocratic estates which were no more than little wooden houses, and Tolstoy's beautiful, silent grave, then just a grass-covered mound in a quiet, wooded spot in the garden overgrown with flowers. In Orel, inspired by that old sense of pathos which had accompanied me throughout the year in Russia, I mar-velled, coming across Turgenev's red Oxford MA gown and hood in a little museum in a town of many mud streets. The tiniest experiences had become huge discoveries.

The Mikhailovskoe trip had given us plenty of freedom to explore. To get there from Pskov we evaded Intourist and took a local bus transporting a crowd of local people carrying quarts of spilling milk. Half-way there the bus stopped for refreshments and we had hot doughnuts and quince juice. Returning that evening we managed to hitch a lift from some locals who believed from our Russian we were Poles or East Germans, or some such friendly nation. When we disclosed we were Western journalists they became silent and fearful, though they still ferried us to our destination.

Then the summer came, quite suddenly and very early, and, no longer a platonic couple, we spent hours in the countryside, swimming in the river Moskva, lighting fires and barbecuing our food and sleeping in the open. It was around this time I wrote a book on Russian food, which reflected much of my sensual delight at being in Russia. We took a short holiday on the Volga, riding bicycles, rowing boats and taking saunas in the bathhouse. There when the heat became too much, we jumped into the river in darkness, the water sparked and the fish swam between our legs. As the life of the senses blossomed intensely for the first time, my interest in Russia revived and I wrote as many reports as the news file would take on non-political aspects of daily life, and for an American newspaper a piece on Freud in Russia. I had long resisted allowing myself to be caught up in day-to-day affairs. I would write about them as if through a back-to-front telescope. I was just beginning to break down that obstinacy and get on with the job when it was time to leave.

Many of us from the West, living in the Soviet Union, agreed that our personalities seemed to have been magnified by the experience. Marriages and relationships were put to a severe test, though some people did not realize the extent of the Soviet influence upon them until they returned home, when they compared their tongue-tied shyness and strangeness with the feelings of soldiers coming back from war.

I flew home, returning in a more conventional, less austere manner than I had arrived, with a charming colleague and some champagne.

Britain appeared to be a distant, rather gentle and kindly place where one naturally led a cushioned existence in mild weather. Life had the texture of soft white bread and the powerful incisors I had developed were now redundant. I was very energized, very grateful, very hungry for more austerity, for what it might teach me. I felt bolder and less fearful, though of nothing in particular. I was grateful to Russia for some revelation I couldn't identify.

My new sympathies showed themselves superficially in a passion for the simple life. A 'green' stage ensued as I went back to work in the London office. I bought a bicycle, pedalled or jogged everywhere, and while a brisk trade went on in automatic washing machines, I bought a mangle. I attempted to write stories about the shock of coming home. The new person I had become must have radiated a greater natural healthiness and suitability for life for within a few months I found myself settling down to quasi-married existence with a companion and small baby.

My ambitions left over from Moscow thus went into abeyance. But I felt the journey I had embarked on was not over and that now perhaps something was being undone or lost. I returned to academic research with a passion, continued with occasional journalism, worked for Reuters in London. As soon as Elizabeth was old enough I decided to return eastwards and explore Soviet communism's other capitals.

There was no conscious rationale behind this, though many small promptings. In Moscow other correspondents had told their tales of more sumptuous, more Westernized communist capitals, which tempted me, and I had always been a traveller. Also I had German, a language I had neglected for some years, and the lands in between were a natural focus of interest. Then there was the continuing parallel: travel was part of 'philosophy', and 'the lands in between' of Central Europe were, like me, deeply affected by Russia and Germany. I was ready to confront my imbalanced personality with an imbalanced, divided Europe, as a further experiment; ready to continue that journey of self-discovery which had begun in Russia and which seemed to depend on seeing myself in the communist mirror. But something had changed. The next journeys would not be so inward. A broader question now fascinated me, of which I could only volunteer to be the tool: what was it to be a Western sensibility coming into contact with the East Bloc? And how in future would one explain to one's children the way the existence of a communist alternative world had affected one's thinking, even benefited it, by making it more aware of its virtues and its gaps? Thus began the extended journey through Eastern Europe which is the real substance of this book.

May 1988

2

Metaphysical Land
Poland 1983–4

In Poland I was kicking against the traces of a new partnership and wondering what had happened to the perspectives Russia had opened up. My routine editorial job in London held little interest and every slack moment was taken up with reading and writing. A little of this was for publication, but a lot to help me master the confused emotions Russia had inspired. Flowing into that turbulent pool now was the existence of my child. I loved to concern myself exclusively with the quality of our day together, yet time had moved me on too fast; too many tasks were unfinished for me to stop being the seeker and become the guide and provider of answers. Beneath the efficient and loving surface it was a time of panic.

Elizabeth at three was too small to travel but we went all the same. In Warsaw we sang songs to ward off the cold while we waited for buses in December. On bad days my only hope of keeping her spirits up and her legs moving was the ice cream shop on Hosa Street, where I copied the local children in asking for 15 zlotys' worth. I don't think we would have embarked on either of our two Polish trips, at the end of 1983 and again in March 1984, had not her father been posted as a foreign correspondent to Warsaw. This story may seem planned, but in reality it began out of a series of coincidences which only later acquired meaning.

In Warsaw immediately there was personal confrontation: the man who was in effect my husband was charged with a job which fascinated and repelled me and one to which he was dedicated. Our relationship became a fierce confrontation. We were in this intense, sad and sophisticated country like two bears in a lair. I wanted to make Poland my own – as I had done with Russia – by filtering it through my inner life, while he sought to understand it – quite rightly and quite professionally – through facts. Our real circumstances also divided us. He had the desk and the secretary and was in residence, while I was the short-term visitor with a small child in tow. I don't mean to make a feminist point here – I had had my turn at the desk – but my exploration of Eastern Europe began like this. It was the necessity of many short breaks and the need to make the most of any unexpected contact with local life which taught me to linger in cafés and make patterns out of the small details of daily living and the tiny confidences which came our way. After a tiring day of pulling on and off gloves and hats and boots I would put Elizabeth to bed and after dinner try to relate these patterns to such literature and history as I knew.

The atmosphere in Poland was not at all like Russia. We were not conspicuous in the streets and strangers were not afraid nor reluctant to talk. I had supposed there would be a police barrier sealing off the compound where Western residents lived, the way we lived in Moscow, but what I saw turned out to be only an occasionally used checkpoint on the road leading to the parliament building, the Sejm. We just happened to live yards away from it. In fact, regardless of political origins foreigners were dispersed about Warsaw, living where they pleased. We seemed free and as if to endorse that sensation, the city was virtually free of propaganda. A mindless Soviet public slogan like THE PARTY IS THE MIND, THE HONOUR AND THE CONSCIENCE OF OUR EPOCH would have been quite out of place. What was more I had spotted a film poster outside the Indian Club in Warsaw depicting a semi-nude woman, a public artefact unimaginable in the officially prudish Soviet Union as I knew it. People in the street here radiated a different attitude to the West, which was not so alien, nor therefore so grotesquely cherished. Poles were neither rude nor badly dressed, and many had relatives in the West who kept them in touch. There was much making-do at a time of economic difficulty, but it was done with flair. And that was what Poland was doing with the imposed political system too, it seemed: making do, tolerating alien circumstances, enduring being down at heel, but not losing native style, self-confidence and sophistication in the process. I think it was that genteel shabbiness which first attracted me.

Elizabeth and I would walk in the Polish capital most days, but in the early mornings I would also go running, to cover more ground, to see what I could discover, to enjoy the many green open spaces which make Warsaw almost rural in parts. I was easily exhilarated by the tiniest find: a statue in the park, bullet marks in an old building, an impromptu tribute of flowers in a milk bottle. I loved hearing Chopin's music coming from within the grimy Chopin Villa and later attending a morning session of the All-Polish Chopin Competition, in which tense teenage virtuosi in subfusc kept the judges busy all day with energetic renderings of Schumann and Chopin. 'Finds' like this were always tinged with nostalgia for a style of life full of religiosity and laden with memories of the war, a style which in the West was long past.

I felt Warsaw had a beauty which was not obvious, and which I therefore admired all the more. A gladiator we passed most days in the park near parliament was dignified and faintly cocky about his perfection, resting one foot on a slain head. The Sejm, with its central dome and pale bas-reliefs, was not an ugly building and made a good contrast with the towering 'wedding-cake' Palace of Culture across the city, a hideous gift from Stalin. Near the university there was a rough-hewn statue of the writer Boleslaw Prus which made him look like Lenin. It was tilted forward and seemed to represent progress. Then there was the spectacle of the boarded-up and decaying Hotel Bristol, originally owned by the musician and Prime Minister Ignacy Paderewski. Hotel guests in the early days of the Second Polish Republic, between the wars, when this was the most chic place to stay, could have looked out in the early morning on the magisterial mounted figure below of Prince Josef Poniatowski, a nineteenth-century military hero, and breathed in the fresh air of the Polish cause.

These finds, passing recognitions of grace, hope, the vanity of time and the dignity of lost causes, were what formed my initial bond to Poland, otherwise I don't know why I was so attracted to what was broken-down, except that it held out the prospect of justified change for the better, like the combination of ugliness and good character in a fairy story. No other country except Russia ate so much into my imagination as Poland, at the expense of my observing its humdrum reality. It made me aware within myself of a kind of obsession with repatriating beauty in the world despite the political reality I found so daunting. Too readily therefore I gave myself up to Polish symbolism, which uniquely hovers on the edge of Polish politics, though as I found on later reading, I was hardly the first idolatrous romantic outsider to fall into the trap.

Walking in the centre of Warsaw one day I found myself drawn to the university buildings. The chandeliers lit in the lecture rooms in daytime and the pock-marked Herculean caryatids holding up the entrance to the university library inspired a magical excitement for a few hours. One reason perhaps was that I knew education had always greatly mattered to the Poles, who had suffered from having their schools and universities russified and germanized. Another was that education, again like fairy stories, effects tranformations from dark to light, from ignorance to awareness, from ugliness to beauty and these transformations, so it was turning out, mattered a great deal to me. I was discovering a passion I didn't know I had, for self-improvement in adversity, or perhaps just showing gratitude for my own education.

In Warsaw the National Gallery is dingy and most of the collection needs restoring, but there's one painting every visitor should see. It's by the Polish David, Jan Matejko, whose vast nineteenth-century canvases recall great national events and military glories. His famous study is rather smaller, of a brooding court jester. It is usually read as a Shakespearean intimation of the cruelty of Polish history. The red-clad minstrel is dwelling on Poland's imminent fall from being a constitutional monarchy exemplary in Europe in the sixteenth century to a small country facing non-existence 200 years later.

No one would deny it is a mournful story. Poland achieved widely admired political stature and lived through a golden age of civilization during the Jagiellonian period of the fifteenth century and the subsequent First Republic, from 1569 until the Partitions of the late eighteenth century. It was a greater power than Russia and it had extensive contact with Renaissance Italy. But the Poland I had come to was divorced from its roots. It seemed threatened with isolation from both East and West. Soviet communism had reversed Poland's greatest historical experience by cutting it off more than ever from Western Europe. Clearly that fact would greatly add to the animosity with which the alien system was received and would inject new force into the established idealization of the old Polish way.

We spent a telling evening at the opera. Stanislaw Moniusko, the nineteenth-century composer who begat Polish opera, was playing at the Teatr Wielki with *Hrabina*. The production, set in the baroque Polish court, was colourful and popular. The music sounded like Offenbach and Rossini in one, with lots of coloratura. Yet it was not the music this fidgety, informal audience was soon deliriously clapping but the scene where a young soldier living in a world of graceful gallicisms is told by his father-in-law how to be a good Pole: to speak and read Polish. By the end of the performance the stage was awash with flowers. Moniusko was a national hero, as was the leading soprano, who received a medal that evening for thirty-five years' service to Polish opera; thirty-five years of singing for the cause. Polish television was on hand to record the occasion. The evening left the impression of an isolated and also intensely self-involved culture.

My solidarity with shabbiness was by now leading me increasingly to 'go native' with only a tinge of self-criticism. Sometimes, to recover from tramping the streets, or just to have somewhere to go, Elizabeth and I sat in the nursery-style milk bars which are a feature of Poland and the Central European countries, eating inexpensive sweet treats with Polish women and children: blancmange with nuts, jelly and cream. Sometimes we stood in shopping queues, the only ones banging our feet with the cold. I enjoyed myself queueing for a carp even as I thought this was an absurd kind of tourism, like Gauguin going to the Polynesian Islands to enjoy their backwardness. We were visiting hardship and I was relishing it. I bought the class II plum jam which was deemed not good enough for export and found to my delight it was refused to the West because it tasted home-made and came complete with stalks and stones. I bought good rye bread and passable international Brie, flat parsley, tomatoes, mushrooms, endives. Suddenly and overnight Poland became my back-to-nature ideal, my vision of self-sufficiency, my unreflected dream of the good life. It made me realize, as a person who had never been tempted by popular counter-cultures at home, that I was nevertheless very interested in alternatives to Western society, in a way of life not super, not pre-packed, not alienated. I liked the spectacle of a society where people were directly in touch with their means of survival and had to seek it every day. Had I been a Pole worn out by queueing and shortages I would have found this attitude infuriating. There were no lemons that month, nor mineral water nor plain yoghurt, and butter, sausage and meat were rationed. For the sake of human dignity I ought to have been less romantic. But there I was, a discontented Westerner, dazzled by austerity.

It was not only urban life which provoked this romantic dreaming. I had similar feelings when we travelled out into the country. One day we motored to Lublin, in the far east of Poland. We drove along the flat, sandy right bank of the Vistula, through an area of what the Germans call *Eigenhäuser*, detached, one-family houses, interspersed with larch woods and orchards. It was a grey, squally day and children and chickens darted forward onto the road with the same unpredictability as the weather. Horses and carts whirred and clopped along the asphalt, their drivers huddled in thick coats and fur hats. The scene had a poignant appeal; a month later I felt I had seen it as a painting or perhaps even painted it myself. The appeal lay in the spectacle of self-sufficiency; that and the secret pregnancy I would wish upon any dormant land. I was correspondingly negative towards anything 'changed' or 'modernized' about Poland.

We stopped for petrol and sightseeing in Kaziemierz, billed as one of Poland's most delightful historic towns. I decided it was also one of those devitalized toytowns which make you wonder why you came, and why history in the form of rebuilding old buildings should have any value. If this was history I would only ever be interested in art and personality. We attempted to buy some boiled sweets for Elizabeth to stave off car sickness. At midday on a Saturday the main grocery store in the picture postcard square was doing a brisk trade turning away customers wanting to buy bread. The shop smelt of curdled milk and compost and sold cheese, eggs, packet foods and soft drinks. Instead of a few ounces of sweets we came away with a kilo by mistake. Local people smiled kindly at us absurd tourists.

We took black coffee and Coca Cola in the smoky café in the square where the teenagers were ordering jelly and cream and the music was vaguely Western; the front window was broken and we should have been colder; a local man came in expressly to tell us we should not have parked in the empty square. We must have been easy to spot. There wasn't another vehicle in sight.

According to the Polish newspaér I was trying to read as we sat there, in Wieden, the Polish name for Vienna, talks were in progress to reschedule the Polish foreign debt. The debt was certainly visible. The unspoilt countryside, the poor-quality transport and lack of cars, the food shortages and the self-criticism in the media were constant reminders: Poland couldn't run fast enough to keep up with the advanced industrial civilizations. The shabbiness was no simple virtue.

Indeed, by the time we got to Lublin it seemed almost sinister. Lublin, almost on the Eastern border with the Soviet Union, was a grey, angular and impoverished modern university town, with tall, solid, flaking buildings. It possessed poignant relics of the Polish-Italian connection which flourished during the Renaissance, but its organized delapidation, gloom and the standard litter of drunks reflected the worst of communism and everywhere there were depressing commemorations of sacrifice. In the main street a monument marked the Union of the Polish Republic with Lithuania in 1569, effectively the demise of the once great Lithuanian Empire which stretched to the Black Sea, and the beginning of the First Republic. Another monument in Polish and Russian marked the defeat of the Nazis and the 'liberation' of Lublin in 1944. The 1569 Union, which incorporated the Ukraine into Poland, inspired the Russian Tsar, Ivan the Terrible, to purge the city of Novgorod, in case it planned an anti-Russian alliance, but in 1944 the balance of power was reversed. The Soviet army, sweeping in across the river Bug to liberate Polish territory from the Nazi occupation, immediately subordinated the area to Soviet might. It set up at Lublin on 22 July the Polish Committee of National Liberation, a provisional Polish government, and used it as a bridgehead against the Polish government in exile. Loyal Poles became Soviet victims. In August Warsaw rose against the German enemy, believing itself about to be saved, and was left exposed. As the Soviet army stood by, Warsaw was virtually annihilated. The Allies suspected Stalin of treachery, but felt they could do nothing.

Lublin was a birthmark on communist Poland. Rape, followed by bungled delivery, not suprisingly produced a scarred child.

It was a cold, grey Saturday afternoon. We passed through the thick arch at the foot of the Baroque clock tower into a network of grey cobbled streets; Renaissance palaces, frescoed with cameo portraits of eminent men and coats of arms; low ceilinged, narrow passageways, hanging lanterns, dark, deep-windowed craftmen's shops with wrought iron trading signs, delapidated pink, sky blue, corn and deep blue-grey stone facings; chipped portals; Renaissance windows which once looked out on a growing baroque city but now looked down on piles of rubble. The old city of Lublin, like a Tuscan hilltop town, had crumbled and had hardly begun to be rebuilt, though there was wooden scaffolding everywhere. It was odd to see these tokens of a civilization so important to us being neglected, really as if a different system of values had taken over. I felt in Lublin what G. K. Chesterton, another conservative romantic, felt in Cracow, that it was an outpost of *virtu*, but also that it was a city overtaken by worldly events, debased and pushed aside, like many nameless, once enlightened, provinces across Eastern Europe.

There I was, peering grossly at disaster. I ought to have been appalled. But Rousseau and Marx explained, both of them against the tide of industrialization and the growth of urban mass existence, the attraction of authenticity. Dominated by my negative feelings about the West I was living emotionally in the eighteenth century and my view of Poland emanated from that nostalgia.

What first persuaded me Poland was suffering was not lack of food but lack of style in daily life, the absence of design. The white and pale blue interior of our cold, dismal local supermarket reminded me of the inside of a refrigerator. In that way Warsaw *was* immediately like Moscow. It was anti-modern. Life was not designed to stimulate the senses and please the eye as well as function. That realization made me bridle. What an omission! Before the war Poland helped create Modernism. There's still a museum in Lodz devoted to Poland's contribution to world avant-garde design. Now an entire human capacity was going ungratified, while in its place had come a false plainness, a surface narrowness, and a dreadful absence of joy.

In this communist Poland I could understand the aesthetic deprivation best, with its extreme negative consequences for happiness,
and it helped me make sense, though not immediately, of some other
small thoughts I had in Lublin. Back in the modern town we had
taken a digestive stroll along the main street in biting wind. We came
to a pizza house, to a puppet theatre, a record shop, and finally a
second-hand bookshop. Grevisse's *Le Bon Usage* was on prominent
display, as well as works by Thomas Mann, the Polish romantic poet
Slowacki and Tolstoy. I liked the international, cosmopolitan aspect
here. It showed a broader world was still reachable. Further down
the street was a plaque to the poet Josef Czechowicz. Czechowicz was
the first to translate the modernists – Joyce, Eliot, Mandelstam – into
Polish. He died aged thirty-six, from a bomb dropped on Lublin in
1939. I had learnt of him from Czeslaw Milosz's wonderfully readable
A History of Polish Literature: 'an imagination steeped in rural Polish
life', 'chamber music made poignant by the counterpoint of dark
philosophical and metaphysical problems'. Czechowicz's life reminded
me of the anti-totalitarian value I was beginning to uncover for modernism in East Europe: first the value of Freud in the Soviet Union,
now the value of avant-garde design on the streets of any communist
city.

But what of ordinary people's real ability to survive in spirit in the
run-down circumstances of contemporary Poland? I tried to remember
to ask.

The waitress in the Hotel Lublinianka, where we had lunch, was
middle-aged and pleasant under pressure and involuntarily I began
to create a background for her. She must have been pretty once and
her legs were still slim and her make-up and clothes careful. She was
unsophisticated by Western urban standards, but not rustic. The
combination of personal dignity and public apathy she radiated made
me think of the entire state of Poland, with its rebellions behind it
like a quarter-century of marital quarrelling.

The Polish Communist Party gazes into the future like a marriage
guidance counsellor trying to be reassuring. It doesn't cultivate a
remote or mysterious image and can persuade some Poles that it has

their real interests at heart. The period of 'national reconciliation' is just beginning as I write.

The waitresss goes on setting down another round of beers, tolerating fat, gnarled, hot fingers on her bare arm. She doesn't care one way or the other, but she would like now and again some small, private joy.

It will be the job of some Polish writer to think about this woman. But which? In the vague way of an interested, even passionate outsider, but still an outsider, I wondered about Polish writers and their view of life around them: how they worked at the present time, a few months out of martial law and still in the shadow of the Solidarity crisis; I wondered what themes preoccupied them and whether they felt a common burden in the fate of Poland. I could never imagine feeling the weight of Britain constraining my heart.

I asked a young professor in Warsaw who spoke French to talk to me about 'the condition of Polish literature'. We sat in his spartan office with too many tables and, relishing the shabbiness of it, I listened. Polish literature boomed during the martial law crisis. Poetry was read in the churches. Marek Nowakowski wrote his acclaimed tales *Report on a State of War* and Kaziemierz Brandys agonized over the Polish condition in *A Warsaw Diary*. The placing of the whole nation under house arrest probably gave some writers and many would-be writers a focus for a perennial, inborn discontent in their make-up; they acquired a subject to which they could lend their intensity and their power of commitment and condemnation. It is a truism that limiting conditions can often encourage literary talent. You can see from so many biographies and autobiographies and fictions that confinement, whether it results from imprisonment, or personal sickness, or a more or less willed withdrawal from worldly concerns, frequently stimulates self-definition just as Moscow had done for me. Artistically therefore the social crisis in Poland was even good fortune.

But Polish literature has long been affected by the narrowing, concentrating effects of exile. During the Partitions, when Poland ceased to exist as a geopolitical entity, literature acquired the burden of defining the Polish spirit, since when it has not been able to escape its tendency to symbolize and allegorize, though often to powerful effect, as for instance in Cyprian Norwid's poem about how the Russian occupiers threw Chopin's piano out of the window of a house in the Old Town in Warsaw.

'The most difficult thing in our literature is to be realistic,' said Professor Zaleski. 'For years we have resorted to historical allegory. Now writers want to be more direct.' Contemporary Polish writers want to be in touch, not isolated, not forced to be romantics. It is all the more regrettable therefore that so many writers, including Brandys, author of *A Warsaw Diary*, should have gone abroad as a result of the Solidarity crisis. Yet in the nineteenth century, after the failure of the 1831 rebellion against Russian domination, the same thing happened. Polish literature seems fated to live much of its life in exile.

As an outsider I'm fascinated by the theme of confinement, of which exile is a form. Exile from one's family, from one's friends, from one's country: all these can be productive. The whole of Poland is in exile under communism. I was in exile in Moscow. The two halves of Europe are exiled from each other. Exile, like occupation, drives us to define our values and I think from here, from the middle of a divided continent, I should like to write a requiem for the Cold War, a kind of bitter thanksgiving. But I can only continue with these notes.

The day we went to Lublin we stopped on the way at Pulawy, a small town whose best feature is the neo-classical Czartoryski mansion and park. I knew of this family from some historical research I was doing in Moscow. The Czartoryskis were aristocrats close to the Russian court in the eighteenth century, but also Polish patriots. They were devastated when the last of the three partitions in 1795 made the area around Lublin a Russian protectorate. Princess Czartoryska lamented:

> My tears flow often when I pass spots which hold memories of my country's past, of this land so dear to my heart, where I have lived since my childhood, where I was a happy child, a happy wife, and a very happy mother and friend. This country no longer exists; it is awash with blood, and soon its very name will be effaced.

In the next generation Adam Czartoryski was one of the Russian Tsar Alexander 1's closest advisers in the brief age of reform after the French Revolution and before Metternich's Continental System. Later he returned to Poland to work in Polish education but was so frustrated by political obstacles to Poland's development he became a leader of the 1831 Insurrection. Defeat forced him to flee to France, where he remained until his death more than twenty years later.

I am drawn to Czartoryski's as a well-defined life: resourceful, thoughtful, constructive, ultimately uncompromising, just as I am drawn to Kaziemierz Brandys's sentiments from exile nearly 200 years later, which makes me understand the way Poles feel outside the system and how they derive strength from that outsideness:

> We lack everything; we lack meat, sugar, potatoes, but unfortunately or fortunately we do not lack any consciousness of our own situation . . . It is precisely that consciousness that produces our instinct for self-preservation, a deeper instinct for spiritual self-preservation; that consciousness of our situation forms our character and our intellect, creating our sense of the meaning of life through the force of simple dreams. What do we dream about? Freedom and justice. What do we want and what do we refuse? We want to be human; we refuse to live like subhumans. Oh, those ideas, 'naive' because purged of doubt. It is they that have shaped our humanity. There is great power in that desire and in that refusal.

Polish weakness in the political world is its moral strength and Brandys and countless other Poles are proud of it. Brandys goes on to define Polish strength as something incomprehensible to Homo Sovieticus, to any genuine dialectical materialist, or to anyone who cannot accept that morality too has power. The message is as important in the materialist West as anywhere.

The waitress in Lublin would not have put her feelings about the alien system with its alien ethical standards into so many words. Nor would the characters created by the finest realist to write about contemporary Poland, Marek Nowakowski. But it is the great merit of Nowakowski's stories that their unvoiced resistance to the alien system is palpable. The morning I was talking to the professor the news came through that Nowakowski had been arrested. 'This is extraordinary indeed,' exclaimed Professor Zaleski. 'This is not

Russia. They do not *arrest* writers here.' In the event Nowakowski was released not long after and pardoned in a general amnesty, but for a short while his detention showed how far the government could move away from the spirit of ordinary people. Meanwhile, said the professor, the government was trying to bring its own spirit into literature, having shaken out the Writers' Union after the Solidarity crisis. It was encouraging mediocrity and kow-towing. 'But I believe literature cannot be more timid than the social conscience,' said the professor, with a controlled absence of passion. 'There was a novel called *A Year in the Coffin*, which attacked Solidarity. It was published in huge numbers and given extraordinary publicity. That's our communist society for you. It was a shameful and pornographic book.'

There it was, a turning point: suddenly my literary concerns and my subjective values had plunged me into politics. They had also made me feel inadequate. The politics of opposition depended on moral discrimination. After talking to the professor I felt underqualified to associate myself with such a cause.

Elizabeth and I met a plump, blonde and glamorous woman in a bus queue. She told us she had been an actress. We talked haltingly about how difficult it was to talk. Her children learnt Russian at school but not very good English. I regretted having no Polish but suggested we might converse in Russian. Akh! Stalin had made her learn too much Russian, not enough English and no German, she said, dipping nevertheless into German to call the other language *Russisch*. She followed it with a homily on the state of Polish history, metaphorically wringing the neck of a chicken. I wanted to ask her if this tension was always in her mind because it seemed too large a historical consciousness to be carrying about with her, of Poland, a modest little country squeezed for centuries between the expanding Russian and German giants and feeling its fate now as cruelly as at any time in history. But had I asked I think she would only have smiled at me, as she would have done at a child. The quirks of Polish history have produced a very sophisticated consciousness in the street.

In the bus, strap-hanging, clutching Elizabeth, not knowing where we were going nor where to get off, my advice was sought by a fellow passenger. All I could offer was a shrug. 'Tourist? First time in Poland?' said a dark woman with a cultivated manner, homing in on my unease. She had worked in Austria as a nurse and travelled, so she knew a little English and German. 'Yes, first time.' 'You must go to St Anne's. It's the only church in Warsaw which wasn't destroyed by the war.' She was getting off at the *Bahnhof* but someone else would show us the stop. She tapped a stranger on the shoulder and briefed him. 'Oh, but I'm a journalist,' I blurted. The succession of my nervous thoughts seems to have been: unnewsworthy Poland, unworldly Poland, metaphysical Poland. How can I begin to understand when I haven't suffered enough? I'm afraid my sympathy won't be genuine. 'Ah, but then Poland is not interesting for you any more,' said the woman. 'It's quiet.'

The time was December 1983. Could I pick up the spirit of the time, or was I constitutionally too remote for Polish concerns? Polish moral strength manifested itself memorably in the rise of the free trade union Solidarity, which three years before had caught the imagination of Poland so fiercely that thirty-six million people came to the brink of civil war. In 1981 membership swelled to three million and included many members of the Communist Party, until pressure from Moscow crushed hopes of radical reform. I wondered what was left and took myself on a short, painless pilgrimage.

I found a Solidarity sign, an S superimposed on an anchor, on a brick wall near a children's playground. Just a symbol, but a powerful one, incorporating Poland's repeated worldly defeats and its ability to survive sustained by national and religious faith. The badge of the wartime Free Poland movement looked similar, an anchor with a superimposed P. The anchor is the Catholic symbol of hope. The strange thing about Poland is that symbols like this really work; they convey popular feeling in a most effective shorthand way. Thus the official guidebook to Warsaw is written in spectacularly symbolic fashion and you cannot read it even briefly without becoming aware of how Poland has suffered:

In 1794 Victory Square was the scene of severe fighting of Polish troops and the people of Warsaw against Tsarist troops. In 1807 Napoleon held a review of his troops here. In the time of the

Congress Kingdom (1815–30) the Square served for military training and reviews held by Grand Duke Constantine [of Russia]. Such
spectacles frequently ended in suicides of Polish officers insulted
by the Grand Duke. After the collapse of the November Insurrection (1832) the Tsarist authorities intended to build on this site a
fortress, bristling with guns, which was to have overawed the rebellious capital. This plan was not realised, being replaced by the
Citadel. At the close of the nineteenth century, a vast Orthodox
church was raised in the centre of the Square – a symbol of the
russification intentions of the Tsarist rulers. It was pulled down in
the years 1924–26. In the area between Tredry Street and Victory
Square stood the Bruehl Palace, the most beautiful of the Rococo
palaces in the capital. During the Nazi occupation, it was the
headquarters of Fischer, Hitler's governor of Warsaw. In 1944 the
Palace was blown up by the Nazis.

There is a kind of madness about the succession of these scenes,
as if History were stamping over Poland in hobnail boots, like a savage
political cartoon come alive.

I toured the Old Town with Elizabeth, the place all visitors go first
in Warsaw to feel the Polish past. The Old Town with its cobbled
narrow streets, noble archways and two splendid Renaissance squares
is where the 1944 siege took place, the last engagement with the
German occupier. The one-sided battle reduced the city to rubble.
The squares with their colourful façades have been rebuilt almost
stone for stone, though without the aid of museum photographs it is
difficult to appreciate how painstakingly they have been resurrected.
Now they are the spot where Warsaw burghers take a Sunday stroll,
and where little reconstructed medieval-style shops sell glassware and
objets d'art. It is possible to make a circular tour by horse and carriage.
Alas, rebuilding is like the way the body repairs a burn. Something
grows back to cover the damage, though it will never be living skin.

Poland is the background against which some distinguished non-
Polish idealists have defined themselves, so I am not without grand
company. G. K. Chesterton was drawn to an agrarian, unmechanized,
slow-moving, Mariolatrous Poland earlier this century, and before

him Marx, with quite a different cast of mind, was equally drawn to Polish backwardness. Marx blamed the aristocracy for the backwardness but allowed himself to be attracted to the result; it gave him the necessary grounds to believe that Polish workers could wreak change and offer Europe a unique display of the establishment of classlessness in liberty.

More recently political idealists in other East Bloc countries have taken Poland as a symbol of justified rebelliousness. In 1956, despite Russian sneering, the Polish workers' rebellion in Posnan became a symbol of liberty. Poland was raised shoulder high in Budapest the same autumn when the Hungarians themselves tried to oust the Russians. In 1980 Solidarity became a rallying cry for democratic aspirations throughout the East Bloc, and underground contacts between Poland and Czechoslovakia, East Germany and Hungary proliferated.

Let me go back to the examples of individual inspiration. I did not know much about Marx's psyche, nor was I prompted now to inquire, but about Chesterton's idealization of Poland I read all I could find. I discovered that wherever he described the charm of things Polish he did so in terms of the Catholic church, to which he became a devout convert, or in a way which recalled the illuminated miniature puppet theatre which was the delight of his boyhood. He had, perhaps unwittingly, brought his more cherished inner experiences to Poland and found or imagined them reanimated and strengthened there.

I can consider my own response like that. This delapidated, suffering country speaks to a part of me which sees in the realms of imagination and personality an unassailable refuge from the world outside, a part of me which perhaps will always insist on the ultimate separation of 'literature' from 'history'. When people first told me of the quietness after martial law, 'the state of war', of people staying at home, of cafés which were now dull places to sit, of popular and politically daring cabarets gone quiet, the negative picture they painted of an outwardly shut-down life evoked in me a secret joy that such a life would not be so bad. I think I could bear martial law, for I have this great capacity for inner happiness which solitude has nourished and which I became so aware of that long, reflective, cooped-up winter in Moscow. Every now and again I would like to test it though, to see if it still exists, and that is another reason, I suppose, for these journeys into communism.

But the other part of me to which Poland speaks is to the campaigner, the believer, the worshipper, and what it shows me is that in a totalitarian society literature is a cause I would be bound to espouse, as it were against my quieter nature, in order for that nature to remain free. I knew this in theory before I came, but naively I had not felt the weight of the reality before.

It is now early in 1984. Occasionally there is still street violence in Warsaw and other cities, on Solidarity-related anniversaries. Some Solidarity activists are in hiding, others in jail. The riot police, whose technique has become steadily more sophisticated to parry world opinion, have rubber truncheons imported from Japan. My friend in Poland redoubles his efforts to report the Polish situation accurately and in painstaking detail. He feels strained by official half-truths. Recently there has been a huge hue and cry over a young demonstrator beaten up and killed, particularly because those apparently responsible have been cleared of charges. In moments of extreme sympathy I see my friend, who has to talk disinterestedly, without showing any emotion, to both the government spokesman and the victim's mother, through the eyes of Dostoevsky. He's playing Christ to that spokeman's Grand Inquisitor. I cannot imagine a more serious role for him and for the free press, let alone for literature.

For my own part I feel a kind of impotence. I am confined to looking about me. The Palace of Culture, a terrible symbol of Polish oppression which dominates the skyline from far off, is an enormous Stalinist erection designed to overawe and make faint all who dare to approach it. Its towering vastness, enclosing offices, restaurants, conference rooms and a swimming pool, seems to distort normal judgement of street distances. It is where the Party meets and other official gatherings take place. It is a formidable exercise in architectural dictatorship, 234 metres of soaring nightmare paternalism, spread over 817,000 cubic metres. The idea of omnipotence is endorsed by making the Palace the headquarters of just about every weighty non-governmental institution. The Polish Academy of Sciences, Polish PEN and the Polish UNESCO Committee are all at home there.

I compare the Palace of Culture to the Citadel across the city. This is a nineteenth-century fortress prison like a giant red brick bunker, greenish and half-overgrown, smelling of urine and rubbish like the pill boxes I played in as a child. Built to consolidate the victor's occupying power after the rebellion of 1831–2 it still stands intact as a memorial to seventy-five years of political confinements, interrogations and executions of Poles by their Russian rulers. The old cells are damp and dark and half underground. On top of the hill visitors can walk the length from the grey obelisk, incorporating a piece of execution scaffold, to the Execution Gate, past a roll call of victims, whose names are inscribed on the gate and on the prison wall beyond. A black prison van looking like a horse-drawn hearse made of giant bat and beetle wings stands behind in a courtyard ready to take prisoners to Siberia. I will visit nothing so horrific until I go to a Nazi death camp.

Now there's nothing nostalgic or appealingly shabby about any of this. With my eyes opening, I can see signs of conflict and coercion all around me. In Warsaw the gold-painted Forum Hotel is like a giant ingot, an invitation to visiting capitalists to invest their hard currency in Poland. I contrast it with the down-at-heel Gong Tea Room, once listed as a tourist venue, but now, on Sunday afternoons at least, a warm, sleepy spot for soliciting in local currency; a place for self-preservation. Another black spot, a non-find in my new mood, is Victory Square, with all its historical significance, but nowadays fenced off with nothing inside. Officially it is closed for maintainance, unofficially it is closed because Solidarity supporters have demonstrated there. But some people see it simply as a model of post-Solidarity Polish life, a big forbidden empty space, not allowed to be of use to anyone.

I went to a play. Slavomir Mrozek's *Out at Sea* (1960) was playing at proprietor-director Jan Machulski's Teatr Ochoty. I set off into the suburbs, clutching my *Falkplan Warszawa*, the Warsaw A-Z, and hoping I would be able to understand something, having read only a synopsis in Milosz. The theatre was a small hall, with rough seating and a set improvised from a huge sheet of tie-dyed canvas and an orange box marked 'made in Poland'. It was a coincidence that all the plays I had to choose from that evening – Peter Weiss's *Marat-Sade* and Beaumarchais' *The Marriage of Figaro* – concerned power.

Machulski, a grey-haired handsome man with many years' experience in the theatre, came out to survey his packed audience ahead of the performance. My foreignness must have stood out, because he summoned me, first in Polish, then in French, to sit in the front where I would have a better view. I had the faint feeling of being in school. He began the evening by reading from the letters of Mrozek, another Polish writer in exile, concerning the human need for authority.

The play which ensued concerned three men shipwrecked on a raft. They decided one must die to keep the others alive, but the options were already closed. The one who would die was the intellectual and weakling, THIN.

Before the execution THIN is already transfixed by fear. He's ineffectively trying to make sense of his fate as MEDIUM lays the table for the feast. MEDIUM'S conscience is troubled, though, and he's delighted to find some tinned food in the bottom of the hamper after all. Thinking the crisis is over he appeals to the man who has emerged as the natural leader of the trio, FAT:

> FAT: Shhh! Hide it this instant!
> THIN: . . . And therefore I have decided . . .
> MEDIUM: To be quite frank I'd prefer baked beans. What do you think, boss?
> FAT: I don't want baked beans. And anyway . . .
> THIN: . . . And therefore I have decided . . .
> MEDIUM: Anyway what?
> FAT: (Pointing at THIN) Can't you see? He's happy as he is!

The sacrifice of THIN goes ahead.

For Machulski, who avows a belief in the 'theatre of moral stances' this play was a rich opportunity to discuss the ethics of power and to consider some of the murkier aspects of Poland's past. An issue which comes up repeatedly in the newspapers is how Poland came to tolerate the gassing of the Jews on its soil. Another implicit issue is the ethical position of Poles who work for a communist government without commitment but with too much fear to voice their disagreement. Here at the Teatr Okhoty was 'literature' not divorced from 'history', nor suffering from the alliance. In short it was a marvellous artistic evening.

Machulski, who evidently also thought so, reappeared after the peformance and tried to engage the audience in discussion. 'There are plenty of men like MEDIUM among us!' he booms. 'Mrozek has much to say to contemporary Poland.' Laughter ripples through the audience, many of them soldiers, but they are too shy or afraid to speak.

A year later, back in London, I wondered what the people in the audience that night for *Out at Sea* thought when the security policemen who murdered the pro-Solidarity priest Father Jerzy Popieluszko pleaded they were only obeying orders. It was the scandal of Poland in 1984. Popieluszko's abduction, sordid murder and the trial of his murderers put the whole ethos of communist Poland on trial. The defence argued that the priest deserved his fate because he was disloyal to Poland. 'Patriots' were justified in hating him.

This was 'communism' at its most monstrous. The defence feigned and distorted the moral values of the other side in order to justify any violence in the pursuit of power. The deliberate obfuscation of the case filled me with rage. This communism was very slippery and quite damnable in the sheer dishonesty of its sham high-mindedness. No wonder Poles in protest had to insist on absolute moral values. At Popieluszko's funeral Solidarity did so unambiguously. It printed its news in red ink to contrast its facts with the black ink lies of the government newspapers.

Freud says that exaggerated conscience and the need for religion are forms of deprivation carried over from childhood, to the extent that the desire for comfort and certainty was thwarted. Certainly I feel the exaggeration though I don't know what is the cause. I am in a strange position now, though, for although I suffered because of my spiritual innocence before, I have suddenly found a positive use for it, which makes me see myself in a clearer light. My long preoccupation with metaphysics at the expense of the outside world makes me associate all the more readily with the problems of this deprived half of Europe, which has also had its desire for comfort and certainty thwarted. My gaucheness keeps me eager to share in the pervasive, self-questioning panic over spiritual values which is fast becoming a culture in its own right over here, under communism. I feel therefore a kind of irresponsibility in going home. Meanwhile, it is only a pity that the same unworldly idealism has spelt disaster for my marriage.

3

Raging Polyglot Land
Yugoslavia 1984

Freud, when he wrote about *Civilization and its Discontents* in 1930, had one eye on Nazism and another on Soviet communism:

> In all that is to follow then I take the stand that the aggressive leaning is a basic, independent human instinct, and come back to the fact that culture finds its greatest obstacle therein. At some point in the course of this inquiry we had the idea that culture was a particular process which unfolds over the heads of humanity, and we remain under the spell of this idea. We should add that it is a process in the service of Eros, which wants to bring together isolated human individuals, then families, tribes, peoples, and nations, in one large unit, humanity. Why that must happen we do not know; just that is the work of Eros. These human multitudes must be bound together libidinously; necessity alone, the advantages of community in work will not keep them together. But this cultural programme is opposed by the natural aggressive instinct of man, the hostility of the one against the rest and the rest against the one. This aggressive instinct derives from and is the chief representative of the death instinct, which we have discovered alongside Eros, and which shares with it in ruling the world. And now, I think, the sense of the way culture develops is no longer obscure to us. It must show us the struggle between Eros and Death, the life instinct and the destructive instinct, as it occurs amongst human beings. This struggle is the essential content of life, and that is why the development of culture can be called in short the life struggle of the human race.

Elizabeth and I enjoyed a short holiday in Yugoslavia in October

1984, and I begin on the theme of pleasure because I was travelling now as a single woman, perhaps one who should have been looking for pleasure.

I arrived tired, and the sight of a genuine holiday resort, a sort of Baden-Baden with palm trees by the sea, where German and Italian mixed with Serbo-Croat speech, was slightly overwhelming. Rows of imperial villas climbed the hillside and expensive modern hotels relaxed on the waterfront. I had not passed through the Iron Curtain this time, merely crossed the modern borders separating three free countries, in a part of Europe where the extent of the vanished Austro-Hungarian Empire is the real dividing line, where local culture matters more than central politics. Inland the trim green alpine countryside, with its neat, individual villas with steep roofs and cool cellars, private gardens, cars in the drive and window boxes, looked disconcertingly comfortable and familiar.

We stayed in the old imperial resort of Opatija, also known by its Italian name Abbazia, which in 1984 was celebrating 140 years in the tourist industry. Our old-fashioned hotel, also called Imperial, had a velvet-pelmeted ballroom with ruched curtains which hung like a row of empire-line dresses, inviting us to play at dressing up. By the time we were installed the hotel's evening routine was in full swing. In the grand dining room a mundane tourist menu was being served, with the food graded by the State; the atmosphere and the service were very relaxed. In the ballroom other guests were watching the American soap opera *Dynasty* with Serbo-Croat dubbing on a colour television, occasionally flicking over to some scenes of urban violence in Italian.

We walked a little and sat outside in the dark and relative cold of the early October evening. The wine was plain and Opatija bay romantic. There was nothing exaggerated or contrived about the lure of the dark water, the lights of the town, and a brilliant moon with a keen face. Elizabeth was drawing what a Jungian analyst would say was a story about her parents. '*Kako lepo citas!*' ('How beautifully you draw!') an admiring male voice commented from the gloom of the café balcony. On her paper the moon turned into a kite hitched to the sun and both were tied to a clown's face, surrounded by attempts at numbers and letters. Beneath us in the street cats ran everywhere, and the bushes hissed as if the entire neighbourhood were calling them to sup. Narrow paths and dark stone steps led in many directions up the hillside.

The cold tin table outside the bar recalled a particular cold spring I had once spent in Italy. My writing hand used to get blue from resting too long upon the marble table top in my bedroom, in a stone cottage in the mountains. The same hand was now quickly becoming too stiff to hold a glass. The sensations came in quick succession, of overwork and physical stiffness and lack of romance.

We took our morning walk by the water, against the tide of East Bloc health tourists, mostly men in uniform dark blue bell-bottomed track suits, already returning from their first constitutional. Elderly Germans with walking sticks, moving not so fast, their women further encumbered by rigid handbags, radiated the smell of Delial sun cream, a favourite German brand, like a continuous reminder of the good life. The smell came back to me as a memory of teenage summer holidays. Germany was materially more luxurious than Britain; meals and suntans were superior, the streets were cleaner, the houses less draughty. As we walked on I had the impression a man called out to me in Russian. For as long as I can remember my sexual fantasies have been tied to the intellectual experiences of my early adulthood in Germany and Russia. In the relaxed atmosphere of sunshine and blue water they surfaced, taking me by surprise.

On the beach we met Tikhomil who had taken his six-year-old son out of school to enjoy the late summer sunshine. Man and boy were strolling along the seaside path above our heads when he stopped to tell me he always looked for the good in people, because most people were good and would respond. For the unnamed others he shrugged his shoulders. He had no time for 'differences'; disliked conflict; abjured 'philosophy'. Life was short.

The Slav roots of his name mean quiet and kind. He is a well-built man in his late fifties, twice married, with a paunch under an immaculately laundered white shirt of lawn cotton and knotted with a silver grey tie. His very straight, very greasy longish hair is greying. When he speaks he reveals the caries that noticeably plagues men and women in Croatia. His teeth, where they have not been replaced with gold, grow in different directions and look like stumps of macaroni, stained with nicotine; and they splay outwards, showing their tops, like shark's teeth on a necklace.

His determination to live in the hope of co-operation is a part of Yugoslav history. He was born near Dubrovnik, in an area Turkish until the collapse of the Ottoman Empire, but has worked for thirty years in the import-export business in Rijeka. Rijeka was under Austro-Hungarian rule until the First World War and, as Fiume, belonged to Italy until the end of the second. The border ran through the heart of the city and though Tikhomil didn't experience occupation he lives, like all Yugoslavs, with the consequences. Occupation breeds, where not nationalism, existential personal philosophies which seek value in the present moment. On holiday from metaphysics I find this intensely attractive. But I should also say it was not philosophy in that sense which Tikhomil disliked, but ideology.

Tikhomil didn't want to talk politics and history, though; he preferred what was happening now. He liked the German tourists, he said, looking around at the strollers on the promenade, and the packed open-air cafés; they were disciplined, and they kept their children in order, unlike the Italians who were forever surrounded by a *Karambol*. *Karambol* comes from the Italian *carambola*, which in turn derives from the verb to cannon in billiards, i.e. to make strike and rebound. Tikhomil's words consistently rejected any experience of collision. He was a kind man with no polemical animus.

I was so pleased we met, and not only because when he happened along the high path behind our patch of beach he ousted a gaitered ginger-moustachioed German who was tiresomely insisting on knowing where my husband was. Tikhomil struck me as the truest of Epicureans, the kind Montaigne described as being most impressive for having learnt to be pleased with their entire fate, not merely to suffer the pain of it, like the Stoics. We decided to turn the afternoon into a local excursion and our first stop was a café in a little fishing village he called 'Spanish', to which the path led from Opatija. The café was a private, not a state, establishment, so that the wine and spirits could be relied upon, he said. We shared a modest 200 cl of Teran, the finest of the local reds. Thereafter we drove absurdly slowly and with much unnecessary hooting at unlikely hazards to a neighbouring village, our two children in the back of the car making a terrible *Karambol* as they became acquainted. We saw the old stone village with its narrow, Italian streets, ate the very sweet tasteless ice cream sold everywhere, which cannot help those teeth so prone to decay; observed the spot where a mariner had fallen from the quay and been eaten by a shark; and eventually retired to another café to drink spirits. It was suddenly cold again, for, although it was only four in the afternoon, by October the mountains block out the sun very early. Tikhomil opened the brown handbag strapped to his wrist and insisted I drank *travarica*, a faintly green distillation which tasted as its name suggests of grass and herbs. It was home-made and especially suitable for women, *für alles Weibliche*, he said. He stroked Elizabeth's legs affectionately.

And where in all this was the Communist Party? I asked. Tikhomil waved a sunburnt, blunt-fingered hand towards a notional, far away Belgrade. One party and no classes. That was good. Not like the Italians, he imagined, where a doctor cannot marry a worker. Classlessness means all people are free to enjoy the same pleasures. This middle-aged man with such positive convictions about his country would have shown me a typical classless person if he could. Instead we saw these private cafés and restaurants of quality, we passed excellent private pensions where I could stay next year, and we looked at the outsides of a few churches, which he showed off as signs of freedom of worship. Tikhomil was not a political man, nor a man of ideas, but a consummate man of pleasure, I decided. Above all he was proud of the possibility that of all the communist countries, in Yugoslavia the pursuit of pleasure had been barely impaired by the imposed social and political system.

It is often said that the miserable dark climates of Poland and Russia do nothing to encourage society to flourish, that they make communism seem all the worse, and that feels true. Certainly Yugoslavia's communism seems eased by the fact that nature here is beautiful. The long summer of sunshine makes its people seem relaxed and unassertive to a holidaymaker. The Adriatic seaboard brings freshness to the stale perplexities and inwardness of Central Europe. Pleasure, desire, appetite: these are obvious but easily forgettable antidotes to politics. Amid the communist countries Yugoslavia seems to act as a reminder; not a great role, but a necessary one.

Opatija, a Slav seaside resort tucked into the angle between the southern line of the Pula peninsula and the southbound Adriatic coast, was full of German-language memories, like the inscription on the house next door to our hotel, 'Villa Doktor Hortenau'. I thought of Doktor Hortenau as we sat in the hotel ballroom watching a television film set in Austro-Hungarian Croatia, full of hunting scenes and characters in green loden and feathered hats. The men who wore those collarless high-buttoned jackets, and the women in velvet hoop-hipped long dresses with laced bodices were greeting each other as if over the fences of the Empires. The men drank beer, swore *Brüder-schaft*, said *Servus*! and *Bene, benissimo*! The soldier who saw a pretty girl said *ma foi, dio santo, kaka krasna*! Technically this look at the past was very old-fashioned and self-conscious. The voices didn't quite belong to the characters, nor the characters to their locations. But it captured another, wanted, life: the easy blending of nationalities in a larger-spirited Europe, the Europe of the old empires, before communism. I noticed that on the waterfront too the postcard industry was thriving on its reproduced sepia cards of Abbazia.

A Dutchman dived, trying to recover a piece of nineteenth-century balustrade he had spotted on the seabed. An amphora perhaps, said his Hungarian wife encouragingly, as we sat on the concrete jetty on our bright towels, gripped by history. The Istrian peninsula, from ancient times right up to the last war, is a rich site for excavations. The diver eventually emerged with a piece of green and yellow masonry shaped like a vase. No mystery remained once we could touch it. This find too obviously belonged to a façade from the row of fine villas behind us, which forty years ago crashed into the bluer than blue Adriatic. Opatija was bombarded during the last war, and Rijeka, close by and strategically important, was flattened.

Still in pursuit of history we went by a stifling, hardly roadworthy bus over the mountains to Pula, in the extreme west of Istria. Pula, known for its Roman amphitheatre, has long been considered an ideal place for an educated Central European to take a seaside holiday and it is still entertaining and instructive. It has communist touches which stand right alongside ancient sights and drive home the reality of modern, divided Europe. Pre-eminent among the relics of antiquity, in a busy square, rests the miraculous, box-like stone temple of Augustus, untouchable in the midst of Slav provincial life.

We walked the concentric narrow Italianate streets around the fortress hill, up to the cannon which once aimed out over the tall masts, protecting the port below. Encircled by the cannon, the old fortress houses a museum of the Nazi occupation which is a treasure trove of old newspapers, photographs, public notices, uniforms and equipment. Of the German tourists who had ventured there two had left in the visitors' book their dates of birth and the words: '*Wir können nichts dafür*'. ('It's not our fault'). Another had signed himself Adolf Hitler, and a third, aged fifty-eight, had taken it upon himself to be ashamed that one of his countrymen could make such a crass joke.

The Pula Resistance exhibition leaves the impression that East European communism, in Yugoslavia's case the non-aligned communism pioneered by Tito, came into being to stop a Hitler ever again threatening these fair lands retarded by alien nineteenth-century empires. When I was in Russia, Moscow under Brezhnev was still pressing home the anti-fascist debt on the basis of that powerful half-truth, and I think it is widely believed here too, almost as a religion. Tito's lasting popularity begins with his leadership of the Istrian resistance to the Germans. It's written up in the hills on the way to Pula. TITO WE WANT YOU, COMRADE TITO, WE PLEDGE OURSELVES TO YOU. Indeed these slogans were everywhere we went in Yugoslavia, painted on walls and roofs and cliffs, wherever they could be seen from far off.

The war is not confined to museums. It is still a vital memory. Yugoslavia was divided by the war and still has problems reconciling the memories of its member republics. Croatia had a Nazi puppet regime and is vulnerable to criticism of collaboration. Those responsible for the imprisonment and murder of thousands of Serbs and Jews are still being hunted. Trials of war criminals continue. When we visited the Croatian capital Zagreb, down one of the charming narrow cobbled streets of the old town, we came across a film being made which re-enacted the Nazi occupation for schoolchildren. Old posters daubed with swastikas were pasted on the walls as ideal Nazi children with blond plaits and Lederhosen ran by. I took some

45

photographs of the set before the woman director asked me to stop. She was afraid I might 'misuse' the photographs abroad. Reputations are vulnerable, history still liable to controversial reinterpretation to stir presently subdued conflicts.

Yet one can give daily preoccupations too much moral weight by viewing them historically. In Yugoslavia forty years after the war the memory is of Fascism, but the national problem is money, a matter more practical than ideological. Under Tito, on the strength of his personal kudos, Yugoslavia borrowed enough money to have a standard of living to rival the West. A man from Zagreb who emigrated to Hamburg twenty years ago remembered in the mid-1970s goods in Zagreb shops being as varied and of as high a quality as in West Germany, but that reality had now vanished. The IMF has moved in to try to mend the debts as inflation soars and shortages are common. People talk about dollars as if they had magic properties; the luckiest Yugoslavs have business to do abroad; the most talented academically seek jobs in foreign trade. The situation brings out a wily cleverness or the temptation to speculate in less educated, confirmedly materialist souls. But it also reminds one of the Western tendency of Yugoslav political style insofar as, unlike the East Bloc proper, it is not afraid to admit it is poor.

We arranged our holiday so that we alternated relaxation with diversity: two days on the beach, a day or two travelling. After Pula we made the longer trip, this time by train, inland to Lyublyana, which briefly took in Zagreb. These exploratory trips involved many hours in transit, chatting to whoever came our way, usually about material things, and mostly money – another sign perhaps that we were in a quasi-Western country. Vlado was a ship's steward who had dollars from his trips abroad, so that a pair of jeans or a ticket to London were in his opinion 'small money', he told us on the way to Zagreb. The Istrians used to do much of their shopping in dinars over the border in Trieste, and he at least still liked to go there, though most people couldn't afford it now. (Trieste incidentally is still the only sensible place to exchange dinars for hard currency.) There wasn't much I could contribute to Vlado's conversation, so I was sitting quietly. He took the quietness to be an invitation and suddenly lurched forward. But almost immediately the compartment packed with schoolboys, who seized Elizabeth's Roald Dahl on which to try out their English. Vlado sank back into his seat and allowed our conversation to lapse too.

Three hours later we were in another train, on our way to Lyublyana. Astonishingly there had been nowhere to stay in Zagreb. Lack of hotel beds is a problem all over the East Bloc, making it difficult, sometimes deliberately, to be a casual visitor, though Yugoslavia normally has a good, welcoming reputation. I was rather nervous we wouldn't find anywhere for the night, but tried to remain hopeful. That way I found myself talking to Vesko. He, also on his way to Lyublyana, was a Serb, a student of electronics in 'grey' Belgrade. He proceeded to tell me: he was proud to be a member of the Communist Party; happy that his country dwelt in the global political middle. Soon we were deep in a very different conversation from the one I had had forced upon me by Vlado. Like Tikhomil, Vesko thought the socialist system best for Yugoslavia, but he also cared for political causes and was an idealist. Unlike the importunate seaman we had left behind, when I talked about shopping he had nothing to say, except that he would like Trst back from Italy. That trilled Yugoslav vowel made Trieste sound a completely different place.

Vesko talked prolifically about his country. Yugoslavia suffered so before the war, having territory stolen from it; it suffered in the war, most memorably with the devastating German bombing of Belgrade; and afterwards it suffered hunger. Vesko recalled five lean years in his family in Montenegro after the war. Though he was clearly too young to have lived through the experience of near famine himself, ideas were enough for him. Communism post-1945 was self-defence, he said, and unification of the diverse Yugoslav provinces was the way to repair pride and international political status. Those two achievements of Tito had defined the modern country, though without such a leader it was uncertain where the same path would lead now. Vesko accepted it certainly meant limited international status for Yugoslavia, whose 'economic and therefore social reality' was different from the West.

I wondered about Vesko, who had to work hard to make ends meet and keep studying. Now and again he went to Venice to buy materials to make filigree jewellery, which he sold to tourists in the Istrian resorts. He had visited London but could barely afford to do so again. The rate of exchange had plummeted. He was not a dissident, but he was a kind of idealist certainly: he was trying to live by his convictions rather than entirely by opportunity. I began to wonder about myself too, taking such an interest in him.

His engineer's Russian reverted to Serbo-Croat under the pressure of wanting to talk, while I held loosely and hopefully on to my Russian, in steady decline since I left Moscow. We didn't have a language in common yet we were having the kind of privileged conversation which happens in fairy stories when the hero is temporarily given understanding of the language of frogs or birds, who later help him to survive. We communicated well until I asked him if he had a wife. No, no, he said, he had to study. He looked embarrassed and clung to the densely printed newspaper-covered book on his knee. I went back to my thoughts about fairy stories, no doubt because I was reading so many to Elizabeth in those days. Soon afterwards we seemed to arrive. We put away the books we had not been reading and Vesko helped me unload my sleeping child on to the platform.

It was midnight. He sniffed the air with distaste and shivered. Akh, Slovenia! After four hours by express train we had arrived in the capital and it was a physical shock after the soft mountain air of Zagreb. I was partial to Zagreb, I said, but he didn't like either city. He was a Serb and Zagreb was Croatian. Croats had killed Serbs in the war. He couldn't stop himself from disliking them.

We began to walk to a hotel he knew. The first was full, the second was expensive. 'They only have one room free,' he said, turning round from the reception counter. 'Tell them we want two,' I said.

When we woke up Lyublyana was grey and raining and Vesko was gone.

Perhaps as a young communist Vesko was bound to bring it up, Yugoslavia's domestic headache, the problem of its diverse and eternally competing nationalities. The conflict affects not only those ethnic groups which have their own republics, but those whose homelands are now outside Yugoslav territory, among them Albanians, Hungarians, Romanians, Ruthenians (Ukrainians), and Jews.

The languages and the cultures of the southern Slavs compete for space and audience, the historical interpretations challenge each other and conflict in an attempt to secure identity. Ideally the idea of communism would overcome this divisive heritage by drawing together all citizens, all workers, regardless of nationality, in the name of international solidarity. But both theory and practice have proved unreliable. The East European experience of Soviet communism has been the very opposite of international. It began under Stalin as Russocentric and has continued so. When Tito challenged Russian supremacy, espousing a cause inimical to Moscow, that of the Balkan Slavs, he was expelled from the fold.

The Yugoslav political ideal remains as an attempt to maintain unity in diversity, to enable relative poverty and wealth to coexist within the same national borders, and to accommodate many cultures and many tongues. The reality involves the most pressing political problem in recent years, the Albanian minority in the South protesting against what it sees as ethnic discrimination and persecution. The post-Tito government doesn't pass the test of openness and humanity this problem sets. Meanwhile tensions persist among the Serbs, Croatians and Slovenes. But it has been Tito's socialism, not Moscow's international communism, which has been holding conflict at bay and tolerating difference.

I can best understand the conflict of nationalities as the babble of languages becoming louder and louder in the excitement of competition. The thought of so much hunger to be heard and so much rivalry is both erotic and frightening.

Rebecca West when she worked on *Black Lamb and Grey Falcon*, a monumental study of Yugoslavia, gathered round her advisers from the different Yugoslav nationalities and watched the sparks fly. But then she wrote – and I think this is a very English response – of her huge admiration for a culture which contained all this diversity of men and women and languages and ideas, and which presented itself even as she sat in a Croatian café as 'raging polyglot intellectual curiosity'.

I too feel in thrall to the babble of the many tongues we can hear and the competing nationalities we can detect here. Not only the

journey with Vesko. I can recall other dozy journeys across the heart
of Europe, changing languages, wondering how far the Italian, or the
German, or the Romanian, or the Hungarian influence would last, or
if anyone remembered his English from school, or his Russian. Often
that kind of linguistic experience is erotic, generated by the sense of
new contact and new opportunity for self-expression. I mean erotic
in Freud's metaphysical sense, but it is the same eroticism that propels
us along, by means of our attractions and repulsions, from day to day.
It is a very keen sense of our being alive by virtue of our linguistic
individuality; but also the sense of a boundless number of separate
people united by the desire to trade words, perhaps only half-intel-
ligible words.

I sing the praises of language, but one of the most frightening
aspects of communism has been the way it has manipulated public
language and the provision of information, as if it set out deliberately
to interfere with the vital forcefield which keeps culture and spirit
alive. You can see that deviousness in the way Tito's expulsion from
the East Bloc in 1948 was announced. Today Yugoslavia's borders
are open and its currency is unprotected, but during the Stalin period
immediately after the war, when the new communist state was still
tied to Moscow, Yugoslavia briefly experienced what the other East
European states have gone on to endure as daily life.

On 28 June 1948 a Czechoslovak Communist newspaper
announced that the Cominform, meeting in Bucharest, had expelled
Yugoslavia from the family of fraternal Communist Parties. Stalin
assumed that the Yugoslav Party would overthrow its leaders ...

Alan Palmer *The Lands In Between*

A political system which makes its declarations like this frighteningly
mocks the natural babble of voices by introducing a deliberate confusion of utterances. Disparate and distant official organs pronounce
with dislocating effect on the reality of lands not their own. Even
though it is history, when I read this passage I feel the same rage I
felt in Poland at official attempts to gain the upper hand through
obfuscation.

In Yugoslavia the crisis years go on being analysed in literature and
film. The debate helps throw light on the plight of the rest of the

East Bloc. To take just one example: the babble of languages coming up against Stalin's attempt to silence the country through political terror is the theme of a remarkable story by the Yugoslav novelist Danilo Kiš, *A Tomb for Boris Davidovich* (1976).

The principal tale centres on an ideologically-inspired murder somewhere in Eastern Europe after the war. Miksha the trainee assassin kills the Polish girl Hanna Kryzewska after a struggle near a railway line:

> Through the clacking of the train wheels and the muffled thunder of the iron trestle, the girl began, before the death rattle, to speak – in Romanian, in Polish, in Ukrainian, in Yiddish, as if her death were only the consequence of some great and fatal misunderstanding rooted in the Babylonian confusion of languages.

It is a short book, a collection of politically related incidents presented as a novel, which I found immensely difficult to understand on first reading. Implying as his background a land forced to become nameless and faceless, Kiš struggles to put the loss of human orientation into words. One way in which he does so is to suggest by the very disjointed form of his book that communism, a political system, has appropriated history and rewritten it like fiction, so that fiction, to distinguish itself as a systematized pursuit on the side of truth, can no longer do the same. The old privilege of being allowed to present a chronological human drama, with places, dates and consistent names has disappeared because its credibility has been wholly undermined by communist-inspired events. The new reality of fiction, which has lost its nineteenth-century empire, is discontinuous, stark, violent and full of deceptions and lies. Kiš's words, and his characters' words, are life, Freud's Eros, struggling to survive destruction, and against which, on the side of death, stand the theory and imposition of totalitarian politics. It is a wonderful book, illustrating the state of humanity unreconstructed by communist reality but terrorized by communist ideology. It is also a picture of the graphic modern struggle in this part of the world between Eros and Thanatos, where what Freud called 'the narcissism of small differences' can sometimes seem like the only way to preserve an identity, and all the more so in the homogenizing communist era. As a Westerner I can only gape at the continuing relevance of large philosophical ideas.

In Lyublyana the rain which accompanied Vesko's departure persisted, driving us into the galleries. In the national gallery a princely St George (Sv. Jurij) was killing a brontosaurean monster. The picture by a seventeenth-century artist seemed to represent political and social progress, not only a Christian triumph over death and destruction. Over the stairs hung a masterly medieval Totentanz. But there was nothing soft in the small, unextravagant, largely provincial collection, except some late nineteenth-century French-style Impressionism, and some small studies of young women, of erotic historical and biblical themes, and Italian landscapes, by a painter called Suvic. Mary fainted as a Roman soldier pierced Christ with a long spear. The pain in the baroque crucifixes was ice cold.

We went from the gallery to the national museum, which was full of photographs of local life. But even there people celebrating carnival week thirty years ago had a Dietrich-like sophistication, a kind of velvety hardness with their short hair, women with hip-belted dresses, and men in sensuous, formal evening dress. It is partly because of the immense contrast with the neighbouring Italians that we think the Germanic world wears its sensuality so uneasily, like this, but for the other part the hard surface is true.

Lyublyana, or Laibach, has to me a German air, and the countryside looks Tyrolean green, the colour of the Austro-Hungarian Empire, a far cry from the parched South and the sparkling coast. It is a baroque city, where some of the houses are painted as if they were wearing Lederhosen braces. Through the centre flows the torrential river Sava, and on the far bank the central market sells nuts, mushrooms, flowers, fruit, grains, vegetables and a huge array of candles. The market reflects careful cuisine and homemaking, what looks like a past culture still intact, an unshabby Poland in fact, though I seem to have exhausted my capacity for nostalgia. At eleven everyone is eating a roll with Wurst while walking along the street, or drinking coffee in a stand-up café, with whipped cream squirted on it from a syphon. In German, in Slovene, in Serbo-Croat, the blob always sounds the same, '*mit Schlag*'. It makes the coffee horribly cold and fatty.

I always notice food and I believe it's a good indicator of culture and atmosphere. Here it was Austro-Hungarian cosmopolitan. In a stand-up food emporium in the main street there was pizza for lunch, and kalamari with a k, and sauerkraut, with so-called local black wine, which is red. Some older women were drinking brandy in large quantities, like the German women tourists in our seaside hotel at breakfast. In a contrasting modern international style the young of Lyublyana, saving their money, and their energy, were drinking black coffee in a side street, in an exclusive smoky black-walled café where they could sit and stay for hours.

We went south after Lyublyana, following a suggestion of Tikhomil's. At 7 a.m. Split harbour was as imposing as any palm-clad port in the world, lying beneath sheer, gravelly mountains and a brilliant sky; the ships made their exciting, tinkling music; TITO was painted on the cliff; we had woken fresh after a night's sleep at sea and were going to new adventures. The liner from Rijeka was clean and the sun very hot as we surfaced for breakfast. A few young bronzed Yugoslavs, having slept the night on deck, were brewing coffee on a primus stove, their sleeping bags hung on a rail to air. Those of us who had dinars to spare drank chicory coffee and ate boiled eggs, apple jam and triangles of processed cheese with dry bread in the restaurant where the stewards spoke German. Yugoslav state catering is characterized for me by that dreadful cheese, while apple jam, which I know from Aeroflot, is a peculiar sign of plain eating. I see the one other English couple on board have brought their own marmalade. The Germans know all this in advance and bring all their own food.

On deck, as we descended the ravishingly beautiful Adriatic coast, I was talking to Igor, who had been drawing ducks for Elizabeth. He had a modern Western mentality but was quite unlike the boastful, ignorant seaman Vlado. A Slovene, he made me eat my words about the Germanic character of that province. He wanted to work hard and enjoy his work and his leisure, but his manner was gentle and relaxed. One of the privileged, in foreign trade, he travelled widely. His task, working for an Italian-based firm, was to make of Yugoslavia a link-builder for private trade between West and East. The job, involving the exchange of chemicals for chemical processes, had taken him to Moscow and New York, to Prague and Milan. It was natural for us to compare experiences but it took us both by surprise to have so much in common.

On the East-West divide, which did not concern him very much, Igor's impressions were of a peaceable way of life among Russian people, much as he disliked Kremlin politics. In America he felt almost the reverse was true. He detected an aggression built deep into public culture. The comparison he made was more psychological than political, to do with the quality of spiritual life, and it was interesting to see this view held by someone other than a romantic, nostalgic Westerner, namely that enforced economic backwardness may have helped preserve the spirit of good neighbourliness and modesty a little longer. But politically Igor believed the Americans and the Russians were both dangerous, and the Russians perhaps more so because their domestic problems were greater. He believed they feared another revolution would so weaken them as to leave the United States supreme, therefore they had to keep a firm hold domestically, which in turn encouraged international tension.

Meanwhile the Americans had colonized Europe with the dollar. Yugoslavia was no exception. Igor expressed mild resentment or perhaps it was just world weariness. At work he was bound to think in dollars, he said: elsewhere he tried to forget they existed. He would have disliked Vlado, for whom he had a word: *dollarist*.

Yugoslavia does not have to aim for economic primacy, Igor says. It is no bad thing for a country to be led even from across the Atlantic, provided the right man is in power in the White House. Again it is gratifying to hear a paeon to modesty expressed by a non-nostalgic sensibility. Politics, he continues, in a definition I should consider appropriating, is a struggle amongst interested parties, which one keeps up with but keeps out of. The Party in Yugoslavia acts to justify its existence, but ordinary people seek mainly prosperity. In Yugoslavia this means more education, a higher level of culture and another leader like Tito. But Igor expresses this ideal more as a hope than as a programme of action. I don't think he is a deeply political man like Vesko, just well-informed. Indeed his soothing remarks and his unstressful company underscore what has struck me from the very first in this country, a political quietism – even among the educated.

*

The low level of education was a problem for me, a woman travelling alone, as we explored parts of Yugoslavia's South. I remembered Igor's words, alongside Tikhomil's, when we arrived in Dubrovnik. In a coincidence of symbolic moments we found ourselves harangued as we left the boat by peasant women calling rooms in Serbo-Croat, English, German, Italian; caressed by cats at the door of our modern monster hotel; followed by little boys whispering dollars and fingering my handbag.

We stayed in what was once a quiet village port at the foot of the mountains outside Dubrovnik. The hotel was brash and large, with a flagship of credit card advertisements in the plateglass foyer; and a vast, turquoise leather reception desk and unstoppable pop music from a local radio station. The German visitors were mostly unskilled in their travelling and clannish in their incompetence, and that made the brashness that catered for them worse. We went by crowded bus or motor launch to the old city to explore.

The cloisters of the Franciscan Monastery in Dubrovnik, the cool courtyard and interior of the Rector's Palace, belong to the Renaissance world, but not to the Reformation. The Gothic remains seem far from home. I, a literary Lutheran, am struck by the strange idea of open-air worship and the alien business of turning to a god other than Dionysus in the heat. Dubrovnik's old buildings boast of prosperity, and intellect, and artistic quality, and well-ordered power, to which worldliness the Fransiscans have brought the message of poverty and simplicity. Dubrovnik has been a great Christian city, a cultural oasis, an equal in the fifteenth century to the Republic of Venice, which in turn inspired the First Republic of Poland. The Turks were bought off from venturing inside Dubrovnik in one of the outstanding diplomatic feats of Western history. When it faced new conquerors in the form of the Croatian-Hungarian kings this fine city perpetuated that same wise and graceful policy of being ready to take second place which began when it first lost power to the Venetians. By that means, that is by following Tikhomil's and Igor's philosophy, Dubrovnik has survived to this day. The old city, still encased in its medieval limestone walls, and in which one can see the symbolic sight of a Christian belfry topped by a minaret, exemplifies the idea that it is often better not to be first. Inside the belfry, sheltering but intact, like Christian Dubrovnik accommodating itself within the Ottoman encirclement, stands the iron figure of the city's patron saint, St Blaise.

Dubrovnik (with the stress on the first syllable) was founded when Epidaurum was sacked and its inhabitants fled a little way north along the coast. They called the new settlement Ragusium, later Ragusa. The modern city houses a port, the university and many fine neo-renaissance villas. Dubrovnik survived, and flourished from the fifteenth century as a centre of wealth, style, commerce and good living, because it accepted domination. To many young Yugoslavs it is their favourite city, because it is lively and offers all the attractions of a capital, while remaining small and on the coast. To a visitor it looks no more than a jewel casket, perched on a rocky fortified prominence well into the sea, home to many cats and exotic autumn blossoms, and fig trees. But it is unusual because ordinary people live in the casket by the hundred, as evidenced by line upon line of spotless white linen of a morning; they live in tall, narrow, cobbled streets full of window boxes with stone carvings of St Blaise, and these houses are topped by television aerials and sunworshipping cats positioned on a jumble of planes of stone and tin. If the soul of Dubrovnik is hard to find today, it is because of the latest menace, dollar colonialism and the collaborationist spirit of the *dollaristi*. The pattern of history suggests Dubrovnik, like another historic city we have visited, Pula, may have to shrink its spirit for a while in order to survive. But poverty is one of the less painful forms of exile, less painful by far than communism. I'm thinking now of the desecration of Lublin.

I'm happy here. All my senses seem to be functioning. What's more Igor has re-appeared unexpectedly. We'll spend the rest of the evening together, pushing aside the dreadful food we're given as tourists, walking by the water, talking and doing an absurd thing: exchanging business cards, in case we ever meet again.

4

Life Under Permissive Communism
Hungary 1985

I had introductions in Budapest, ready-made subjects to contemplate. The very first evening I met Imre, a strikingly handsome poet and activist, youthful at forty, a sort of banner dissident. He gave me a useful introduction to Hungarian life over an egg and paprika sandwich in a cosy café divided into rustic cabins. We had been there about half an hour, chatting. 'You won't find anything spiritual here,' he said in his excellent English, guessing accurately at my thoughts.

Certainly this café didn't make me feel I had escaped from the tyranny of Western fashions and expectations. The style seemed Western. I began to inveigh against the commercialization of privacy, which had reached this far into the supposedly closed East Bloc. I had begun rather to like those aspects of a closed society which lent dignity to my solitude. By contrast these cabins were a way of saying in our Western language of design: look, I have a lover, a friend, someone I can cuddle up to, share confidences with, look at me! Goodness knows what went on in Imre's head during this tirade. He looked puzzled, and throughout my stay we agreed on very little, though there was a mutual fascination and empathy and a dim recognition that we might yet have something in common, so we met again several times.

It was March 1985 and the weather was still grey and cold. We stayed with a charming couple in middle age with whom we could exchange no more than two words. But they loved having a child in the house and every day, after obligingly walking in parts of the city with me, Elizabeth would settle happily into a late afternoon routine of Hungarian children's television and tea. Actually it was an uncomfortable time of the year to visit with a child. Large chunks of ice floated down the Danube. The winter of record cold had dragged on. Why had we not waited until Spring? our hosts asked. The solid, nineteenth-century city of Pest, the business, commercial and government centre, looked its worst. The ground was patchy with traffic-spattered snow and the grand boulevards were unmercifully exposed to chill winds. The buildings needed cleaning. But, anyway, the architecture struck me as too eclectic to be pleasing as a whole. I liked this corner and that building; a neo-Gothic courtyard in an apartment block; a shopping arcade reminiscent of Paris or Milan. But the total product was confusing. A change of season wouldn't have helped.

Buda, the older hilltop village across the river, was more manage-able in size, but in spirit a toytown like Kaziemierz in Poland, not a place one would go to do anything but sightsee. The view over the Danube bridges and the parliament building on the Pest side was worth the climb but truly early March was not the best time of year to visit this eighteenth-century royal settlement, with its palace, and fine churches, and a number of historic houses. The buildings were all preparation and scaffolding, and might as well have carried notices saying that until the season began there would be no life in them.

Dodging the roadworks and construction sights we strolled round the top of the hill, along the gas-lit avenue, skirting the backs of the houses. Elizabeth and I walked the round once on a Sunday morning after a snowstorm, on our way to a concert, when the pace was set by the middle-aged; and again on what everyone hopefully proclaimed was the first day of Spring; certainly it was the morning when the new season's toddlers came out. Afterwards we had coffee and cake in a famous café, Russworm's.

My daughter at four and a half was now grand company. Despite the cold her spirits were high and she was impressively at ease with strangers. I felt grateful to her for her introductions: fifteen minutes here talking to a waitress, half an hour there with a student, though these fragmented contacts didn't lead anywhere. Seeking shelter we did a lot of sitting in cafés, smoky black-walled new ones like those we had found in Lyublyana, or velvet-curtained older establishments. Nothing happened. The Hungarians have something akin to Anglo-Saxon reserve. Among the educated young, few speakers of French or German or English come forward. The older generations, those who experienced the war, are more cosmopolitan, but shy.

In a well-known café near the opera I eventually spoke to a man whose studiedly casual clothes made him stand out as a Westerner. He spoke to the waitress in German. It turned out he wrote for the West German stage, 'the vaudeville business', and came to Budapest regularly to get away from the telephone and to live cheaply. It was a way of shedding his mundane responsibilities when he needed to concentrate on his work. 'A big city like all European cities,' he complained. 'It's noisy, congested and all anyone ever thinks about is money. Forints.' Yet Hungary gave him pleasure, in the form of a woman who would apparently never run away. He began voluntarily to talk about his girlfriend. 'I have a friend here, who keeps an apartment for me. She's all I have in the world.' I let the idea of the always available woman in an apartment without a telephone slip away as if it were irrelevant. Actually it was a marvellous fantasy to pin on Eastern Europe. I concentrated instead on the familiar business of leading a marginal existence. I too dislike the frantic world which only *dollaristi* can love unequivocally. But again, like Hans, I do not belong anywhere else. There are a number of us, displaced souls, wandering round the East Bloc, looking for an antidote to the West. I wasn't ready to admit that to Hans. I didn't want sympathy from possibly a kindred spirit. I protested that having only just discovered this comfortable, semi-Western, politically unharassed retreat I rather liked Budapest.

I set about finding some things to do with a small child. We both remembered with pleasure attending a children's concert in the Filharmonia Hall in Warsaw, and hoped for something similarly warm and musical in Budapest. We ended up enjoying a magical afternoon at the puppet theatre. The stage stretched the breadth of the theatre, the puppets were lifesize and the very basic lighting and colours were brilliant. Moreover the play, *Tom Thumb*, was easily accessible without language. A giant had enslaved Tom's parents but Tom rescued them by pushing the giant over a cliff. Everything about this production pleased me and I was happy Elizabeth was well entertained. That the spoken language had been unimportant was an exciting thought; besides which I have a great liking for the aesthetic boldness and simplicity of the nursery. On the way home, after a friendly drunk gave us tickets for the metro, we felt very buoyant.

Another icy day we went to the zoo, which was under snow, leaving only the hardiest inmates – polar bears, snowy owls and penguins – on show. That unexpectedly was where I had my first sense of Hungarian politics. The zoo is in a tourist quarter near Heroes' Square, and that is the place where the giant statue of Stalin was pulled down by joyful rebels in 1956. Only his boots were left behind, a sight commemorated in a number of famous news photographs. I remember them vividly from books. Their story is one of the outstanding events of the eleven-day revolution, with all the makings of a classic. It could easily be rewritten for the puppet theatre. Yet though the children would like a good story about the felling of another giant, the peculiar thing about Budapest is that unless the giant had a moustache and were called Joe or Ivan hardly anyone would notice or care. There is no obvious political reality to confront. Hungary isn't free but its exact condition is hard to pin down. It has a history of easy compromise, first with the Turks, then with the Austrians, now with Moscow.

When I met Imre he had just moved, he hoped temporarily, into a kind of commune. He was there, living off a mattress on the floor with a couple of boxes of belongings, and his small daughter, and two women and another child. The building was splendid, with an interior courtyard and huge, broad stone steps leading from floor to floor. Inside the apartment the atmosphere was genial, busy – everyone had visitors – noisy and concerned; actually it was quite unbearable as a place to live. We sat drinking tea and vodka in a large, empty high-ceilinged room with an old tiled central heating oven. Imre had to finish typing a samizdat declaration and give his daughter a bath before he could talk to me. I felt charmed by the transitoriness of his surroundings. There's a German word for this, *bestimmbar*, which means open to change in a positive way, as opposed to being merely indeterminate and vague. It dearly needs importing into English, as a highly cherishable form of hope.

Imre told me by way of an introduction to his work that some time ago he had published a book in the West about censorship in Hungary. Later, when Anna was asleep, we went to see a woman who had a copy of the German edition to give him. A relative living in the West had sent her a parcel and we called to collect it. Having already turned in for the night the woman, in her late fifties, answered the door in hair curlers and a dressing gown. She poured us all a large sweet vermouth while we chatted. The book was hidden under the bed. Imre sipped his drink reluctantly, explained that he was driving; they talked about his books and her daughter who was a friend of his. He had an absurdly young romantic aura about him which the woman was clearly enjoying. Since he and I were out together I wondered momentarily at my own amorous feebleness but let it pass.

To my surprise Imre and I were often talking about politics, a subject of which I had long considered myself afraid, because I could only conceive of it as being something chaste and knew it wasn't; chaste because I presumed it subordinated and sublimated the personal to and for the general, public good. Perhaps this is only to say, though, that in observing the reality of politics at home in the West I could find no way into the political sphere for myself from literature. Since I had been travelling in Eastern Europe I was more ready to change, but still the only conceivable bridge was poetry, something I sensed more than reasoned in Poland. But here was Imre, passionately committed to the idea that politics was change, as radical a thought as I had ever encountered in Poland, where politics was morality.

'Politics is the desire for change!' he declared grandly as we sat there with the vodka and the tea. I told myself, perversely afraid of him, that it was true. Dissent and the pursuit of consensus were both ways of expressing disagreement with the prevailing authority, differing only in the degree of discontent. But still I found it hard to accept both were 'politics'. Discontent in the East Bloc was a matter of rejecting a world view, an entire philosophy of man, which is why it seemed to me closer to the imaginative life than to politics.

Why did I find it hard? I had to keep asking myself that question because when Imre introduced me to his friends they were also very political. Ironically the two we saw most of were British and young women, by which I mean ten years younger than me. They had set up home in a pleasant Budapest suburb, out of a desire to experience East Europe first hand. Hungary was the only East Bloc country which would allow them the liberty of residence and to earn money by working for International Hungarian Radio.

They were fresh from the disenchantment of university and a secure English middle-class background. 'At home we would have been just two more unemployed arts graduates,' they said. They worked for a Westerner who was a communist and had lived in Hungary for many years. He was a broadcaster who, as it happened, also covered sports events for Reuters. I couldn't help smiling.

Perhaps it was a generation gap. My new acquaintances talked about personal relationships in terms of a 'discourse' and about their undergraduate course in art history as a study in capitalism and the institutions which supported it. They concerned themselves with 'the position of women in Eastern Europe' and believed peace, simply peace, was a viable political cause. I couldn't fathom why they were so political.

'Don't you want children?' I asked one day.

'We can't separate our personal hopes from our political hopes,' they replied.

For a moment I thought I did understand. They didn't want to be egotistical, which is the cardinal bourgeois personality sin in the revolutionary socialist book. They wanted to represent all women, and marry History. Well, not quite.

Darkness at Noon came to mind, that book I abandoned in the train to Moscow but have since read and reread in the light of the Mrozek play I saw in Warsaw. It's about the inhuman consequences of banning egotism. In turn it reminded me of Zamyatin's *We*, the first anti-totalitarian novel, and the most far-reaching, a book in which Eros is firmly lined up against Central Planning.

We met again several times. Apart from my liking and admiring them, one thing we had in common was that we'd all come to Eastern Europe to find out something about ourselves. We were looking for insight and a clearer perspective before going back. We shared it with Hans the vaudeville writer too. We were all looking in the communist mirror for answers. I believed one of the girls was having an affair with Imre too, another way of finding an answer. I have heard it is not an uncommon phenomenon for Western women to feel erotically attracted to East-bloc dissidents, because these men seem to personify

History. There exists the dissident groupie, though the description did not apply to my friend.

The distinguishing feature about Hungary is not its difference from the West so much as from the rest of the East Bloc. This week I find myself collecting images I cannot measure, having experiences and conversations, not knowing if they are significant, wondering if my lack of exhilaration amounts to boredom with the ordinariness of it all, the easiness, writing little in my notebook. It is a world very much to hand, and yet I cannot reach out and grasp it. The smooth surface of Hungarian life is encouraged by the absence of domestic conflict and the growth of a little wealth. (Hans and others tell me forint millionaires are increasing.) Meanwhile the rules and conventions of communism seem hidden.

Superficially Budapest's aspect is Western. There are discotheques (albeit with rosy apples as bar snacks), smart shops in the centre with Cardin-labelled clothes, restaurants with careful menus and service. The central market contains by other East European standards an enviable supply of meat and fruit and vegetables. It's a treat to walk past stall after stall of garlic and onions and dried peppers, knowing that this is just what is required for perfect Hungarian cooking.

More obviously in Hungary than anywhere else in the Communist Bloc, East has decided to run with West, though disliking so many aspects of Western life myself I'm not necessarily impressed. Marx urged such a compromise on the non-proletarian classes on the eve of the putative proletarian take-over of society, and the present Hungarian situation judged on that pragmatic model looks like a celebration of Western profitability. But it's not exactly a display of high principle, unlike in Poland and in Russia where there are still idealists loyal to socialism, or even Marxist-Leninism, who are only unhappy at the way the ideology has become corrupted in practice. Here most people are quite happy to renounce their Hungarian communist selves for something wealthier and more stylish. The official ideology clearly has no moral or economic hold. The same might be said of Poland except that again the atmosphere produced by Polish pride and the high political profile of the Catholic church gives anti-communism a more moral colouring than here and tends to marry it with the cause of national unity. The business of returning from communist exile is much more dramatically and spiritually presented.

But there are gaps in Hungary's extreme pro-Western stance, and it's not only that there's a shortage of black shoe polish and washing powder. It has something to do with the atmosphere in Gundel's restaurant where we decide to lunch one day because I'm attracted by the name of the most famous Hungarian gourmet this century; something to do with pretence and self-delusion.

Gundel's has been restored recently in an effort to boost the tourist trade. It is warm, comfortable and spacious and the waiters are polite and the food good. But state tourism aims at the insulation of the Western tourist from Hungarian reality and the effect is of being in a no man's land. The more efficient the service the stronger the feeling of disorientation. A bored, uniformed commissionaire at the wrought iron gate leapt to attention as we walked in. Inside other men and women whose job it was to be helpful opened more doors, took our duffel coats, brought canapés, menus, drinks, and finally huge plates of robust Central European specialities, in this case stuffed peppers and meat-filled pancakes. The airy circular room with pastel-coloured furnishings buzzed with hushed conversations in German and seemed to be hosting mainly business meetings. We must have looked an odd pair, mother and daughter, informally dressed to say the least (with the duffel coat and what went beneath it I hoped to disguise our Western-ness), and both reading. I had the acute feeling I was only there because of the accidental privilege of my Western money and freedom and sat feeling uncomfortable at being treated as a Hungarian top dog.

Imre says that Hungary lives deliberately superficially, acting *as if* it were part of the West, without the moral and political substance to make such a claim true; and that it lives that appearance *in spite of* knowing it's not true. I think he is describing the malaise of an intellectually and spiritually disaffected population, too tired to accept or protest publicly against the falsehood it is forced to live under official communism. If this is so it's a debilitating state of affairs, for though 'as if' and 'in spite of' are not acute problems they're chronically undermining of the sense of self. The situation is not that different from the one in Poland, in fact, but it is very differently expressed.

The self-images of Hungary I catch in Budapest are shadows and caricature. The day I arrived I asked the taxi driver if he spoke English. *Nem*. German? *Nem*. French? *Nincs*. Russian? He laughed. That was one image the people of Hungary have of themselves, I decided: their function was to laugh at the Russians.

Three tall fat military men of familiar ursine bearing, with briefcases and fur hats were waiting on the Metro station one morning. I tried to get near them to overhear their conversation but they were determined to stand alone. A Hungarian woman sized them up with the hint of a grin. In 1985 there were 65,000 Soviet troops in Hungary and though they were little seen, their presence was never forgotten.

I went to a jazz concert at the university. The tall, fuzzy-haired, stoop-shouldered leader of the band opened his patter by comparing the uncharming and cavernous plate glass venue with Leningrad station, which made everyone feel he was a good Hungarian. The music he played was tremendous, though at the end the students clapped as if they were under observation for their ability to show restraint.

This will often happen here. Life, because it can afford to be fashion-conscious, will look Western but the underlying reality will be quite different. A self-image official Hungary courts now is the one we read about in Western newspapers, of a country moving close to a market economy under communism. It is a good line, because it displays developments in Hungary which Westerners can understand as progress, making it seem a good place to lend money and take holidays. But individual Hungarians are rightly more sceptical.

We had gathered in someone's apartment for their children's English class, at which Elizabeth was to be guest of honour. The children and their teacher had the living room, while we parents crammed ourselves in the kitchen, sitting on the table and the rubbish bin. It was a nice moment which in a small way makes a distinction between the people of an East Bloc country and ourselves. Collecting Elizabeth from a party in Britain I've never sat with other parents and talked seriously about the world. Our conversations have always been about small, immediate things and I cannot imagine that the prospect of discussing the condition of Britain with a foreign stranger would be greeted with anything but fear; fear of exposing our own ignorance, or of being taken for a serious person. Perhaps I am lucky these hospitable Hungarian people are making an effort for me without warning. But it is also the way they understand their jobs – we have several teachers, an economist and a film director among us. They feel obliged to keep abreast of the national situation and to speak.

They begin to explain. 'We are politically dependent, we rely on another Soviet-bloc country – Czechoslovakia – for 90 per cent of our gas – under those subordinate conditions how can our prosperity, as they call it, seem anything but tenuous?' declared the economist. 'No one knows how far the reforms will go, the limits have not been fixed, they'll only be felt once they've been transgressed.' Another man says: 'You can give company shares to employees, but is it real if their total value represents only a very small fraction of the economy? You can sanction individual enterprise by allowing people to do private overtime at their work place, but does that weaken the strength of communism as a system of political control and as a Russian imperial tool?' I remember the English girls have been quite impressed by the shares for workers programme, but all I can find here is scepticism.

The government reply to scepticism is to ask Hungarians to look around. They can surely see that they're relatively well off. At least Hungarians have plenty of food and good international credit, unlike the Poles. At least they don't have dissidents who have to be tried and imprisoned and who give the government a bad name. At least it is not as difficult, unless one *is* a dissident, to travel in Eastern Europe, and, for those who can afford it and get the right invitations, to go to the West. Hungarian literature and music are not hemmed in by the crude application of prescriptive socialist realism as they were in the years immediately before '56. There is a serious housing shortage in Budapest, but perhaps it is not as bad as in East Berlin.

The trouble with this kind of relativism is that it does not answer grievances. It leaves a kind of void, in which judgement becomes impossible, because there are no absolute standards by which to orient oneself. Comparisons are odious because by means of them any complaint may be made to look unfounded. They may also be used to teach. In 1968 when Czechoslovakia rebelled against Soviet domination, Hungarian troops were sent in as part of the Warsaw pact invasion force, a useful reminder of the lesson of '56, lest it be really forgotten.

So Hungary remains uncertain where the extent of domestic freedom ends and where Russian control begins and therein lies the power of the government. Because of '56, and because of the crushing of Solidarity in Poland, Hungarian people are cowed and dispirited. What it is to live in Hungary today hardly anyone can say, other than that he has food, and a roof over his head, and is more or less happy in himself.

The country Hungary would most like to be is Austria, a case of idealizing an older brother. Their cultures have been close for over two centuries. Austria was a senior partner in power, a setter of fashions, a source of wealth and prestige. Once an empire it now flourishes as an independent, neutral, Western, capitalist country. I heard several Hungarians curse the post-war settlement at Yalta between Roosevelt, Stalin and Churchill, which set them so fiercely in the East Bloc. The declaration Imre was typing out the night I visited him at home was on the Treaty's injustice. The fortieth anniversary of the post-war settlement was approaching.

I was surprised. The Hungarians do not feel they have much in common with their East Bloc fellows. Coexistence under a similarly imposed political system does not necessarily encourage solidarity. Though they take their holidays in Romania, a beautiful land they once half-owned, they bear the Romanians a huge grudge for that reason. Romania acquired Transylvania after the First World War and has always regarded itself as the rightful owner of territory on which Dacio-Roman culture has flourished since before Christ. Hungary has a different account to offer of Transylvania's history, based upon the argument that the Dacian culture died out early on. Hungary accuses Romania of persecuting ethnic Hungarians within its present borders. Dissident opinion is close to the official viewpoint on this sole, very important national cause. It is worth noting because Transylvania is the only issue which makes Hungary think of itself with pride and a sharp sense of injustice.

Hungarian opinions vary on the Czechs and Slovaks. Territory has also been ceded to Slovakia this century. More Hungarians are capable of loving the Poles, to whom Hungary once gave a good king. They love them for their bravery at the same time as they now patronize them for their apparent political naivety. In 1985, with Poland two years out of martial law, and riven with suppressed conflict, Hungarians are tempted to say we told you so. The relationship between Poland and Hungary particularly shows up the weary, middle-aged, disillusioned, unromantic nature of the Hungarian compromise.

Inevitably those words bring me to our hosts. They lead a quiet, publicly narrow life, shunning newspapers, going now and then to a concert, enjoying a glass of good wine on Sunday and a walk in the country. Imre, who began as a good communist, calls them relics of the old Christian middle class. Overnight communism transformed their lives, forcing them, like the Czartoryskis in eighteenth-century Poland, into spiritual exile at home. Zoltan, who lost two brothers in the Revolution of '56, can see nothing more likely ahead than a third world war to restore old borders. He reads Maxim Gorky and accepts Gorky's view of Russians as a race of congenital liars. Their disease has spread, he maintains bitterly. I ask for a newspaper, so I can see what's happening in Budapest. 'All lies!' he says in German, shaking his head. He doesn't keep one in the house. Instead we look at his photographs, of holidays spent in Romania and that part of Czechoslovakia which used to be Hungarian, near where he was born.

What is at stake, I feel from talking to Imre and Zoltan, is possession. It is necessary to a sense of individual well-being on the part of human beings and even mature nations to feel joy and pride in the possession of an integral self. Such possession is neither bourgeois narrowness, nor covetousness, nor indeed egoism. As a form of self-preservation it may manifest itself sometimes as aggressive, but that does not make it wrong or unnecessary.

Freud criticized the communist drive against private property, against the family and against the nation. Fifty years on we know he was right to argue that those social and political ideals were untenable, because all three have dried up inside the shell of what is still called 'communism'. He could see why. They failed in Central Europe because of the prevalent 'narcissism of small differences', a cultural phenomenon communism has not only failed to suppress but which it has also failed to exploit. As anyone who wanders about East Europe knows, and as all my journeys confirmed, racial and national prejudice is rife and the enforced communist fraternity by contrast is hardly given a thought.

This is Freud writing in *Civilization and Its Discontents*:

> A scientific critique of the communist system is not my business, I cannot investigate whether the abolition of private property is advantageous and serves its goal. But I know the psychological assumption behind it to be a boundless illusion. To abolish private property is to deprive man's aggressive appetite of one of its instruments, certainly a strong one and certainly not the strongest. In the differences between power and influence, which aggression misuses for its own ends, nothing has been changed either. It is not created by property, it reigned virtually unfettered in the earliest times, when property was still poor, and it reveals itself even in the nursery . . .
>
> It appears that human beings do not find it easy to renounce satisfaction of their aggressive leaning; they don't feel comfortable if they do. The advantage of a smaller cultural circle, which gives this drive a way out in hostility towards outsiders is not to be underestimated. It is always possible to bind together a greater number of people in love, as long as there are others left for the expression of aggression. I once worked on the phenomenon of how neighbouring and otherwise closely linked communities mutually curse and deride each other, as do the Spanish and the Portuguese, North and South Germans, the English and the Scottish, and so on. I gave it the name of 'the narcissism of small differences', which does not really explain it. But one recognizes in it an easy and relatively harmless gratification of the aggressive leaning, which makes it easier for members of a community to cohere . . . It was no unintelligible coincidence that the dream of Germanic world domination summoned up anti-Semitism for its completion, and it is conceivable that the attempt to build a new communist culture

in Russia finds psychological support in the persecution of the bourgeoisie.

Yet there *is* a form of possession communism has successfully suppressed in many cases and that is self-possession, the integrity of the personality and the nation, the value the personality might otherwise attach to representing its inner drives authentically in the public world. Here in Hungary for instance an enforced life of double values over forty years has been immensely destructive of personal and national well-being. It is what both Imre and Zoltan rebel against. Deprived self-possession is exactly the nature of the malaise in the East European countries.

There was a message of tortured intellectual vitality in some difficult, cerebral music I went to hear at the Budapest opera. A young composer, Attila Bozay, had written an uneasy work about love, exploring the tension between spirit and flesh. The opera, *Csongor and Tünde*, was unquestionably serious and obsessed with the problem of self-deception. The subject was woven round the love of an earthly man and a fairy, the substance of an epic poem by the nineteenth-century national poet Mikhaly Vörösmarty. Both the music and the production were overtly sexual, though the music seemed to flinch from the power of the emotions it portrayed. The couple came together after a series of ordeals and spiritual trials, which involved Tünde finally renouncing her fairy existence.

Though visually the production was painful – it was like seeing Hans Werner Henze performed in the costumes of *Babes in the Wood* – the subject was high-mindedly conceived and substantial, a far cry from the banalities of dialectical materialism and Pavlovian psychology. It was too much for the rudely inattentive audience in the highly restored, massively gilded neo-Renaissance opera house with its inexplicably nasty red and grey plastic seats. The mostly middle-aged public wearing evening dress in dated, inelegant styles took the occasion to stand about before mirrors. The young present were too young, running about, being social. Two minutes before the climactic Richard Straussian end people began rushing out as if they had last buses to catch, not a real need at 10 p.m. in municipal Budapest.

Those who remained broke into ritual applause. I had the sense of alienated public behaviour, of dues having being paid, and not much felt or enjoyed, and I went home sadly.

I talked to Zoltan about my exaggerated reactions. I felt personally offended, as if I had been forced to witness blasphemy. You could exploit a public like that, I said. As long as they can't understand it, and it has a national connection, they'll support it. Out loud, with evident relish, he began to recall the Party people he knew, the kind we guessed had made up most of the audience. All their politics were only for gain, he said, and when they retired they threw their Party cards in the fire. There was, I realized, this lovely aggressive pride in large differences which ran in Zoltan's veins and helped him survive.

Why do I come? In search of self-justification? Certainly in the East Bloc there is instant moral virtue in standing 'outside'. But I have to ask myself if I would be a 'dissident' if I lived here, one of those who is 'outside' by virtue of his personality and beliefs, who cannot bear the self-alienation imposed upon him by a prohibitive, spiritless official system and is finally driven to make his position explicit. I doubt my courage, though I had the feeling in Moscow I would have been taken away anyway, as it were for the look on my face and my failure to say the right thing. So again, if I imagine myself transplanted to a totalitarian society I see it would be impossible to avoid politics. Merely to have a personality would be a negative factor in the state's eyes. Or would they see it as an opportunity lost? Imre is one of the few who does set some store by socialism in an untarnished form. He was a zealous communist as a young man, brought up in an active communist family after the war, before disillusion with a system which did not live up to its proclaimed ideals set in. I too, with my capacity for idealism, can imagine being regarded by the Party as a lost sheep.

That is why so much impresses me about intellectual dedication here and why I love meeting those like Imre who have something large and valuable beyond their own enlightenment and profit to work towards. I can't emulate them but they remind me of what I loved about nineteenth-century Russia.

Before I came to Eastern Europe I knew the history but had never before felt the reality of the nineteenth-century Russian *kruzhki*, the little bands of men united by their intellectual and moral dedication and their position outside the mainstream. In fact there's no better instance in the world of the marriage of politics and poetry. The literary imagination and the way of life of each *kruzhok* member was in those days deeply affected by the causes of freedom of speech and social equality, and involuntarily the *kruzhok* is the institution I refer to in my head when I see Hungarian intellectuals today. Imre and his colleagues painstakingly record the subtle facts of censorship and the vagaries of daily life in the face of all too rounded, Panglossian official claims.

As in Russia and Poland, defence against obfuscation is vital where Hungarian history is concerned. Hungary fought on the German side during the war, but it rose up against the post-war Russian occupation in the autumn of 1956. Most Hungarians know by heart the course of those eleven exalted, terrible days in late October and early November, from high hopes to bitter disillusion, in which the Russians were defeated and actually began to withdraw from Hungary. Thousands died in the fighting and 2,000 were hanged afterwards. The personal memories are legion. The role of the intellectuals was also crucial in the early days of the rebellion, so they have another plaintive reason not to let the memory die.

Today the authorities barely concede that 1956 happened. My guidebook to Budapest, from the state publishing house Corvina, gives it one line and the belittling designation: counter-revolution. During my stay an exhibition in Buda was in progress to mark forty years since the expulsion of Nazi German forces by the Red Army. But this history of the city, in a museum which called itself national and historical, omitted the most important event of the post-war era and the exhibition was justifiably empty.

One feels a ferocious impatience in the face of such muted dishonesty. I had the same feeling some months after my return from Hungary, when I had time to investigate the Hungarian position on Freud. There was a well-publicized interview in an English-language Hungarian cultural journal with the leading Hungarian Freudian, Imre Hermann, which made clear Hungary was very proud of its connection with Freud (via his colleague Sandor Ferenczi and the early popularity of analysis in Hungary) and regarded him as a natural son. What was unacceptable under communism was his espousal of aggression as an independent human drive. So here was Hermannn offering a suitable reinterpretation, arguing that aggression only arose from unnatural deprivation, the implication being that if society were better, human beings would not need to be aggressive. This seemed to me to miss Freud's positive life-preserving meaning entirely and indeed to contradict it fundamentally. But on the other hand it was also a kind of subtle, ambiguous manoeuvre to show the world that at least in this communist corner the ideas of Freud were still being debated actively. Hungarian psychology was constrained but still alive. Its practitioners were half-free to voice their thoughts and reveal their interests. I noticed too that Freud was available in German in the bookshops, in an edition 'for the Socialist countries' but a *bona fide* selection nevertheless.

But one feels rage at the very need to dissemble and spin webs of half-truths like this. Communism being an intellectually-conceived movement, the threat it presents comes from the potential inscrutability of deep falsehood; words dressed up to disguise their real import. This passion to undress masked words is what Brandys and Mrozek feel about Poland, why the Solidarity supporters contrast their red newsprint with the black and white of the official media, why Zoltan won't have newspapers in the house and why another friend of mine in Budapest, Johannes, having published books abroad critical of Hungarian society, is without a real job. Now I understand more of my disappointment at *Csongor and Tünde*. The relationship of art to occasion I witnessed at the opera was in fact a model of the relationship which exists here between life and government. It's comic, it's fake, but in the end it is also overwhelmingly spiritually flattening. The potential inscrutability of communist words and gestures calls out for dissection and I admire all forms of intelligent protest against it. In Johannes' case I feel enormous respect for his makeshift life, which is only hard to accept because it's a form of martyrdom.

What I admire about these intellectual protesters is their boldness. Generally in the East Bloc the issues of freedom and duty and truth are faced more directly and with less intellectual convolution than they have been in the past forty years in the West. We find these concepts problematic precisely because they have become only concepts, no longer central to our lives and writing, and because we have elaborate ways of deconstructing and bypassing them, whereas in the East Bloc the same ideas are experienced in daily life. Life seems to exclude them; their absence is palpable, so they must be kept alive in thought, and the very fact they must be thought about is a voluntary moral act as well as a political necessity. A thought, as in Russia, makes a life.

In this sense Johannes has a job for a lifetime. He lives with his dog in a vast, light, book-lined top floor apartment he has designed and restored himself. He loves Russian literature and opera and, to a background of Haydn the morning I visited him, we fell easily into talking about Russia as a most powerful culture. We could talk this way knowing neither of us meant armies or warheads, but Dostoevsky and Mussorgsky. Coming from opposite ends of Europe we admired, envied, perhaps also feared the Russian intellectual tradition for its strength.

In the end though, as if looking for a bridge for our better understanding, we came round to talking about a Polish novelist writing in English, Joseph Conrad. *Under Western Eyes* is a marvellous depiction of some of the murkier byways of Russian power and some men's fanaticism and violence, and of how incomprehensible both the conservative and the radical Russian political mentality of the late nineteenth century – the consequences of which we are still living with in Eastern Europe – are, in essence, to a quiet, apolitical Western liberal. Such a liberal, Conrad's narrator, suitably ascribed the profession of teacher of Latin, is vulnerable, just as all of us outside Eastern Europe are in the face of a political ruthlessness we don't readily understand.

After a week here talking to men committed to live by their intellectual conscience I ask: is it a fantastic dream to think that one might, in coming to Eastern Europe, make up a little for what Western literary awareness has lost in potency, without losing sophistication? Is that dream not one potent reason too why Conrad is such an esteemed writer in the contemporary West? And finally, should that dream not be made explicit for what it says about our pent-up literary energies?

Zoltan and I used to watch the television news together. The interim

Soviet leader Konstantin Chernenko had just died and it looked likely in March 1985 that he would be succeeded by the apparently Western-oriented and reform-minded Mikhail Gorbachev. That prospect was welcome in Budapest, if only because of widespread fear of what might happen when Janos Kadar, the man the Russians set in power on 4 November 1956, stepped down. Zoltan said the possibility of a neo-Stalinist beast taking power in Hungary depended on the climate in Moscow. For his own part he was frightened by a political speech made a few weeks previously by the then Budapest Party leader Georgi Grosz. It had glorified the role of the Hungarian government in its suppression of '56.

I write now in retrospect: I couldn't help recalling his fear when, in May 1988, Grosz succeeded Kadar and what appeared to be a wave of irreversible liberal reforms began to sweep Hungary, encouraged by the onset of the Gorbachev era in Russia. My new-found political instincts make me highly sceptical and probably insufficiently hopeful. It may also be that I was more inspired by Hungary's suffering aspect than by that part of it which was so eager to join the West. I think now, perversely, that if the East Bloc dissolves, humanity will have gained much in terms of freedom, and I will be happy for all my friends; but we in the West will have lost a valuable focus for our aspirations and a source of self-criticism.

5

From the Danube Station
The Banat 1985

Not all obstacles to happiness are political, of course. It depends on which initial path one takes in life, the literary or the revolutionary – a sociologist friend once suggested to me these were the two possible attitudes when one was a teenager – depending on what first appears the greater bane, dislocated personality or unjust society. To echo the title of a long, nowadays unread novel by the Russian socialist Alexander Herzen, one casts about in early adult life, not quite knowing *Who is to Blame?* or what. It's only when the literary and the revolutionary gradually become less exclusive points of view that one hungers to understand simply what is.

In my early life I did not suspect any obstacles to happiness were political. I remember as a teenager in Munich not only my sorties with Viktor to discuss existentialism but also a series of meetings with Mattei, the son of an exiled Russian Orthodox priest. Mattei was a rebellious figure who seemed very strange to me with his wild, uncut dark hair, his large quasi-Mongolian features and the impressive way his huge lips enunciated words in Russian, German and English. His bearded father, who under a mass of black cloth hid the traditional embonpoint of the Russian church, seemed much quieter and more retiring though I guessed in essence he wasn't. The priest's wife, Mattei's mother, appeared calm and generous and welcoming; in some way she was probably suffering.

I was already a great devotee of the problems of art and personality. I had behind me a love affair with a married man in Germany, who was, as they say, twice my age. It had been a traumatic time, but one for which I was grateful, for without the insight to be gleaned from both secret and realized passion I doubted I would ever have understood literature. The anno domini of my feeling for and dependence on literature coincided with finding myself, to my own astonishment and confusion, in love, and this was very much my emotional baggage for some years afterwards and was probably heightened by returning to Germany.

Mattei, who was only a few years older than me, would send me Constructionist postcards across the city of Munich reminding me that the problem of unhappiness lay with inadequate social conditions. Invoking Pasternak I argued my point of view in what I hoped was a disguised, general way. There might have been another way of representing my thoughts, but in those days I would never have allowed myself to confide in someone who apparently took an opposite view of life. I said nothing about myself.

With more information of the social documentary kind I suppose Mattei would have seen me as a natural outsider, coming from an unintellectual but well-intentioned family where my father was particularly keen on the benefits of freely available state education. I would resemble the classless *raznochintsy* of the Russian nineteenth century, men who like Mattei himself were the sons of priests or teachers; men who bore the burden of education as a new, unexpected blessing and as a source of torment for the separateness it caused; men who fought for change in a world which barely had a place for them. But these were activists – or to use the 'writing' word, publicists – and even if it described Mattei's view of himself I was far from that.

In fact in Mattei's eyes I was probably decadent. I didn't, unlike him, aspire to socialist or communist goals and I didn't feel unambiguously indebted to a society which I felt, while I was still at school, was trying to force my modest talents into a conventional mould, stratifying individuals only to homogenize them within their stratum. I wanted to work hard, but my industry was neither a commendation of society or of myself. I just happened to be made that way, which is to say I was always more concerned with answering to myself and setting my own standards. Like the nineteenth-century Russian social democrats Mattei was adamant about the sanctity of work, any work, as a means of social contribution and economic honour, but I couldn't follow his example. When I was down to my last three Deutschmarks he gave me the address of a place where I could go and label envelopes or fold boxes, the advantage being that the hours were flexible and the pay regular. But I preferred to make my way as an adventuress, dodging from job to job: looking after children, selling records, being a waitress, but never with anything secure ahead. 'You must ring them up and tell them you're not coming, so that they can give the job to someone else,' he said disappointedly. I'm afraid I didn't and I hardly saw Mattei, a rare personal encounter with theoretical socialism in one person, again.

I sank back into literature and also into a very unsuitable affair with far less a person than Mattei, but which I didn't have the strength to abandon. I learned to drink wine too, for this, at nineteen, was Europe! The affair I viewed as an endurance test, the price of not being lonely and vulnerable; the price of the flesh. I thought: 'There is such a thing as an efficient material life, but I don't think I'm part of it and one day I'll be strong enough to say so.' I read an early Russian socialist novel, *What is to be done?*, by Nikolai Chernyshevsky, about the efforts of a rational couple to organize a marriage which would leave them free to give their best to work and society. That the marriage failed and the woman fell in love elsewhere seemed quite appropriate.

But my dearest book was Theodor Fontane's novel of adultery, *Effi Briest*. It illustrates in the first instance the unfairness and intolerance of Prussian society at the end of the nineteenth century. The girl Effi is married while still a child to a much older man. Later she has a trivial affair. Her husband understands but society will not let him forgive the dishonour, so he casts her out of the house with her child and she dies in penury. I learnt nothing about how to be a good woman in society from this reading, but I felt with Effi in her few days of happiness and have gone on sympathizing with passion as the key to a real existence, if not necessarily a productive one.

1985. We had been three weeks in Italy, relaxing. The drive from England, meandering through France and Switzerland, crossing borders with a minimum of formality, was one of the pleasantest I remembered and everything combined to make the forthcoming journey East a wrench. We left the car in Como and at the railway station I felt close to tears. 'I'd like one and a child return to Timişoara in Romania, please.' 'Romagna? Some place in Emilia Romagna?' The official began searching in his directory. Some confusion was caused by my pronunciation of Romania but we finally got underway.

The twenty-four hours to Belgrade, with changes in Milan and Venice, passed relatively smoothly. It was still light when we sidled close to the Adriatic at Trieste, where gypsy women got on the train with small children to beg. Bedtime brought a babble of petty needs in various languages. We began to improvise because the steward spoke only Serbo-Croat and I discovered my travelling companion was mute; actually he was monolingually French, rather shy about it and very nice when he overcame his shyness and talked about life in Marseilles.

When we awoke we were moving steadily over the endless yellow Pannonian plain. The shimmering golden carpet was daubed with tiny patches of colour from workers' overalls. We longed for the good unsweetened black coffee which was already far behind us. Two hours later the white skyscrapers of New Belgrade looked startlingly pure in the sun, as if they were merely the model for some future city.

The older part of Belgrade where we spent the rest of the day was busy, spacious, much lived in, relaxed. We bought provisions of sausage, yoghurt, bread and tomato in a dreary supermarket where no one would believe we were English, then watched the schoolchildren in the park playing volleyball, and the old men playing boulevard chess. The art gallery had an exhibition of Braque, for which there was not enough time. A central bookshop featured in its window Joyce and Moravia, and the translated novels of one of today's best-known Czech novelists either side of the divide, Milan Kundera. His presence was particularly striking. Kundera, a fierce critic of Soviet communist society, would not be tolerated officially anywhere *inside* the Bloc. But here it was even possible to buy a book on the Czech human rights movement, Charter 77. We were returning to Eastern Europe only very gradually.

'We have democracy. What's wrong with us is the economy: inflation, 100 per cent price increases since last year, the same the year before. What we need is more private enterprise,' said the Yugoslav taxi driver, proud of being self-employed. He told me the story of how he had trained as a locksmith and done lucrative stints in West

Germany as a *Gastarbeiter*. His German was still bad. What did I want to go to Timişoara for? 'We have democracy, but Romania is bad. That's Russia.' He puzzled, sighed, and finally began to whistle.

I wasn't consciously seeking immersion in hardship this time, nor certainly political enlightenment. The idea for the journey came to me on a walk across the Buda hills where the kiosks were selling warming tea with rum and spiced wine. My German lover from my student days used to drink *Tee mit Rum*. (They drink it in the Gong Tea Room in Warsaw too, where I had also remembered him, fleetingly, with less ambition than now.) Klaus was a Schwabian who, though he lived in the green, rolling country south of Stuttgart, had been born in the Banat, in modern Romania.

The Schwabenland in Germany is the scenic, rural, fertile country which produced the great dialectical minds of the late eighteenth and early nineteenth century, the philosophers Hegel and Schelling and the poet Hölderlin. Since Marx was so affected by these minds you could see it as the environment he had to shrug off to make his own mark upon life. The Schwabian summers are long and hot and many of the villages and towns are called by names ending in *–ingen*. Schwabians soften and slur their German, so that their spoken language sounds a world away from *Hochdeutsch*.

No doubt the stiffened tea helped Klaus get through our many discussions of German Romantic literature. He had a particular passion for the poet Lenau which I would always remember. But what made the greatest impression on me was his own life story. Klaus was a farmer's son drafted into the Romanian army around 1942, when he was eighteen. He was shot in combat with the Russians almost immediately and spent the rest of the war in a prison camp, where he immersed himself in the German classics. He had briefly died of his wounds and he claimed the experience ever after intensified his pleasure in living, though it pronounced his fondness for solitude. When the hostilities ended he fled to Germany, where he married, and became a successful architect. I liked to think of him embodying the post-war economic miracle. In a few years his money sufficed to buy his parents out of the communist Banat in old age and bring them to Germany. Where had they come from? I had always wondered about Klaus's birthplace, which I pictured quite wrongly as mountainous. In those days I had never heard of the Banat.

We set off for the capital of the western province of Timiş on the only train of the day. All services from Belgrade to Romania leave from the Danube Station, a ten-minute bus ride from the centre. It was a terminus with a country air, not the sort of station where people amuse themselves with paperback books or newspapers, or bring out work from their briefcases. We sat under a sun umbrella on a level with the platform, drinking coffee, and watching the occasional horse and cart roll up. When the train came in there was a great deal of toing and froing with sacks of vegetables and baskets of eggs.

The journey over a mere 150 km of plain was scheduled to take four and a half hours. By now I was becoming an experienced East European traveller and had remembered to bring food and a plastic bottle for water. We sat with an elderly Romanian woman, travelling home to Cluj with her granddaughter. This dark, pretty girl, handsomely equipped with all an affluent Western child's unnecessary paraphernalia, had left her mother in Italy and was still crying when we boarded the train. She went to school in Padua and acted as my interpreter all the way to our Romanian destination. A young man, speaking Romanian when he had to, sat with us. His presence gave off heat and took up space, otherwise it hardly impinged. But an unvoiced feeling amongst us all on that hot June day declared there was no room for anyone else.

Then the Serbian family came: beautiful, tall, shapely, sensual women, with brown skin, black hair, dark eyes, swollen bellies and high cheekbones. The younger one, in her late thirties, had delicate silver studs on her nose, while her mother, still lightly built, wore a headscarf, a dark blue skirt and a pale blue shirt with the sleeves rolled up, under a tight, sleeveless black pullover. Her husband had none of this grace. Gradually they invaded the compartment. First the children sat down: the younger woman's greasy-skinned teenage daughter, an unkempt, animated creature with long brown hair and fashion jeans with many odd pockets, then the tall, thin youth with a black moustache, all in denim, who was her husband. They held each other's thighs and joked and asked for my address and whether they could get work in London. When the young man got out with much

81

kissing at a station still in Yugoslavia that was the signal for the rest of the family to pile in. The older husband instantly offered himself to me in lieu of my apparently missing mate.

The crisis came as we prepared for the frontier. I had wondered why such a short journey on the map should take so long. We took more than two hours to clear customs, in the midst of which Elizabeth wrapped her arms round the Italian girl and declared she wanted to lie down with her 'like a man'. (In English this, fortunately.) The older Serbian woman unloaded some debased East European chocolate from her bag and thrust it into mine. Next came two cartons of Dunhill cigarettes. The younger woman contributed another carton. Her mother pulled out a wad of dinars from her brassiere and pointed at my handbag. I stashed it all away hopefully and with that absurd feeling of specialness which comes from being party to a secret about to be put to the test. It crossed my mind that the Romanian grandmother might betray me.

On the Yugoslav side of the border they routinely checked our papers. There was a pause, then a cleaner came on the train and swept up the dogends. 'They think the Serbs are dirty,' said another young man, part of the family. 'They come in to disinfect.' Ah, so Romania stands for *Ordnung*, I thought, realizing I too thought these particular Serbs messy. The brisk Romanian officials had a purgatorial air about them as they opened every suitcase. 'You're all hiding something, come on now, undo the bag.' Customs officers, like taxi drivers, are proud of not having been born yesterday. They spoke in blustering, impatient voices. The Serbian woman was told she would have to pay tax on her chocolate and began to sulk. A young man in overalls asked us to get out while he lifted up the bench seats. Another unscrewed ceiling panels to check the hollow compartments under the roof.

The threat posed by contraband was probably the least serious. Markets at which Yugoslavs and Romanians exchange goods thrive on the Romanian side of the border. As for stowaways, one doubted there were many going into Romania. Drug smuggling was the real problem. They didn't find anything in our carriage that day.

I was treated with an excess of politeness. Would I mind standing outside with my little girl for a moment? Did I perhaps have pistols or porno in my luggage? By trying hard to confirm the impression I came from civilization I managed to hang on to the Dunhills. My carrier bag was the last bag, the only bag unsearched. 'Food,' I said, looking tenderly at Elizabeth, who might conceivably depend on me to provide. The blustering guard waved a hand.

The wooden train was retired from international stock and still had its 'Don't lean out' signs in Romanian, French, Italian, German and Russian. At last it began to move again. The older woman continued to sulk. Her husband said that ten years ago the border was virtually open. People like them, who had family in Romania, could come and go without passports. The ordeal and the anger made everyone hungry. The younger woman unwrapped a huge roll of sausage, with tomatoes and bread, and then begged from me a plastic aeroplane knife she had seen me use. Her kinfolk fell upon their food. The younger woman fixed her eyes on my water bottle. 'Ne mala voda?' As in Russian 'little water' meant vodka, I guessed, but no, it wasn't that, just ordinary water. She took several swigs. I gave them the knife. When I got off leaving the plastic water bottle behind they took that too.

In East Europe international travelling instantly becomes an experience of conflict, a near existential catastrophe, as you submit to border searches and questions of identity and intent. I knew why I hadn't wanted to leave Italy.

The train slowed. Everyone shook my hand. 'We're grateful, Madame,' they said, in some language or other, as they made sure they got everything back, except the stick of nasty chocolate. The husband picked up two of my bags and shuffled behind me as we waited to get off in the darkness of Timişoara station. 'You're not afraid?' he breathed down the back of my neck. Oh, yes, sir, yes, but mainly of the dark and the possibility that you may think my luggage is also disposable. His family, saying they wanted to help, were gone in a flash and mercifully he followed. Alone, safe, and with all our possessions, I looked for a taxi.

Timişoara is a city of 125,000 inhabitants. It is the capital of the province of Timiş with roots going back eight hundred years. Of its more recent historical claims to fame, the original Tarzan, Johnny Weismueller, was born there, and it was the first town in Europe to have electric street lighting, in 1864. The latter fact is widely advertised as a tourist attraction. The next point defies subtlety. In 1985 not a single light was on outside Timişoara central railway station at midnight. Nor did a single taxi wait. In the gloom small groups of men loitered, with private cars, demanding large quantities of lei for what might or might not turn out to be a ride into town, all of 2 km. They surged towards us and fell away again, once, twice, like a dream. The third time I nearly yielded. But no sign, no meter, no papers, no common language, only much wanted dollars in my bag. We felt our way nervously to the tram stop, where I talked to anyone who would listen about the need for a HOTEL ... Why, there was one across the street, only in the darkness it was invisible. It had no illuminated sign and only a small door. But inside, at the end of a long, yellowwallpapered corridor without pictures, was a man behind a desk, open for business, who spoke most charming French. '*Ça va aller?*' I said, hoping my words would have the same effect on him as his very existence had on me, and happily they did.

This wasn't a hotel for foreigners but because of the artificial exchange rate prices were still very high for a gloomy, mediocre room with plywood furniture and a silent television. We slept top to tail in a single bed to economize. Next morning when I turned on the tap to wash there was no water. I caught Romania at a bad moment, after an unusually severe winter resulting in an acute energy shortage. But something else called economic mismanagement had been biting visibly into Romanian life for the past three years. Huge sacrifices were being demanded of every man and woman to pay off interest on the national debt.

Setting foot outside I hoped I would be able to speak German to get about. Germans have been settling in Transylvania, of which the Banat is part, in a series of migrations since the Middle Ages, and, because they are skilled and hardworking, they have always been welcome. 'Their dialect is very corrupt,' said a Romanian lawyer scathingly as we downed a late breakfast of fried eggs and presweetened tea. How curious that we'd come to see the Germans. Still, he would have a word with his friend the manager to make sure we were all right over the next few days. I looked like a good girl.

'*Zum Zentrum? La centre de la ville? Il centro?*' Won't anyone respond?

People in the wide street with its traffic of trams and buses seem quiet and tired, dressed in cheap synthetic fabrics either drab or garishly-coloured. We made it to the centre though, accidentally without a ticket, and found a spacious, airy, unhurried oriental-looking town. Before the Austrians came in the early nineteenth century the Banat was Turkish and the population of the Banat area, including the Western Carpathian mountains, is still very mixed, comprising ethnic Germans, Romanians, Hungarians, Austrians, Szeklers (a tribe of Hungarian descent), Jews, Serbs, and many smaller communities. The architecture is similarly mixed. Two fine squares of pastel-coloured neo-classical buildings, no doubt from the Austrian days, were on the verge of decay when we inspected them close up. Here and in other side streets most of the traffic consisted of horses and carts. There were German bookshops with a dull and heavy political stock, and a German theatre. We bought an ice-cream but austerity had made the cone so thin it wasted away in our hands. Next stop was a beer garden, where the waiter brought sweet syrup in water for Elizabeth and offered to change my money. 'Come to my car at four o'clock. We sit inside and exchange notes. No one ask questions.' The rate was good. Sixty lei to the pound sterling instead of sixteen, but I didn't like the system.

Timişoara is full of green spaces, especially along the length of the canal. We were walking there wearily after lunch, taking a shady path away from the sun. Too late I realized this was a haven for the sexually homeless, but the face-saving thing was to carry on, hoping Elizabeth wouldn't cast her eyes too widely about her. We walked a bit faster and two nice girls who spoke French told us the way to the open-air swimming pool.

The pool is quiet except for a few foreign students. While I swim an agriculturalist from Senegal counts the lengths and a Lebanese doctor more subtly encourages Elizabeth. In exquisite French the agriculturalist then tells me the story of his life and wonders whether I would like to write it up as a novel. He could call in on me in London and see how it was coming along. This was alarmingly quick off the mark. Samy from Lebanon whispered in my ear to beware of Africans and offered to be my bodyguard. The African, who had a friend with him and sensed competition, retaliated by hanging round the changing room. 'Palestinian terrorists,' he whispered in his turn. 'You recall the bomb in Bucharest just a few weeks ago? Well then. The Romanian security police have their eye on Arabs. You don't want to be associated with them.'

I suggested a drink all together that evening. No one was keen, but everyone turned up. They sat in a silent row on a bench outside the hotel room and waited for me to emerge. I was delayed because there had been a flood. The tap which had been dry had suddenly spouted forth in the middle of the day and the drain in our basin couldn't cope with the flow. The French-speaking receptionist looked irritated but I gathered these disasters were common during the hot water shortage. Eventually I did emerge and surveyed my consorts. 'Oh well, if you're not free,' said the African, tight-lipped, and he and his sidekick walked off. Samy, Elizabeth and I went to an old-fashioned cabaret with acrobats and fire-eaters and girls in G-strings, where we dined off pork and chips in surroundings of mirrors and chandeliers and polished wood. Samy and I danced and the close dancing struck a sensual chord with Elizabeth, who had not seen it before.

The next morning I hauled us out of bed to catch the 6.15 a.m. to Lenauheim. In a brief stop at the tourist office the previous day I had discovered this place name on the map and knew instantly it should be the destination of my pilgrimage. The Schwabian village was about 30 km away and we were taking the only train of the day. It is on the map for visitors because it has a museum devoted to Nikolaus Lenau, who was born there in 1802, the son of an Austrian imperial official. The name Lenau spoke to me because he was Klaus's favourite poet. Otherwise I could hardly have known of this insignificant settlement of 2,000 people, with only a cinema and a supermarket. I set off absurdly excited and pleased to have wangled a packed breakfast. Things had been going well in the hotel, despite the tap incident.

'Do you know what the Bible is?' said an old woman at the station. 'Do you read it?' 'What's the name of your daughter?' 'Elizabeth is a Biblical name. The Bible, you know, is the book of the Christian faith . . .' This woman, who had introduced herself as a Saxon German, looked doubtfully upon my Christian credentials, but showed us with a glad smile to the right train, where thanks to a kindly ticket collector we fell in with a host of potential friends. 'They're English!' he said, throwing open the door, and everyone moved up.

Among them was a man in his late sixties, a retired veterinarian, Doktor Becker, who spoke Romanian, Hungarian and German fluently. I perceived him as a token of the days when the Banat belonged to the Austro-Hungarian Empire and our conversation immediately struck a harmonious chord. We talked about the Banat and the nature of my visit and he was quick to say Hungary would not get this much-desired territory back from Romania, however much it campaigned. He apologized for his German, the dentist had just given him new dentures. Actually it was perfect. He had studied it in Vienna and still spoke German at home with his wife and children. Born before 1918, when the Banat was Hungarian, Dr Becker had worked for an Austrian pharmaceutical company before the war and enjoyed driving fast cars. After the war he trained in veterinary medicine to get a job with the new communist and Romanian State.

'The women want to know what you're doing here,' he said. 'They find it strange you should come alone. Romania is very backward in these matters. A woman belongs to a man. I've told them your interests are literary.' I began to laugh. We talked excitedly as if we were old friends.

'What was his name? Did this Klaus T. ask you to marry him?'

I shrugged evasively and Dr Becker and I passed on to the subject of mad poets, of which Lenau was one.

'Even Goethe was a bit batty,' he said. *Auch Goethe hat manchmal einen Vogel gehabt.*

We turned to the badness of the world. He reflected on the fate of Klaus's parents. 'Ach, fancy selling people like that! This country lives by extortion.' I wondered how much badness there had to be, how many shortages, to make ordinary people want to leave their native country, knowing they might never be allowed to return. The pain can be constant, and still most people won't go. Only the young go, before they create families and put down roots. They go to the Federal Republic of Germany, where as Germans they are guaranteed citizenship, though it is not an easy transition nowadays and stories filter back of their loneliness. When the whole of Europe was in turmoil, when Klaus left and Becker's sister decided to stay in Vienna, it was easier to fit in and start again. Becker himself had no desire to leave now. He was too old and he wanted his immediate family around him most of all. All the same he would have liked to see his sister again, but the authorities kept refusing him a visa.

'But your lives are not all milk and honey over there,' he said matter-of-factly, without pride. News of the Brussels football stadium disaster, in which forty Italians were killed by stampeding English fans, had just filtered through to Romanian newspapers, three weeks late. The item was briefly in his Romanian newspaper that morning and moved him to defend the communist media. 'They try to encourage a philosophical view of current affairs. They try to avoid creating fear by not delivering anything sudden.' Yes, I could see the point of that.

He turned to talk to an elderly woman in the compartment. When she got off his eyes followed her admiringly. 'She's a good woman, that one. I'm so fond of her.' I liked him for liking to gossip. He was better than any newspaper.

The talk was of the social problems caused by the presence of so many African and Arab students in Romania and about the friction among Romania's own numerous nationalities. Dr Becker declared how enviable East Germany was among the East Bloc states for having just one race within its borders. 'We Romanians are well-known racists,' he quipped, but he was serious. He began to plan my next days' trips for me, taking out a huge train timetable and a map. As he did so his briefcase gaped open, full of bread.

Lenauheim has, as I say, 2,000 inhabitants, a supermarket and a cinema. The station consists of a small house, a broken bench and a tree. Dr Becker and I embraced and he helped Elizabeth down from the train. 'What time do you go back?' I called to the friendly ticket inspector in what I hoped was an approximation of Romanian. He smiled and smiled and in the end embraced me too. I felt like a pilgrim.

A strong warm wind blew across the broad dusty street where the rest of the arrivals walked and we followed. At the far end stood a small, neat, well-kept Catholic Church, build in 1783 and dedicated to the incumbent Austrian Empress Maria Theresa. Golden, bungalow-style German houses with ornamental facades and the names of their original owners carved above the door ranged in varying states of decay either side of the road. The Schmidts and the Müllers and the Schneiders were gone, and Romanians, or some said gypsies, had moved in to replace them. But the village was still mainly Schwabian. I called out *Grüss Gott!* to all and sundry, as I had learned to do with Klaus in German Schwabia and received a steady stream of replies. Nevertheless 1,200 Schwabians had emigrated since the war. As Dr Becker had told me in parting, with his kiss: '*Das deutsche Reichtum hier geht unter.*' 'The German Empire here is coming to an end.'

It was not the same as witnessing the flight of the Germans from East to West, or of Poles to Hamburg and Russians to New York. This was a civilization dying out, a chapter of history coming to a visible close. The Schwabians colonized the Banat in the 1770s. A painter named Stefan Jäger depicted their trek in oils and a copy of that painting now hangs in the Lenau museum. More than a tribute to the poet who spent only a few weeks of his early life in the village, that museum, with its sign in German and Romanian, was a memorial to a lost culture.

The original commemorative plaque, in German and Hungarian, had become an exhibit inside the light, two-storey wooden house. It was a charming building, with an open gallery running along the outside of the upper floor, overlooking an orchard. Romanian Pioneers (children in the communist youth organization) were playing there when we arrived, and when they went the house with no other visitors became unnaturally silent. I heard a horse and cart pass and I bent over the tombstone of Magdalene von Niembtsch, Lenau's sister, who died in 1802, the year of his birth. '*Sie blühte kurz und schön,*' it said, 'she blossomed briefly and beautifully.' Because the village itself was a museum and a graveyard, there was double irony in visiting the exhibition. With the sound of more hoofbeats outside the window, the past seemed to be alive outside. The air smelt of camomile and geese wandered everywhere. Most of the water was fetched from standpipes in the street and only two cars passed during our visit.

The Germans are neater and more reticent than the Romanians in the way they live. The German woman who looked after the museum, plump, dressed all in black, was anxious to talk but held herself back. She assumed I was a teacher, or had come to study the local dialect.

Her own German was very pure, despite the prediction of the Romanian lawyer in Timişoara, evidently no sympathizer with the Schwabian community. I mentioned Klaus's family name. 'People of that name used to live in the village of Triebeswetter,' she said. 'We call it today in Romanian Tomnatic.'

In a dream I might have imagined seeing men everywhere with Klaus's dark features, small stature, brown eyes, bronzed skin; men wearing his collarless jacket with the green loden band round the top and buttons to the neck, and plus fours. But the reality was odder. I found a little replica of Klaus instead. He was one of the museum's extensive collection of dolls. For more than two centuries every Schwabian village in the Banat maintained its own distinctive costume and every village from the past is now commemorated with a pair of dolls. The woman set the mechanical dolls dancing for us, to Elizabeth's delight. I considered the waste of Romania's precious electricity and wandered off to look at the mockups of old German interiors, photographs of Banat life and the original plans advising the immigrants how to build their German houses. I suppose I was hurt at what my passion had come to.

But then while Elizabeth and the plump museum keeper went to eat biscuits in a back room I read the extracts from Lenau's works and letters around the walls. A passage from one of his letters had been rightly magnified:

> *Ja, Freund! Ich will leben, arbeiten, handeln; doch ich entscheide für wen und wozu – ich will noch was tüchtiges leisten in der Kunst; ich will arbeiten für die Welt und mich veredeln für meine Freunde.*

(Yes, my friend! I want to live, to work, to play an active part in the world; but I will decide for whom, and to what end – I want to achieve something sound again in art; I want to work for the world and ennoble myself for my friends.)

We left the museum and walked the length of all Lenauheim's remaining streets, peering in the windows of the closed supermarket (opening hours 0700–1100 and 1600–1800). There were eggs, powdered chicory, tinned fruit, preserved vegetables and plain biscuits. Samy had explained that most of the locals grew their own food, kept their own pig, tended their own fruit trees, and the bakery would probably be in a private house. As outsiders it looked as though we would have had to beg to get anything to eat. Fortunately there was enough left over from the packed breakfast as we sat on the seat, by the tree, waiting for the returning train.

The journey back to Timişoara was a disaster. Was I interested in their dialect, said a man in a beret, with gold teeth, whose son had emigrated. He was travelling with his daughter, who had about her the pathos of a young person who had decided to take no risks with her life. She was plain, un-made-up, tall and pale, with a long face and dark hair, and wearing a full-skirted red and white floral dress belted at the waist and black high-heeled sandals. She worked as an agricultural bookkeeper in Lenauheim, she revealed in a very quiet voice. Her father, who described himself as having been in industry, was more extrovert, young for his age, a man who did not find it difficult to smile. He surely had some hold on her, I thought. He talked about the limited opportunities in higher education for those who wanted to study in German. There were German schools, but no German-language university existed. His daughter may have decided to stay in the Banat under the illusion that he needed her to look after him, or he may have convinced her she did not have enough education to go.

A problem loomed. There hadn't been time when we changed trains to buy a second return ticket in advance. A different ticket collector entered, accompanied by a young inspector with a revolver and a truncheon. I explained my case. He snapped. Ninety lei. A fine of £5 for incompetence. The money didn't matter but I wanted to question the fairness of the punishment. He snapped again. He spoke no foreign languages. Someone halfheartedly offered an explanation on my behalf in Romanian. He wasn't interested. I sat bathed in sweat, only just resisting the temptation to tear up his penalty ticket in his face. Inside my head I was still fighting for ground to stand on long after he had gone. My fellow passengers shrugged and lowered their eyes. It was an absurd situation, for the steely-eyed young inspector resembled some model character from an early Soviet novel, or a perfect young Fascist. And what right had I to be shocked that he wasn't interested in communication? When he left, my travelling companions breathed silent kindness, became wellwishers again. But the spirit of the day was ruined.

Provincial Romania was shocking, demanding. To get anywhere in the countryside we had to get up by six and not expect to do anything else with the day. That Friday evening we washed clothes in cold water, Elizabeth slept and I made notes under a feeble light. Samy called but I postponed a rendezvous till the following day. Why had I come to this town where all was hardship?

We packed a great deal into the next day, which was as sunny as the last and when I might have expected everything to look better after ten hours' sleep. The central market had vegetables and herbs and pulses but only very maggoty apples. The souvenir and bric-à-brac stalls sold cheap jewellery Elizabeth pounced on, also cup and jug sets for drinking the national liquor, *ţuica*, and some earthenware pots full of holes. 'Go on, Samy, ask them what they're for. You're the one who wants to buy me a memento.' 'They're for giving chickens a drink of water,' he said soberly.

His English was as exceptional as his kindness. When we failed to buy either fruit or *ţuica* he proposed a tour in the car. We drove a few minutes in a residential area, then he stopped and called out across the gardens. A woman who also kept a pig in the backyard of her bungalow appeared with a huge bag of half-rotten cherries and strawberries. As for the plum brandy, we first asked the basket weavers and the flowerpot sellers, then we stopped a few cars in the road and asked their drivers, then we knocked on half a dozen doors. Eventually two litres of very fine *ţuica* were procured in unmarked bottles from a private cellar beneath a high-rise block of flats.

We could have driven out into the country every day. For me that was the most desirable thing, but our driving was hampered by an acute petrol crisis. 'Anyone spare us 10 litres?' That at least would have made the emergency light go off. We spent the rest of the morning touring the town, looking for friends who might have the precious juice to offer for dollars. Even then, did everyone have a syphon in the boot? I wondered. Despite Romania being a substantial producer of oil, everywhere there were queues of dormant cars unable to proceed on a regime of 27 litres of petrol a month. The line of those waiting driverless outside the main filling station for their day to come tailed back at least a mile. The oil was going into Romania's rundown heavy industry or abroad.

We struck lucky at a café which was a favourite haunt of the Palestinians, who sat stirring Turkish coffees, eating pastries, and arguing over Middle Eastern politics. They had come to Timişoara to study because admission procedures were not too stringent in Romania, which badly needed their fees in hard currency. The town was full of their large foreign cars, like Samy's BMW.

The encounter with the BMW was curious. We had been riding in an almost identical car the week before in Como and there petrol cans had also loomed larger than usual in our daily life because every night at the villa where we were staying thieves came and drained the tank. It's a moot point whether the brochure should have warned us that we were on the front line of the class war. It turned out we were the only villa for miles around without an electric fence and an Alsatian dog. So, think of it! In Italy one white saloon was immobilized because individuals were thieves, and now here was Samy's BMW stationary because the thieving state was exporting all the petrol it could and giving the rest to tourists for hard currency. The temptation arose to shout what price either Europe.

But finally we drove into the country and swam in the river. We drank Romanian Coca-Cola, which smelt like disinfectant, and Romanian beer, which Samy claimed was too light for a man. We played football and ate the ubiquitous pork and chips in our swimming costumes. The secret of Samy's fluency in Romanian was his past marriage to a Romanian girl. He had even converted to Romanian Orthodoxy, out of indifference towards all religion. He liked to see his son as often as he could. He had one more year of a five-year course in Timişoara to complete.

It was relaxing for all of us to spend the afternoon in the sun, but our problems wouldn't go away. There wasn't enough petrol to get back. We stopped in some woods and Samy produced a set of German licence plates. 'We'll have to pretend to be tourists!' 'Watch out,' I said, 'there's someone coming!' A local man wandered over, but he thought we were German tourists already, so we continued operations while he introduced himself. His father was a *Reichsdeutscher* but the connection went back further. The family had come to Romania two hundred years ago, in another German emigration east from Alsace. He spoke five languages and despised the idea of nationality. 'I belong to no one but my family. My wife is Russian, my son-in-law is a Serb, my mother is Hungarian.' We chatted vaguely about grand ideals. I like to think of myself as a European but this man saw Europe not as the free place I did, when I enthused about open borders and the comedy of little linguistic misunderstandings. His Europe was a serial victim of power-seeking. It had a weakness which returned in every generation to ruin ordinary lives. 'What do you think of this country, eh? First Romania had Hitler, then communism. It's all the same. It's all Hitlerism.'

My spirits were sinking very low. Here was the Banat, which consisted of cornfields stretching as far as the eye could see, and vineyards, and pastureland, and there was no bread in its villages and no cheese. In the capital there was just a little pork and sausage. Everything possible was being exported to earn dollars to keep the country afloat. Because of Samy's kindness (he showed me his wardrobe full of lei) I realized rather late that at the official rate the cost of plain food in restaurants (pork and potatoes, chicken livers and rice) was prohibitive.

After securing some more petrol we stopped in a wine village to drink the local red, which was excellent, but then the lights inexplicably went out for an hour. Was there no respite? The shortages were blamed on the draconian domestic regime of President and Communist Party leader Nicolae Ceausescu, who together with various members of his family, after the manner of Napoleon, had headed this Balkan country of 22 million people since 1965. In 1985 the plight of Romania was not sufficiently realized in the West. The Americans still granted Bucharest Most Favoured Nation trading status. Nor was Moscow unhappy. The orderliness of the Romanian people continued to look dependable. Unlike the Poles it seemed they could be made to endure severe conditions without complaint.

Westerners ask why Romanians have been prepared to endure so much in recent years, their worst experiences under communism. The simple answer seems to be to be that Romanian ways are radically different from the political habits of the other East Bloc countries.

*

94

Not quite occupied by the Turks, they nevertheless endured hundreds of years of subservience to them via the rule of despotic hospodars, Phanariot Greeks from Constantinople, who paid the Porte for the privilege and exacted harsh dues on the Romanian populus in return. The Romanian well-to-do learnt to ingratiate themselves with this ruling class and eventually became one with it, swelling the ranks of corruption and exploitation. The pattern today looks similar. Where the Turks left off, Soviet communism has taken over. The hospodars are the Party cadres. If this is a more or less common view, it is nevertheless a dire spectacle for the co-opted neighbourly countries which might otherwise look forward to political emancipation, like Hungary, or back to it in the hope of renewal, like Poland. The rest of dissident Eastern Europe has hastened to separate itself from the problems of Romania, and for slightly different reasons from its Balkan neighbour Bulgaria, because it considers their fundamental situations alien.

Samy, who refused to see anyone downhearted, proposed dinner at a 'charming' restaurant with local specialities, but it was catering for a special function that evening. We had no choice but to repair to the big international hotel in the centre of town. Inside the vast dining room the students were celebrating the end of their examinations. I would have liked a quiet evening but the room was crowded. A Romanian girl with a broad flat nose and an American accent learnt from pop songs joined us with her Palestinian boyfriend. Getting steadily more drunk on Banat Riesling the boyfriend began trying to kiss Elizabeth while Samy kept asking me why I didn't talk. With my finger I traced the filigree pattern of the silver foil dust covers over our empty plates. I had never seen such an object before and focused my attention on it hard when I was not reproaching the student, who did nothing but laugh. Suddenly from a few tables away came the sound of scraping chairs and broken glass. 'A Yugoslav,' said the girl in disgust, 'a Yugoslav causing a drunken rumpus.' The band, in local costume, went on playing Banat gypsy music at deafening volume. 'I've got to leave, Samy, I can't stand it any more.' Of all my trips it was the first time I had cried.

Fascism advocated abandoning the comforts of a 'bourgeois life', which was materially abundant and replete with pleasures, because it was deemed to create soft men and women. There is something in that toughmindedness, if, like self-censorship, it is a free choice. But these East European citizens yoked to communism at its most harsh and materially deprived today do not have any choice about not being 'bourgeois'. Their deprived reality is shocking. All post-war societies East and West have their rightful places between the 'bourgeois' and 'non-bourgeois' extremes. For myself it's where I'm going to aim.

You could tell the foreigners on the station next morning by the neat packs of hotel sandwiches they carried. Recognizing each other, a Swede, two Spaniards and ourselves, we stuck together, fought together for our seats in the train, fought off the demands for lei from the inspectors, and regaled each other with horror stories as we trundled back to Belgrade. The Swede had been elbowed out of a ticket queue by a party member, whereupon he had broken into the 'Star Spangled Banner', to the man's acute embarrassment and the amusement of the entire railway station. The Spanish girl, a slight, gentle, immaculate woman, wondered why the Romanians did not make more use of the marijuana growing wild on the railway track. I thought of Klaus and his parents on the other side of Europe, not necessarily happier, but safe. Unlike those they had left behind they were not without hope.

6

A Reasonable Schizophrenia
Czechoslovakia 1985

To return to the withdrawn ways against which I am defining myself on these journeys into communism, and to return to them because each journey makes me see them in a different light: I have long stumbled over the business of political sympathy. I could understand such sympathy as reasoned support, but not as something felt. If I was to *feel* sympathy I would somehow have to be directly involved. I remember as a student that I had no interest in the world of public responses and mass media and would only believe what I was in touch with.

This might seem like an impossible route to broad understanding, for how could one ever come into contact with enough new objects, but hardly consciously I pursued it, taking my beginnings from what touched me. I visited new countries, I encountered different person-alities, works of art, observed certain reactions in myself. Out of this came the conviction that the point of enlightenment, the point where an idea touched sensual experience, was poetic, and that this kind of poetry should concern me. August 1968, viewed from the French countryside, stands out in my mind as a political event because I have of it a poetic memory.

I was a teenager staying on a farm in Normandy that summer and August is lodged in my mind because the people I was staying with, strangers wrapped up in their own lives, were suddenly, unusually and disinterestedly aggrieved at Russia's invasion of one of its satellite states. The Czech invasion broke through the barrier of homogenizing newsprint and signified something extraordinary. The mother, father and uncle of my French companion were so disturbed by the news from Prague that until noon they went about their tasks in near

97

silence. I wish I could remember our table talk later but perhaps there was little of it. Afterwards in my memory I formed an attachment to that silence. I believed then, and continued to believe for many years after, that my hosts were stunned because an idea had been murdered; the idea that a freer, more reasonable life could be led under the insulating roof of Soviet communism. The impact of that tiding seemed to me outstandingly emotional and personal. Men and women with a vivid memory of war stood speechless, as if the radio were describing a new variety of corpse. Even now, looking back with more scepticism, knowing my overweening, often inappropriate faith in the power of ideas to change the world, I am not disinclined to believe in the poetry of that memory.

I have the same search for the poetic bridge between dreams and reality in mind as I come to Eastern Europe nearly twenty years on. Coming to Czechoslovakia, my foremost desire is to know where the idea of freedom touches daily life. The question which takes shape is: how much does freedom matter to the average man or woman, I mean freedom to criticize authority, to share in collective decisions and responsibility, to travel, perhaps marry abroad, and to pursue intellectual and artistic interests out of elective affinity, not political or national piety? But even in the way I ask my questions there is the homely comparison implicit: how much are these men and women like me?

'Elective affinities' is a less familiar expression in English than German but one which I often want to borrow. Goethe's novel of that title is about the conflict of formality and creativity, order and romance, reason and inclination. To pursue interests out of elective affinity is to be free the way I am today to roam about Eastern Europe and interpret what I see through the filter of my knowledge and memories, as well as in the light of political developments. It's a freedom – for poetry – which makes me see the best side of the society I come from.

Prague is the intellectual heart of the East Bloc, where reason struggles to analyse what the playwright Vaclav Havel has called post-totalitarian life. To go there after rural Romania was to travel the greatest distance between possible forms of communist life. In 1985 the shops were well-stocked, and no one needed to go cold or hungry. There was no food rationing, unlike in Poland across the border to the north, and there were no forced cuts in fuel and electricity supplies as in Romania further south. We took a bus and then the modern, efficient metro from the airport and walked across the centre of the city.

Crossing the Old Town Square, following the busy, winding streets to the black, Gothic Powder Tower, we fell in with the unsluggish, moderately pressurized crowd of shoppers and workers, eating bread and sausage or doughnuts with poppy seeds and honey from a take-away stall. The roomy coffee house on the corner beyond the Powder Tower was immediately imposing, being a tall, broad, recently restored art nouveau building, gilded and richly coloured. It had cakes and sandwiches and newspapers on sticks, and good coffee, and music, and ruched curtains and red plush, everything a tourist might have expected of a turn-of-the-century Central European refreshment palace. In front of it the wide street led to a well-stocked department store and immediately opposite work had just finished on an important station for the new metro line. We stopped though, in a milk bar a few streets away, one of those establishments of bright and childish decor, mainly catering for women and children, such as we had found in Warsaw. It was a place to eat ice cream and get away from the tobacco smoke. Then we sought a hotel.

Do you have a room?

(Man in his fifties) No, fully booked.

Not even for one night?

No, nothing.

But surely you can't be full on a Wednesday? Just a single room?

(Smiling) OK. passports please. Room 312.

Phrasebooks for communist Bloc countries should include sympto-matic situations like this under the heading *At the Reception Desk*. For though Czechoslovakia visibly has almost everything, only the invisible things matter, and one needs to become attuned. 'What did the hotel receptionist want?' I asked a Czech aquaintance later in the week. 'Dollars,' he said, 'or a kiss.' My naivety. I hadn't considered giving him either. But I shouldn't have forgotten, because this was just how it was in Russia.

We walked the streets some more the first afternoon, down to the river Vltava, and the Charles Bridge, having a present to deliver to a friend of a friend. We were walking with other mothers and children, watching the swans and the fishermen, the sunset and the boats, and photographing the tall, ornamental apartment buildings on the embankment with their heavy, eternally fashionable wrought iron jewellery. Trams, fussy and noisy like steam trains, gave us all the late Romantic music we needed as they crossed the bridges overhead. Elizabeth was the better reporter, unsentimental. She noticed the odd things, and the ugly things. Away from the water we were looking at the clothes in the shops, which did not reflect what people wore, and were dull and unstylish. 'Like in Poland,' she said. 'Why?' 'Because they have a funny government which won't let them buy what they want to.' Communist Czechoslovakia felt more rigid than either Poland or Hungary, though the propaganda was almost equally discreet. My daughter, not quite five, spotted a red star on the hillside across the Vltava and more on this and that building. 'What are the stars for?' she asked, surely believing they were something to do with childhood. 'To remind people of their government,' I said. 'What's government?' 'People who tell you what you can do. People who make rules.' 'What are rules?' 'What you're allowed to do.' We had got on to one of those escalators of questions which plague busy parents but which are in truth a delight. Then she said: 'You make rules for me. You're my government. And I'm yours when I sometimes won't let you play with my toys.' I was astonished and boosted at the sudden companionship she could now offer me. What was she telling me, that we all need a taste of power sometimes to feel whole again? There would be power for some in good clothes. It wouldn't be a bad start. Clever girl, but lucky girl too to have been born in a world where liberal instincts are well rooted.

Eventually in the dark we found the apartment we were searching for, in a solid spacious mansion built at the end of the last century to reflect bourgeois continuity and splendour, rather like where Imre lived in Budapest. We knocked on the door and a timid young woman with a child opened. She wanted to be polite and friendly but clearly she didn't want us to stay. The living room, truly the place in which everything was done except cooking and washing, had a clear corner where she and her son were playing with toys. Her son received the chocolate we brought in silence, as she did the tea. A stranger commuted across our path into another room, adding to all our constraint. This too reminded me of life in Moscow, where too many people were compelled to live cheek by jowl and 'like everyone else'. I remembered the tale an elderly woman writer had told me about the way she and her husband, also a writer and critic, lived when he was alive. They loved to spend hours in discussion with friends and would often invite people round and detain them till the small hours. Their neighbours, with whom they shared a kitchen and bathroom, became increasingly agitated by these habits. One day my acquaintance felt bound to ask them what was wrong, to which came the fearful reply: 'Why the bloody hell can't you live like everyone else?' Mindful of the real fear, we left the Prague apartment within minutes.

There was a drunk in the street, a capless young soldier, whose clownish movements and bawling made the tram queue tut. We watched his antics and the faces of the crowd for a few minutes, then made our way to the opera. I asked too much of Elizabeth to get her to sit through a mediocre, rather mawkish *Eugene Onegin* in pastoral costume, viewed from the top of the packed house. She made a brave try, but after Onegin's first visit had captivated Tatiana but reduced one of us to tears we had to leave. We stole outside and chatted to the old women knitting in the cloakroom. These Czech *tricoteuses*, full of kindness and common sense, were a pleasing human contact. In a country which seemed to be leading a secret double life I greatly took to the idea of them: they could have a stage role as the chorus explaining the play of communist daily life. Actually there wasn't much we could say to each other, given my lack of Czech. But I wished them well in German and they smiled and waved.

They could not still our hunger, though. We were looking for proper food, not the endless sweets and fatty snacks which make the Czechs a conspicuously overweight people. As we walked down the street, the Jalta was one of those grand, half-empty restaurants, like Gundel's in Budapest, whose prices are less forbidding to Westerners than the formal airs and graces they assume. But we had to go inside by this stage of the evening. Jalta, or Yalta, of course is the Black Sea resort where the borders of the present Soviet empire in Europe were drawn. I will always think of Imre, sitting in Budapest, bathing his daughter while considering how to revise them. This restaurant wants to cater for the post-Yalta East Bloc establishment, I decided. The Cyrillic sticker over the doorhandles: *Zdes' govoryat po-russky*, (Russian Spoken Here), would make a nice souvenir.

The blond young waiter with an agile, amused, ironic face – he would have been perfectly cast to play Thomas Mann's Felix Krull – shook his head. 'Italiano, Arabico, yes, Russky no.' All right, we'll try and order something to eat in English. What about some salad? *Salad?* he blinked. 'Yes, Madam.' Meanwhile there were no diners to listen and no dancers to smooch in the semi-darkness to a highly amplified 'Stangers in the Night'. A near-plastic man singing blandly while also playing a Hammond organ was staring into space. The *maître d'hôtel* looked bored. In a better life he wouldn't have had as his only customer a Western woman in a sweater and trousers who ordered a glass of wine for her child and a scant cold meal. In a proper bourgeois world he would have money and she would stick to the milk bar. I was pleased to imagine a healthy superiority complex to get this miserable aloof fellow through the evening.

The night was melancholy after I drank both glasses of wine, and it was unavoidably hot. The heat in the hotel could not be regulated from room to room and I had to throw open the windows in October. I fell asleep considering the overproduction and waste of hot air, a too obvious metaphor for the state of the Czech economy.

In the morning the little restaurant in our hotel had no natural light and smelt of last night's beer, though the strong bread and good jam were tokens of something brighter. I asked for a newspaper and the waiter laughed incredulously, bringing me one called *Work*, almost entirely taken up with the publication of the latest Warsaw pact communiqué. He listened to football results and polished glasses. Outside under a blue sky in brilliant sunshine the gilt on the coffee house was gleaming. Prague looked wonderful.

Life is as comfortable in Prague as it is in Budapest, and Prague is more beautiful. The Czechs agree, but say Prague is not as good as Vienna. 'Austria was once our economic partner!,' they exclaim, reminding us of the history we have forgotten. 'We built up a profitable urban economy in the nineteenth century. Bohemia and Moravia developed remarkable strength for Central European states. They industrialized rapidly and to a degree which threatened Austria's economic supremacy in the Empire and made possible the growth of an educated, cultured, politically aware bourgeoisie.' The Czechs can fairly lay claim to a distinguished history, for though they never achieved the autonomy they sought under the Hapsburgs, they sent deputies to the Viennese parliament, acquired the habits of western liberal democracy and achieved prosperity. After the Versailles settlement in 1918, when the republic of Czechoslovakia was created, Czechs and Slovaks together sought to establish a parliamentary democracy. They have slipped back since the war and the memories die hard.

Outsiders, though, enjoy Czech culture all the more. Prague, a city of 1.2 million, is an oasis in the leisure wastelands of the Soviet Bloc, where lack of money and experience often prevent the final polish being applied to hospitality, let alone to the inspiring presentation of history. The first university in Central Europe was founded in the mid-fourteenth century in Prague, with Jan Hus as rector, and architectural styles across the city, beginning from the Romanesque, testify in fairly harmonious conjunction to six centuries of a kind of permanence. They are the result of Czechs seldom having fought battles on home ground, and Prague being not too much scarred by fire, flood and the perennial desire to modernize. Prague rose to its most recent intellectual prominence under the Austro-Hungarian Empire as a ghetto of German-language and Jewish culture, and as the national centre of Czech art and music. The very name evokes a rich cultural atmosphere. The tradition is cosmopolitan on the side of reason, and proudly national on the side of the heart. The Hus epoch contained the roots of the national idea which became articulate and reflexive in the nineteenth century, when the Czechs won freedom for themselves through their art, and through the music of Smetana and Dvořák. Since then the glorious experience of self-determination has never been forgotten. The present situation galls because the cultural and political traditions are inseparable. The Czechs know what they have achieved in the past and they expect for themselves affluence, intellectual culture and liberal democracy in the future.

We spent the morning walking, looking at buildings, and slowly climbing the Hradcany mount, taking in the visible signs of the Czech legacy. Lunch was a silent affair in a small hotel with a thin East German couple and their thin child who did not speak to each other, still less to us. The waiter had refused to seat Czechs with us, though they were willing and I had welcomed them. Afterwards I had the idea we would call on the International PEN representative, who lived in an antique block in this exclusive part of town, next door to the European art gallery. In London PEN warned me she would not be straightforward to approach but I was sorry not to find her at home. (Is it not extraordinary for an international writers' organization to have to say: beware of the communist representatives of art? I wanted to put her to the test.)

However the European art gallery was such a telling contrast with Warsaw that it more than filled out the afternoon. It also suggested that galleries must invariably be a litmus test of the nation's wealth and health. Czechoslovakia's European art collection is in excellent condition and absorbing. One can see works of the fifteenth-century German master Lucas Cranach the Elder, and a famous Dürer *Madonna of the Roses*; works by Klimt and Egon Schiele; a superlative Picasso collection; and tucked away at the end of a corridor, a selection from the nineteenth-century Russian realists, Levitan, Vereshchagin, and Shishkov. Best of all is Ilya Repin's study of a headstrong, plump-faced, very handsome Pushkin.

Something out of the ordinary was happening inside a bookshop back in the centre of the modern city near Wenceslas Square. About thirty men and women were crowded round a table on a spacious, almost elegant mezzanine floor. Two middle-aged favourites of the Poetry Lovers' Circle were signing copies of their books in a simulated domestic atmosphere. I was instantly mindful that the playwright Vaclav Havel, whom I admire, and who must be at least as well known as either of these two, had spent time in prison for his writing and continually courts the possibility of rearrest. Did these writers have him, their fellow, on their conscience? It was painful to see so much fuss being made of the allegedly inscrutable creative process, in a society which did not value it.

We walked across the Old Town Square in the early evening, after dark, and found it fenced off by a wall of slack-postured soldiers, some of them laughing, some chatting to girls. Passers-by were amused or mildly irritated at having to make a detour round the obstruction. Some of them walked through the human barrier and the military policemen forgot to notice them. Others stood and watched. The young soldiers began to arrive by the company. From out of a side-street they marched in formations of sixty men practising two degrees of stamping, until more than a thousand of them had lined up. We had happened on a dress rehearsal for the induction ceremony of new army recruits. The following Saturday the young men would take their oath of allegiance to 'Socialism' before a red-spangled podium outside the Gothic Old Town Hall.

Watching them now in the dark Elizabeth began to sing: 'The Grand Old Duke of York, he had ten thousand men . . .' A youth in training shoes and jeans and an anorak made a remark I couldn't understand but which set everyone around sniggering. From a slow-moving open jeep four buglers sounded a fanfare to no one and two top officers saluted. The crowd tittered. 'I wonder who's on the podium?' said a woman. I too wondered who was enjoying, for one brief hour in the dark, the fantasy of being a communist military dictator.

What is irritating, even enraging in this country, is the way art, artifice and reality have been blended to such a degree that the absurd can come upon one as readily in the street as on the stage. It is all the more irritating and astonishing because it is a manufactured absurd which clearly belongs only on the stage. Last night's rehearsal was symbolic of a whole way of life. But it's probably only thanks to the theatre of the absurd that we in the West can readily imagine such a life: in which all occasions are only dress rehearsals for a reality which will never come; in which all fanfares are sounded to absent ears, salutes taken to invisible men, oaths sworn in empty formulae to incredible authorities. But here people live like that! You see, even as we stand here on a bright October morning, who's this coming along a side road, if not an old man with an old pram full of red flags. He's pausing at intervals to set them in place in readiness for Saturday. Poor fellow, a refugee from a Western play, and not even aware of it!

Under these extraordinary artificial circumstances life saves itself by going offstage. Forced to be actors, people return to the audience as soon as they can, and take the chance to jeer at their forced selves. Their real culture must be hidden. It must go underground for protection.

When I go into the tourist information office I see that the assistant has a sheet of paper on which the nature of every question is logged together with the nationality of every questioner. The last topic column, in which there are no ticks, is politics. What about my question about the parade? I want to ask feebly, just for the sake of asking something and setting the superficial official procedure in motion.

I've only been here a few days, but nowhere has the social schizophrenia endemic in Soviet communism stuck me so forcefully as in Czechoslovakia, which, surviving like all its East Bloc brothers on a 'black' economy, also needs a 'black' ethical code to live. Black morality is not wickedness, simply the possibility of an alternative, silent, unwritten code of values, containing more or less truth, goodness and charity, depending on the practitioner. This is why it is impossible to foresee how a hotel receptionist or waiter will behave. In human terms he is absolutely temptable to behave badly, or well, depending on how he perceives the situation.

We had an incident over some jam. I brought my customary enthusiasm to class II stuff in a bowl the first day, but the next day that was only for the staff, who brought us commercial packs of sweet red rubbish fit for export instead. To get the real thing again was a struggle, because any challenge to the given state of affairs is perceived as an attack on the individual administering it. The government is very sensitive and passes on its prickliness to its subjects. They, having conformed, I got the impression, will defend conformity to anything. Well, I got the jam, partly because the waitress was naive and offered me none of the plausible excuses, like having run out of real jam or its not being included in the deal, but by then my appetite sufficed only for the newspaper.

Western visitors to Czechoslovakia risk suffering in a minor degree the worst kind of communist official behaviour, because as tourists they are trapped in the spider's web of socialist appearances. Unpleasant things happen in banks, hotels and restaurants because men and women who only want to be functionaries can succeed brilliantly by merely barking out their uncompromising terms. Their manipulation of appearances, their hiding behind them, is a tiny bid for individual power and the only way to succeed. I know this from Russia and it says something for the hidden severity of the Czech system that the Russian instance should immediately come to mind. At every door you must knock at least twice to gain entry, once officially and once according to the black code, after which someone might open it. In Russia I occasionally saw people deliberately create for themselves the opportunity to exercise authority, sometimes followed by clemency. Afterwards Elizabeth taught me it was the sort of game children play when they come home from school and beat up their dolls to 'teach them', because having been taught all day feels like that. I am happy to say she has long since moved schools.

In short, this communism doesn't bring out the best in human nature. Hiding behind surface rules reflects the coward's desire to do the simple, acceptable thing. The desire to conform is especially strong in dealings with foreigners, however, for unorthodox connections can bring a great deal of trouble. Those who work in the media, foreign trade and all politically sensitive jobs, including those dealing with foreign tourists, are obliged to report on all foreign contacts as a condition of employment. And this is the civilization which talks of internationalism and global fraternity! Sometimes I feel my coming to Eastern Europe is wanton. I am a germ someone might catch. But if I believe this and people here believe I'm right, they're condemning themselves to a life of parochial isolation. It takes courage to remain internationally in touch, against the threats built into the system.

By mid-week we had seen a fair bit of Prague, the capital of Bohemia, and thought we should get the feel of the Moravian city, Brno, to compare. We made our way to the railway station, originally art nouveau, but recently revamped. A new high-tech main hall which looks modelled on Beaubourg in Paris has swallowed most of the old building, though the turn-of-the-century stained glass has been preserved. The new exterior is an experiment consisting of rust-red tubing and spirals and rounded towers and turrets of glass. The architecture pretends to be ultra-modern. The station is surrounded by pleasant strips of green in an otherwise unscenic part of the city, and it makes a diverting impression. But it doesn't take long to realize that this is all a Potemkin façade. Inside the station the bureaucracy remains old and absurd. When we arrived in mid-morning the queue for the train tickets and the one for compulsory seat reservations had intertwined and together these two filled the entire booking hall. Every passenger had to queue in both. At this rate it was going to take hours to get to Brno.

A big-built, dark-haired man just ahead of us in the queue stooped to retrieve a baby's rattle and handed it to the baby's mother. This seemed to me an unusual gesture, one the *tricoteuses* would have approved of. We began talking. (Was that the point of the gesture, though, on second thoughts? Still, given the fact that contacts with foreigners are discouraged he would still be taking an admirable risk. Depending on his job he knows he ought to file a report on anything that passes between us. What a political bother it is in this country to be picked up, apart from all the usual bothers.)

But Gustav didn't warrant my suspicions. He was a proud Slovak and seemed just to want the opportunity to say so. He was a man both melancholy and enthusiastic, who made no secret of trying to live a virtuous life. It was a life he enjoyed nonetheless: being an international volleyball player, a European, and the father of a family. He gave me his card and an invitation to meet in Bratislava. All this seemed very acceptable.

We had been queueing about an hour already now though and outside it was a clear, sunny day. Gustav took my suitcase and suggested Elizabeth and I might like to get some fresh air while he continued to line up on our behalf. The train was delayed and it was going to be hours yet, they said, so we did. In the meantime the train came. We returned to find the ticket hall empty. All I could think was how pleased Gustav must have been to be put to the test. He so much wanted to show me that people here could be civilized in their relations with Westerners and not just after their money and material goods. And indeed we found the bag and the ticket safe with the cashier. A train later we finally set off for Brno.

In Brno I hoped to meet at least one signatory of the human rights document, Charter 77. This handful of people are not celebrities, they don't have 'at home' days, and they often have nothing to call a press conference about; moreover they don't like being telephoned as their telephones are invariably tapped; so it is not easy to track them down. We had left the parade rehearsal in Prague only to make one long fruitless journey already out into the suburbs. Now in Brno we would try Jiri. We bought a map and walked to his apartment, but again without luck. It was cold and far to walk and I felt sorry for Elizabeth and a bit for myself. On searches like this there always seemed to be more drunks and the streets were darker and colder than in the centre of the city where we had our touristic place and were welcome. I have no nerves for adventure. It wasn't fun and the cause wasn't even mine. But the attraction was the prospect of finding old and familiar ideas from German literature alive in a Central European town. Only love is so obscure, I can now remind myself.

After five journeys into communism I have come to understand that, as in Russia, and as in Poland, the Czech dissident position is not primarily political. The leading Chartists are thinkers, philosophers and artists who have turned their attention to the nature of political life and the possibilities open to Czechoslovakia. Their views are not identical, but they are bound together by intellectual honesty and the readiness to debate. To me they are a fine model just as Imre and his friends were in Hungary. The intellectual energy of independent minds is being funnelled here into a social, ethical and aesthetic theory of a wider sweep and depth than anything presently in our own domain. To take just a couple of instances: Havel writes about Czech society in terms of Faust's pact with the devil. Jaroslav Sabata reawakens interest in Kant's *On Eternal Peace*. Moreover there is great concern with Europe as an entity. One current theory is that the Soviet hold on its satellites can be relaxed only if peace is assured, and for that the continent must be reunited, beginning with the Germanies. Such a theory ties Czech thinkers neither to East nor West, but to the cosmopolitan vision of Kant and the Central European Enlightenment. This is how independent Czech thinkers define their contribution to world *politics* even now: they want to remind the

West of the individual goals of reason and happiness which set the continent on its modern path.

The more I contemplate myself in the communist mirror and explore Europe East and West, the more this cosmopolitanism attracts me. So I think I can feel with the Czechs the oppressiveness of the Soviet cultural invasion which signals the opposite philosophy.

In Brno we lodged by chance and somewhat ironically in the Hotel Europe. It might have been different had we met Jiri, but alone we had the impression of being far from home. We visited a popular restaurant on the main square, where we ate stewed hare and dumplings, and choked on the thick tobacco smoke as we took in the black African faces of students at the city's agriculture and veterinary schools, now speaking French, now fluent Czech.

(This, incidentally, is a phenomenon to be found in all the East Bloc countries, Africans, Arabs, South-East Asians who spend as much as six years of their lives in a provincial communist town, and learn to speak fluently a language which is never likely to be of use to them again. They also learn to hate communism for its deprivations and lies.)

Outside, Brno life seemed temporarily and patchily glued together by Western pop music and propaganda: greetings to the Soviet sister town of Voronezh; praise for the great years of Czechoslovak-Soviet friendship and for the Czech-Slovak Federation. Isn't all this false bonhomie unbearable? Advanced communism had retained all the worst aspects of bourgeois life, I thought. Feeling frail that evening, not able to get into conversation with any of the Africans, I wondered where we should take cultural shelter in a city which seemed utterly without pretensions to Western Europe, despite the fact Mozart stayed there and it was the birthplace of that most vibrantly exciting composer of the twentieth century, Janáček. These biographical associations were simply incongruous, uncheering facts, virtually meaningless; meanwhile our only delight, an old shoeshine machine, of the sort I had not seen since my early childhood, refused to respond to any coins.

The next morning felt better after a walk past the massive Janáček statue and through the autumn park, where we watched the squirrels. Then to Elizabeth's chagrin, but my eventual delight, we began a longer, steeper walk. The Berlin architect Ludwig Mies van der Rohe built a house in Brno, the so-called Donat house, in 1930. It stands oddly inconspicuous today in a residential suburb full of large, detached patrician houses. The house is white, angular, low-rise, featureless, a blank sheet of paper on which the guttering draws a few careful geometrical lines. On the right-hand side there is a kind of open window which you might think was some sort of transition from residence to rear garden, or perhaps a sun terrace hidden from view. You have to stand back to see the joke of it. The 'window' frames the old town below so perfectly that the whole might be a painting of a distant Renaissance landscape, the blue sky and trees and towers beyond the temple. And so you have side by side extreme modern functionalism and effortless classical perfection, a competition the beauty of nature would win hands down if you did not remember it was the ascetic eye of a talented modern man which had put it in perspective, both literally and metaphorically, by making it architecturally useful.

Afterwards, back in the city, I queued up seemingly for hours to buy our bread and cheese for the train, was bumped and jostled, and was jubilant at having secured this unexpected vision. Wasn't it a triumph for such an intellectual statement still to be standing? A triumph for the experimental, individualistic freedom of modernism against the belief that society is better off without such imagination?

I have already recorded a number of experiences in this book which have made me jump up and down with rage at the frustration of imaginative freedom, but also, because that value has been at stake, I have almost as often jumped for joy. Some meeting of private memories and preoccupations and public events has invariably happened to make life seem richer, wittier and more humane. Visiting the restoration workshop in Moscow was one joyful example. Communing with Dr Becker in the train to Lenauheim as if he were the reincarnation in this Europe of the child life of my friend Klaus – Klaus who now lived his adult life in the other Europe – was another. Yet another memorable hour was seeing Mrozek's *Out at Sea* in

Warsaw and being reminded of Koestler's *Darkness at Noon* and, at the black heart of things, of Dostoevsky's Grand Inquisitor in *The Brothers Karamazov*. In relation to this last work I never understood with my heart as an undergraduate what it took for humanity to break down, but now in retrospect I did. I felt the truth of what before had only been an idea; and the result was elation.

Moments of enthusiasm and enlightenment like this gave significance to my Western travelling in the East Bloc and I relished them as a way of hanging on to humane and poetic values. When they happened my happiness – that imagination was functioning – was instantaneous, unreflected and physical, and no one should believe that just because I am dissecting my heart now that it was tranquil at the time. The East Bloc drives its citizens and visitors to look to their imagination for succour; in a Westerner's case it makes him take notice of imaginative values he might otherwise take for granted and reinforces their social importance. It's a privileged and moving experience to go through.

On that basis I feel I can say with authority that the greatest intellectual tragedy which could befall Czechoslovakia would be to be forced to become, under Soviet rule, a member of a different cultural continent. Left to their own devices the Czechs would probably explore and exploit their central position between East and West. But coerced they feel 'asiatization' threatens them and dissident policy is designed to counter it. I can't judge from long experience, only record that when we walked about Prague, and far more when we explored the Moravian capital, we sometimes had the impression of being abroad in a different commonwealth. Different is not to say bad. But the Czechs do not want the European element in their culture overwritten by international Soviet socialism, because the new philosophy is not so enriching. Vietnamese communism hails passers-by from posters in Prague shop windows, and along the capital's main thoroughfare lie the Soviet Club and a vast Cuban house of culture. Such new points of reference don't overshadow more traditional ties with Germany and Austria, but they are still an attempt to redraw the cultural and political map. The shift in emphasis is unwanted because it seems alien and also backward.

But we're in the train, seeing recede the infamous Spielberg prison which the Nazis built in Brno, and eating our hard-won bread and cheese. In the daffodil yellow and spring green buffet car, flower-bedecked, where we go for a drink, I am overwhelmed by the pleasantness of the decor, gentle and childish. It is like the milk bars, as if that is the only way interior design can be practised to please nowadays and not seem subversively modern. The waiter, too, is nice to us, until we refuse to change money.

In about two hours we reach Bratislava, the Slovak capital, seat of the autonomous Slovak parliament, the Slovak national theatre, the Slovak national museum and other national institutions. The strength of Slovakia's autonomy and equality in the Czechoslovak federation seems instantly doubtful. There lurks an inferiority complex, a consequence of the Slovaks having spent so much time, like the neighbouring Hungarians, under the Turks, instead of enjoying the more enlightened national past of Bohemia and Moravia.

Whoever has ruled the Central European lands has had to face the nationalities question, Freud's 'narcissism of small differences'. The first republican government in Prague under President Tomas Masaryk did what it could to create a unitary state, but potential for division between Czechs and Slovaks lingered. The Slovaks, linguistically and geographically so close to Bohemia and Moravia, but a more backward people, continued to work largely in the fields and the vineyards while Bohemia and Moravia industrialized; they belonged to the Hungarian rather than the Austrian branch of the Empire. Only this century did Slovak nationalism gather pace, and only then as a challenge to centralist rule from Prague, which sadly undermined the strength of the new democratic state. When Hitler invaded, Slovakia became a puppet Nazi state, whose Catholic church collaborated, while Czech democracy was martyred. The Slovak shame has been difficult to live down, and economically, too, Slovakia remains the poor relation.

At the reception desk:
  Do you have a map of Bratislava?
  (Young woman) Only to look at.
  (Self, after looking) It's very difficult to manage without a map. Can I buy one somewhere?

Not until Monday (two days hence).

We're leaving on Monday.

(Looks in drawer and finds another map). You can have this one if you like (smiles).

(We smile too, puzzled. This receptionist surely can't want a kiss.)

I called Gustav from the hotel, to emphasize to him and to anyone else listening that our contact was above board. Here in Bratislava he worked for the Post Office and I was lucky to turn up on a Sunday, when he was free. He hadn't lost interest in showing us around the city and within an hour he was there and we set off. He brought along his fifteen-year-old daughter, Eva, a very thin and pretty girl who was a pupil at the prestigious Foreign Trade School and already spoke excellent English, German and Russian. It's curious, having approached from Prague, to remember that their home town, Pressburg as Napoleon knew it when he conquered Austria, Pozsony as it was to the Hungarians in the nineteenth century, lies only an hour's drive from Vienna. The distance in spirit is much greater.

The four of us walked along the Danube embankment in brilliant sunshine and autumn haze, admiring the graceful space-age bridge across the river and avoiding substantial and sensitive issues. Our daughters walked along a wall, holding hands, exemplifying the balancing act, though none of us had far to fall. 'Odd, isn't it,' Gustav said. 'Eva has never visited Russia. It's odd to have to learn the language at school, but not to be allowed to travel there for fear of bringing back disappointment. It's odd when Czechs learn that Russia is the pinnacle of what they are working towards and then they are not allowed to go and see for themselves.' Gustav broke off. I shouldn't get the wrong impression. Home was good, the simplicity of the people, the good air and the beauty of the mountains. Slovakia was also coming up in the world, whatever the self-regarding *Prazaki* thought.

Under communism Bratislava had become the seat of a nominally autonomous Slovak government federated to the Czech government in Prague; money had been poured in; and central government and party posts were about equally divided between Czechs and Slovaks, Gustav elaborated. He must have viewed my near silence with suspicion. I found the Slovak capital a strange mixture of provincialism and international aspiration. Bratislava's winding old streets and wine taverns and the French grocers and the antique shops had only holiday appeal, though its citizens seemed to feel in touch with the larger world. They were proud of having six television stations plus Moscow to bring them the news, also many Western radio stations, and three standard languages. Gustav boldly compared Bratislava with its Slovak, German, and Hungarian to Basle in Switzerland, with its French, German and Romansh. He was Slovak, his wife was half-Hungarian, and he spoke good German. Did not his family exemplify the broader outlook? The cosmopolitan self-image made him happy.

In the church at the foot of Maria Theresa's forbidding fortress, from where she administered these former lands of St Stephen, we watched a christening. Gustav splashed holy water on us as we entered and left, but didn't profess to be holy. The faith in Slovakia is traditionally strong and passive, not a source of political strife, but neither way did it interest him. We went to the clock museum, where we saw pictures of Napoleon in Pressburg, but after we had made the fatiguing, unpicturesque ascent to the fortress, boredom threatened us all, and it was a relief to get into the wine tavern, loudly tuned to Austrian radio. 'Everyone listens,' said Gustav dismissively, more worried that our sample of the local wine was too cold. He took my glass in his huge hands to warm it, which captured Elizabeth's attention, then he asked to see my palm. 'I'm normally afraid of talking to Westerners, I fear a *Blamage*,' he said happily, still holding my hand in his big warm paw. That word, the same in German and Czech, means for the Czechs getting egg on their face in front of Westerners. It's true, it was a happy, relaxed meeting for us and neither of us had anything to fear. But I had to have my hand back if there was truly to be no compromise.

Gustav's difficulty was that he was a genuine egalitarian, mourning the growth under communism of a new 'high society' with money, and of a rapacious middle society in pursuit of it. He shook his head, one eye permanently wept as a result of some infection. Look at Hungary over the border, he said. There the gap between rich and poor was growing notoriously. For a non-bourgeois, which is what he was and what one must be in East Europe to protest against the comfort-seekers who travesty socialist beliefs still seriously held, it is a sad thought. Gustav disliked the tourist establishments catering for Westerners, and the surly cum obsequious manners they bred, because they epitomized the materialist ethics of the new communist bourgeoisie. He declared again he wanted to show us that East Bloc citizens – Slovaks at least – were not 'primitives' only after our Western money, but cultivated people.

To be cosmopolitan, well-educated and free! The Czechoslovak dream has not been a dream of power, but one of integrity in peaceful coexistence with the great powers East and West. After the First World War that idea grew, which Gustav still cherishes, of the Czechs and the Slovaks becoming 'a kind of Switzerland' and today by the same token some Czech idealists have a yearning admiration for Yugoslavia. Gustav enthused over a second glass of Romansky. 'It's important to talk to strangers and travel the world!' He was pleased that Eva was so clever at school and hoped a career in foreign trade would give her the same break in life that volleyball had given him, with the possibility of travel from Modena to Mongolia and the chance to earn enough dollars to allow family holidays abroad. But she wanted to be a writer, an ambition which worried him. It suggested an unhealthy life of black coffee and cigarettes. He could think of other reasons for discouraging her too. 'It's difficult to get published here. You need the right contacts.' She agreed and they smiled at each other and said in chorus: 'Volleyball's no good.' Gustav ordered the stimulant. It was the right decision after all, he must have reflected silently, for then he declared: 'You see, no one *has to* do anything in our household. Each one of us is free.'

We'd drunk *Brüderschaft*, we were friends. With no spilt egg in prospect, we waited for a tram back into the city and I asked Gustav about relations with the other East Bloc countries. 'A man is not free to choose his brothers,' he replied in the same dull voice with which he spoke of the Catholic faith. He really didn't want to talk about politics. He dropped us at the only restaurant I was able to name. (Elizabeth and I had fallen for its smart appearance and tables outside.) We wanted to try it, against my better judgement, and Gustav's, though as a patriot he was placated by the idea that we should eat well in his country. We left, promising to write.

It was an extraordinarily unfriendly lunch. We didn't represent the wealth of the West and everyone was disappointed. In fact the relationship was reversed. We were poor and looking for something we could afford from the East. Afterwards we wandered through the attractive winding streets of the old town, peering into the closed antique shops, and the shoe shops. Elizabeth needed winter boots and the best and cheapest for children came from here, or from Poland. We eventually bought them in Prague. Then, as we walked over a particularly scenic bridge and under the archway of the old city gate, in the company of all the burghers of Bratislava, we heard a commotion overhead. I blame no political system for this absurdity. A huge, bare-breasted, grotesque old woman, a contemporary Tiresias, was moving rhythmically back and forth at a high window next to the Maria Theresa tower, shouting abuse at the Sunday strollers: down with the bourgeoisie and its pleasures! She was an archetypal crone, more of a vision than a reality, though she reminded me instantly of the crones who stand for reality in Zamyatin's *We* and who help defend Eros against Central Planning.

Gustav was not a dissident. He saved his political philosophy for his family. But the signatories of Charter 77 keep the silent dissenting majority like him in mind. Back in Prague we finally caught up with one of their spokesmen, having knocked on his door in search of good conversation. Every day in Czechoslovakia began with that expectation, as in honesty, if one had more energy and more leisure, it would do in London. Pavel spied us through the glass eyehole. I knew that he worked at a blast furnace, that he had spent nine years locked up for his political activity and beliefs, and that he spoke good foreign languages. Wearing a dressing gown and pyjamas he opened the door. 'Excuse me, I have a fever. Don't you speak French? My German is . . .' The face, plump and intensely handsome, belonged to a man in his early forties, and it was one the makers of Gauloises could market. He was a man of great presence, who seemed to enjoy being ill because it gave his powerful personality an extra boost. You could put him on the stage as a dissident and he would be a fine character. All his personal characteristics told the political story and its ironies.

Pavel's student years in Paris equipped him with a natural French accent and a lasting infatuation with Trotsky. Meanwhile his beauty and charm made him believe in himself. So nowadays he hogs the limelight in the dissident movement, colleagues say, and wants to do everything and see everyone himself. He can take everything seriously, and therefore everything in life cynically, but he is not bitter, only passionate or mocking or contemptuous of other people's lack of knowledge and understanding and experience compared with his own. He loves to discuss, but is even happier offering a monologue.

Pavel's discourse, full of historical facts, is informative but not enlightening. One could have read it in a book, though preferably not one of his authorship, for when he writes for the cause his prose is unbearably and almost incomprehensibly laden with political and sociological abstractions.

We sat talking for an afternoon, than another afternoon. Elizabeth played with the baby. Pavel and his wife, because of their political commitment, are professional entertainers of Western strangers like me, who call because they are curious, or have a message to bring, or want to write a newspaper story. About a dozen of us come every month, and more from the West than from the East Bloc, because it is made hard for East Bloc citizens to travel, lest they establish cross-border links. Pavel's wife says life is not so bad, hardly austere. She sometimes doesn't recognize Czechoslovakia in what is written and published abroad. Even when people come they only see what they want to see. We got down to what I wanted to see. I mentioned the name of one of Pavel's colleagues I had visited. Pavel's lips suddenly tightened and he looked at the ceiling. How could I have said the name when I *knew* they were listening? His skin went grey in anticipation of something horrible. The man's carefully built-up cover was probably blown, Pavel's deathly appearance said. He scowled. I couldn't speak for shame and left.

'Oh,' laughed Benno, the man in question, as I confessed later in the week with visions of his going to prison swimming before my mind. 'Don't worry about that, it's my job. Anyway Pavel mentions people's names all the time. He just wanted to assert himself.'

That the East European dissident is not primarily a political phenomenon remains true, but Pavel is an exception. He is probably one of the country's few real political men. He likes power. You can see how he might behave in power by looking at his family, for they adore him but are careful to obey. He expects obedience, loyalty and an altogether quieter public performance from his plump, pretty, at least equally intelligent wife, and good behaviour and school work from his children. The entire family is learning French. He teaches the children himself while his wife goes to classes.

His best lesson is his enthusiasm and the kind of happiness he radiates in having, besides a delightful family, an honest cause. I encourage the Lenau-ish idea that as a dissident he has to set the example of an independent mind to keep political and moral integrity alive. He is all agreement until I call them spiritual values. That expression makes him shrug like a pseudo-French advertisement. He's a materialist. Also not a man of words, I think, but there's no sense in quarrelling over semantics. Whatever he calls himself he is made the very opposite way to the shallow official culture in which he has grown up.

My next acquaintance, Jaroslav, was less of an individualist and less concerned with his own charisma. Another family man, yet who always seemed to be looking after the children alone, he was a keen English scholar, very fluent, and surrounded by all varieties of paperback books. He too had signed the Charter and rejected the double life. The price was a menial job, but it was not too painful a sacrifice, because he would rather have been a window cleaner than a counterfeiter. He had a bronze cast of the head of President Masaryk propped up on the living room floor, a hero officially ignored, rescued from a demolition site for a bottle of Johnny Walker.

Jaroslav and I drank wine and chatted about children and his 'sociological' hobbies – comics and collecting chewing gum wrappers from all over the world. He was interested in the fringes of literacy – quite a fashionable interest in the West too. More absorbing were the stories both he and Pavel told me illustrating Czech social schizophrenia. Both were aware of the drama implicit in the situation of people who have renounced one half of their lives. This was Pavel's story, a parable of frustration: 'I knew a man once, he was an election chairman, then overnight he couldn't take it any more. He got up and pasted anti-election posters everywhere he could. I met him in prison.'

Jaroslav spoke of cleaning windows for people who were once his social equals. Some of his former college friends now work at the Foreign Ministry. When he cleans their windows both sides are aware of the choices they have made. The socially divisive choice-for-life, Jaroslav explained, brings with it a style, a set of friends and either the means to raise a family in comfort or the need to scrimp and do several jobs. One might feel one had made the wrong choice but it was difficult to turn back in bitterness or guilt. Jaroslav was cleaning windows in the apartment of a successful woman television director one day, of his age, who suddenly recanted, declaring she should be cleaning his windows. An incidental point here: the Czech window cleaner, working from inside the building, is less easily turned into a comic voyeur than his British counterpart. He is more a strange visitor, a potential intimate witness, a man likely to stimulate inner discontent. He would be useful in a play.

Another subject which greatly interested me in talking to Jaroslav was the difficulty of bringing up children in Czechoslovakia's spiritually divided circumstances. As we talked he was getting the children to bed, helped by Elizabeth, who despite being the youngest present was staying up and proud of it. The two older children were reading a translation of Tolkien in samizdat. Officially there was not enough paper to publish all desirable literature. It's the same argument they use in Moscow to account for the shocking absence of the nineteenth-century classics from bookshops. I've never believed it. Then we got into a conversation about schools, the kind I might have had with another parent in London or Budapest or anywhere. I recalled Pavel and his wife had complained of the severity and inefficiency of the schools available to them, and the amount of extra teaching which had to be done at home. The children of Pavel and Jaroslav and others like them were lucky, because their parents were able to give them what they needed. Yet clearly their families faced an extra problem: how did they teach their children to acquire the dual set of values necessary for their integrity in this schizophrenic society? And how could they help them make like-minded friends? Not much can be done, except by example at home, as with any desirable upbringing anywhere. But there do exist in Czechoslovakia underground scout troops. The official scouting movement, akin to traditional Czech Sockel or 'gymnastic clubs' in the same morally and socially educative vein, has always been popular, indeed so much so that it had to be banned in favour of the communist youth organizations in the wake of the withered Prague Spring. In the underground troops the children wear different badges, and follow a different code of values from visible society. The parents of would-be new entrants are carefully vetted.

On our way home from Jaroslav's, as we waited for the underground train, there was a line along the edge of the platform and Elizabeth was running her foot along it, testing the feel of the rule. Of course she was oblivious of the personal freedom she displayed, but other people seemed to watch her with pleasure. I reflected how lucky we both were that her feeling for freedom had been so easily established by an unfettered upbringing. I hoped it would be rock-hard by the time she approached adulthood and faced the threat of losing it.

We made a final trip, by coach, to the spa of Karlovy Vary, known to Austrians and the world as Karlsbad. It is like an inland Eastbourne, a once chic, now shabby, unfashionable and elderly resort, surrounded by mountains and unspoilt wooded countryside. The place has been socially lowered rather than liberated by its loss of style. The town is arranged along the banks of the river, which narrows as it moves into the birch forest. The stone statues in the woods are of great musical and literary figures who once recuperated in Karlsbad. The healing iron and sulphur water they took spurts up from wells all over town, either enclosed in summerhouses decorated with white- and blue-painted Victorian cast iron, or freestanding in the streets. The main sources are enclosed in a frightful modern plate glass leisure shrine dedicated to the Soviet cosmonaut Yuri Gagarin. To relax as well as to receive treatment holidaymakers go to the grey, modern building of the thermal centre, which incorporates a dance hall, a concert hall, bowling lanes, well-stocked shops and restaurants and a snobbish expensive hotel Gustav would have hated. Glamour-ladies with long cigarettes, gold lighters and bright lipstick sit listening to Western music there, and drinking cappuccino with cinnamon, while mostly older women in trews and woollen hats cluster along the riverside avenues, drinking from Karlsbad's peculiar jug-cups. The narrow design of these cups is meant to minimize spillage, and all the shops have souvenir models for sale, or you can rent one at the spa centre. Both bought and hired varieties may be chained up by the handle overnight in a huge open-fronted cuproom for a small fee.

All this is familiar, bourgeois territory, the essence of middle-class Central European life. Where the river bends and the woods begin stands the imposing predecessor of the thermal centre, the Proto-Freudian Kurhaus, 'built 1893–95 in the glorious reign of his majesty the Kaiser Franz Josef I according to the plans of Viennese architects'. Statues either side of the door show Caritas and Youth protecting age. The whole would recall the ornate Victorian Post Office at Ipswich, except for the motto: HEALTH AND CHARITY. The atmosphere is not that of a hospital, because the battle is not full-scale, the sickness not unwavering and acute, but dimly one is made aware of a continuous struggle taking place for the survival and fitness of the body and the spirit. For me there is the ambiguity of *The Magic Mountain*, Thomas Mann's ironical study of the bourgeoisie and its discontents, in the smell of sulphur water indoors, in the sound of a distant vacuum cleaner passing over the red carpets, in the sight of the reception desk staff in white coats. The atmosphere is one of genteel relaxation, faint boredom and guilty convalescence. It belongs to quite another world than communism.

Then a motorcade screams past Soviet-style, accompanied by police with flashing lights and blaring horns. No wonder the real Czech bourgeoisie had gone underground, leaving only its faded appearance behind. All bourgeois cultures today have lost their way, caught between modern necessity and the attraction of the traditional, but in its sphere of influence Soviet communism has been most disruptive of the bourgeoisie in the Czech parts of Czechoslovakia, which have a most substantial tradition to displace.

Outside Karlovy Vary, in the forest, along one of the many marked, measured, but still delightful trails, there is a shrine to Friedrich Schiller, which quotes the eighteenth-century German historian, moralist and poet as saying, at the summit of the bourgeois path:

A nation which does not joyfully risk everything for its honour is worth nothing.

7

A Time for Reading
Romania 1986

'Strangers in the Night', arranged not for the Hammond organ but for the mandolin, eased the Tarom flight to a halt in Bucharest. It was early January 1986. Since the previous year, Romania's food and energy shortages had intensified and, remembering the arduousness of Timişoara in midsummer, I had left Elizabeth behind. My packing was done with survival in mind: coffee, ham, candles, matches, a torch, a penknife, a spoon, paper and pens, scissors, toiletries, a map and many packs of Kent cigarettes. A British newspaper had reported that Kent (no other brand) was the only viable currency; the coffee and ham I was persuaded to bring as presents for the starving. I began to picture myself as explorer, relief worker and missionary.

'Heh! Buna sera! Which hotel are you staying in?' I'm in good spirits and when the prepaid car doesn't arrive it doesn't seem to matter. Everyone official is doing his best, and smiling and not being at all officious. The men are very noticeable, kissing hands and generally affecting courtly deference. They have flowers in their buttonholes and no hesitations. The physical type – thick, dark hair, high cheek-bones, brown eyes – appeals to the northern sensibility and maybe vice versa. I remember Graham Greene on his only trip much admired the women. I believe instinctively in a kind of sensual sophistication in Romania.

As if to corroborate that impression an unexpectedly comfortable and civilized world passed obscurely by on the way into Bucharest, an Arc de Triomphe followed by a wide boulevard of graceful villas, some functional, some Wagnerian and fey, all built around the turn of the century. Later I found out that these salubrious, leafy streets, close to the park reserved for the exclusive use of President and Mrs

Ceausescu, housed the world's embassies and the city's important personages. But the present taxi driver spoke too little French (and I no Romanian) for us to converse even to this degree. We quarrelled over the fare, which was my misunderstanding. I was confident I knew a lot about travelling in communist countries by now, but my jumpiness belied it.

At 9.30 p.m. I felt hungry. The hotel restaurant shut at nine and the only one open was at the Intercontinental, which became my destination. In the centre of the Romanian capital there were not many signs of life in the dark, muddy, virtually noiseless streets; just the occasional grinding of a tram and a couple of men, inebriated but still wearing their caps. I walked for about fifteen minutes, passing not more than half a dozen people. After that the muzak-filled Intercontinental, the usual five-star establishment for foreigners, was proof against any intrusion from outside. I walked unwittingly into the dollar bar with its German snacks and *Bier*. 'You can eat here, but you don't really want to pay in dollars. In the Madrigal room you can pay in lei,' said the waiter sympathetically and showed me into a circular, pink dining room with white painted chairs, pink cushions, pink table linen and a red carpet. I sat down still wearing my weatherproof jacket, feeling like a farm hand in a boudoir.

The waitress pretended the restaurant was closed. 'It's five past ten. You don't close until eleven,' I insisted. (If you've travelled in Eastern Europe and survived you don't need lessons in self-assertion.) Our struggle was graciously conducted and very soon some soup arrived, a salad of endives and tomatoes, cheese and egg, and a pleasant white wine called Florea or Formosa. I sat wondering whether endives, which grow indoors in the dark, might not solve the problem of fresh vegetables in the East European winter while the spirit vinegar dressing brought back memories of impoverished mushroom-preserving in Moscow.

The few remaining diners were Romanian and peered at me curiously in my outward-bound clothes. 'Buna sera!' said a bloated large man in a suit, with a floral buttonhole, as he walked out with his party, not expecting an answer. Perhaps I might learn some of this language, which sounds an attractive mixture of Romance and Slavonic.

There were few street lights on even outside the Intercontinental, and my short cut back over the grass was unintentional. 'Buna sera!' called a voice behind me. 'Hallo, Hallo, buna sera!' Romania was going to be erotically bothersome, I felt. I walked faster. A young policeman finally, angrily caught up with me and demanded my passport. 'Merci,' he rapped, then after a moment's glance, 'Bonsoir.' He sounded a little sheepish in his schoolboy French and our eyes didn't bother to meet. He and the eerie emptiness of the streets, the lack of traffic and the difficulty of getting a late meal sufficiently conveyed the idea of Romania as a police state with an evening curfew. Back in the safety of my overheated room with its vast ancient television set and noisy refrigerator I reflected on my first impressions. My textbook talked about the historical gap between the *pays légal* and the *pays réel*. But communism was supposed to bridge the gap.

At breakfast it was good to see the restaurant open. I was required to sit alone, away from the Bulgarians and the Vietnamese, because of my political origins, but the staff were friendly enough. The New Year celebration, the most important date on the Romanian festive calendar, had just ended and they were taking down the decorations to the sound of vacuum cleaners. I downed a slice of omelette and some weak tea and made a few telephone calls with the help of the reception desk. There hadn't been a Bucharest telephone directory since 1977 but they didn't mind phoning inquiries and even holding the paper while I wrote the numbers down. So much co-operation everywhere and so little expected! It was as exhilarating as the cold sunshine outside. Whatever else was wrong with Romania it wasn't under the same strain as Czechoslovakia. Despite obvious frustrations, the Latin temperament seems to make communism, a northern discipline, warm up. A north European myself, I'm also feeling rather buoyant.

The twin elements of Romanian cultural identity, Romance and Slavonic, have been fiercely contended. The Stalin era threw the emphasis on Slavonic traditions and as late as 1965 the official name for the country was Ruminia, to play down ties to Rome and the West. The proximity of the Slav world has introduced Slav peoples and manners during more than a thousand years, yet Romania remains proud of its Dacio-Roman origins and of the culture which evolved under Turkish suzerainty. It was then that the aristocracy began to emulate French civilization, following the example of the country's Phanariot Greek overlords. Francophile culture and manners flowered under the pre-war monarchy and filtered down, to the extent that today most people in the street can manage some French and educated older people speak it fluently. Some of the hotel staff also speak Italian. The educated modern culture derives mainly from the West. The collective dream of the citizens of Bucharest is to be another Paris, though the folk culture, reflected in the most sophisticated art forms such as those of the sculptor Brancuçi, is Balkan. I could become happily absorbed in this refined, reflective heritage. The country and the culture instantly appeal.

Immediately beyond my hotel were several streets of art nouveau villas with wrought iron balconies, fancy eaves, curiously shaped wings and windows. The architecture was individual, animated and elegant. Bucharest has charms for anyone prepared to believe that a trip to the savage commercial wastes of Oxford Street would exact a greater toll. The charms are deceptive as to the quality of contemporary life, but that does not stop them being passingly true.

It is a little-known place. I could not have dreamt what I was missing before I came. Western newspapers are not as in touch with Romania as with most of the other East Bloc countries. Much that has been written recently reflects a fear of a repeat of last winter's record cold, in which many died indoors, but it doesn't quite describe the present misery nor the small but persistent compensations. During my stay the weather remained relatively mild, with some rain, the temperature around freezing. The worst that could be said was that the uneven streets were muddy, with their potholes and tramlines full of water. The greater fears were not instantly visible.

In the old parts Bucharest looked like a village and its streets as if they led from a farmyard. (Precisely this area has since been demolished under President Ceausescu's much criticized rebuilding programme.) Only in the spacious turn-of-the-century residential areas like those I had admired on my arrival did the civilized urban environment appear untouchable, though upon closer inspection most of those large houses had been divided inside. Meanwhile a huge flat expanse of mud, punctuated by bulldozers, was all that remained of the newly demolished Jewish quarter around Calea Vacharesti, though a senior member of the Jewish community assured me that Ceausescu's notorious plans for rebuilding the capital by demolishing most of its old sites contained no hint of anti-Semitism. The remaining Jewish synagogue, the Jewish theatre and the Jewish museum had armed guards to protect them against possible terrorist attacks.

Romania was unique in the East Bloc at this time, and therefore vulnerable, because it had diplomatic relations with both the Israelis and the Palestinians. One consequence was that bomb attack in 1985 which the Africans I met in Timişoara had tried to exploit for their amorous ends. From the sea of mud the way led down towards the indistinguished river Dambovica where the Head of State had started building the projected largest Presidential palace in Europe. When they look at his plans for this city, the Paris of the Balkans, the Babylon of the Apocalypse, some call Ceausescu whimsical and others mad.

As I went on my way all the supermarkets I passed were largely empty. Long queues emerged from narrow doorways for bread and chicken. The central market, another site scheduled to be demolished, had some eggs, soft cheese, apples, fresh herbs; some root vegetables and leeks; red paprika powder and wheat-coloured coriander seed, heaped into little dunes on the stone counters. Elsewhere the stalls were piled high with raw wool, and knitted coats and hats. These provisions were hardly enough to keep warm and feed a capital city of two million inhabitants. Yet a curious thing I soon found out about Romania was that provision-gathering did not mainly take place in shops. It was explained to me that connections with the land were still very strong and a lot of food was sought there privately in exchange for goods or services from the town. With the economic emergency the barter system was spreading. Western experts call it a reversion to the medieval economy.

At breakfast next day I had my eyes wider open. On the back table of the restaurant, by the door, packages appeared and disappeared according to who arrived in the doorway. The hotel kitchen had good cheese, sausage, eggs, pork and cake. It was not greatly varied, but if you had a friend, or a relative, or an ex-pupil among the waiters or the catering staff it was clearly easier to collect it from the back of the dining room than waste hours waiting to be served with poor quality sausage in a shop. You would be called upon to perform a return favour soon enough.

At 10 a.m. shopping was largely over for the morning. Queues for some goods began in the middle of the night, with people rising and turning in according to the old peasant clock. Western newspapers make much of this middle-of-the-Western-night queuing as a sign of ultimate hardship, but I suspect it is a country habit relatively recently brought into the towns, shocking enough in the late twentieth century, but more so to us than to Romanians themselves.

The date was Monday, 6 January. It meant nothing to me but by mid-morning the churches were filling with Orthodox believers. Outside Sfinta Vineri, at the beginning of the Calea Vacharesti, it was as busy as a bazaar and inside was full from black wall to black wall with bottle-carrying worshippers and ablaze with gold leaf and candlelight. I wrestled with my guidebook to find out what was happening while a woman began a commentary in Romanian on my behalf. Soon we had set up a talking circle quietly rivalling the service. We were standing elbow to elbow alongside a tomb, where the inscription to the prince who founded the church was in Cyrillic, the script still used in Russia, Serbia and Bulgaria. Did I know what Cyrillic was? the woman asked. Everyone began to assert he did, but the words were hard to decipher and left several pairs of eyes pinched and thwarted. The Romanian church abandoned Cyrillic more than a century ago and the script went out of secular use in Romania even earlier. The virtues of the prince remained undisclosed to us.

On the prince's tomb lay a bunch of dried herbs. I sniffed. The woman rubbed the leaves between her fingers. It was very pungent basil. Today was the anniversary of St John the Baptist's baptism of Christ, and it was the convention to bring basil to be blessed and to take away Holy Water. The gypsies outside were selling the herb tied up with red cotton for one leu a bunch. The congregation clutched empty bottles which would be filled from enamel buckets in the vestry. Each with a single little bottle, they looked as if they might have been in hospital, and the crocodile which curled round the outside of the church recalled the bread queue. The images were dislocated in my

Western head but I didn't want them to be so. In the austere context of communist street life the church was a warm, roomish asylum of luxury and solemnity and elegance and tradition. The atmosphere was powered by the rich iconostasis, the comfortable, cosy proportions of the interior, the carpet on the floor and the enamel stove. Surely I could accept it without demanding that my Protestant expectations of worship be fulfilled? Yes, but with distrust. The Romanian Orthodox church belongs to the East Christian world. Like Russia and like Bulgaria its spirituality presents a spectacle and a hurdle.

The Romanian woman gave me a hug and I took stock of feeling both high and sated. It was good to be in this strange country, making contact with strangers without the help of words, but disconcerting. One was never quite sure what was the *pays réel*.

I reverted to browsing. A small market sold wooden implements and pottery, chipped jugs and huge mouse traps. From behind another table a wizened old man was displaying fresh herbs and bunches of dried herbs for making tea – camomile and a pink one I didn't recognize. He looked on my investigations agreeably and told me the local names and pointed to the parts of the body they benefited. This one for the heart. (Sick organ or lovesick state? No way of asking. Does he think I'm lovesick because I'm on my own? Actually I think it's true.) The main herb was lovage, which smells like the fenugreek in curry, but tastes milder. The Romanians frequently cook with it. I bought some apples. Did I have any shampoo? asked the apple seller. The Kent cigarettes were weighing like stones in my pocket so I took the opportunity to pass some on. I had no idea how I was going to get rid of them. The apple-seller looked overwhelmed.

Lovesick? The instant eroticism of the airport lounge persisted. But thoughts about erotic hunger, magnified by being suddenly free of the responsibility of a child, fairly quickly gave way realistically to physical hunger. I felt ravenous when I passed a café selling spit-roasted chicken, with bread and salad. The under-manager was fetched to explain in French that that was all they had. I pulled apart the juicy, tiny whole bird in my hands with frantic delight, and washed it down with some more Florea or Formosa. Only the pile of sharply pickled tomatoes was beyond me. '*C'était bon! Merci, monsieur.*' Everyone waved. Life couldn't really be so pleasing and simple. I would quieten myself down by going into the museum of the history of Romanian communism.

This was a mainly dull, empty exhibition, explained only in Romanian, but for an hour I couldn't think of where else to go. The basement was full of jewels, with many relics of the monarchy, all now belonging to the President and his wife. As I conjured with their invisible presence these two reminded me of Ferdinand and Imelda Marcos of the Philippines.

The attendant, a slim man in his mid-twenties, reminded me to walk round the exhibition clockwise, and then lingered.

'Do you speak French? Where are those jewels that went to Russia in the twenties?'

'Over here, madam.'

'They gave them back then?'

'Of course.'

'Are you a jewellery specialist?'

'No, I'm a modern historian.'

'That's a long way from jewellery.'

'That's true. But that's life.'

This was a sad encounter. I hung around for a bit, we exchanged a few meaningful glances and half smiles, then I left. We wanted to talk and go out for a drink, but we couldn't because I was a foreigner. This is where invisible Bucharest, the real country, finally begins.

Apart from chance encounters I had introductions to literary men and women in Bucharest, established novelists, poets and translators. They were disillusioned and almost to a man or woman afraid, even those in official positions. The fear was of unforseeable reprisals in a country which had turned within twenty years from being the East Bloc's most cavalier, free-wheeling state into its most repressive.

In 1986 Romania was drained economically, in part because of the huge demands made upon its resources by Russia and by the Russian-led Comecon group. It also needed to pay off its crippling hard currency debt to the West. Oil, of which Romania was a substantial producer and exporter, had helped for a while, as we saw from all the stationary cars in Timişoara, but recently the price had fallen drastically on world markets. Material conditions in Romania were deteriorating daily. The *de facto* curfew saved heat and light and human energy for the next working day while much of the food from the land was exported for hard currency. A novelist made the point: 'Everything good we make is exported, except literature.' But he wanted me to understand the real cause of distress. 'The food problem makes us greedier than we used to be. We eat more now, but we're not really short of food. The real problem is the compromise and the waste and the ugliness.'

I can't talk about this man or anyone else I met directly, for fear of reprisals if they are recognized, but this is approximately what I found.

Victor held his head in his hands and mourned the cult of leadership in which the President and his family indulged. The term dynasty was in common use and every day the press carried formal photographs and tributes. For a sophisticated country to be at the mercy of these antics was painful indeed. The intellectuals pursed their lips fastidiously; less tortured men and women laughed. Political scientists in the West see in the cult something of the Ottoman tradition of leader worship, but they say it has reached original proportions in Romania under Ceausescu.

Of course it is a difficult country to lead, essentially under Moscow's thumb. But Ceausescu's domestic politics, perhaps as a consequence of that ultimate attendant humiliation, have become so unpredictable and inscrutable that their very secrecy seems to have engendered social decline. In the days when Romania was the most independent member of the Soviet Bloc, outspokenly critical of Soviet economic and foreign policy, the atmosphere was quite different. When the Russians invaded Czechoslovakia to put an end to the Prague Spring in 1968, Ceausescu was famous after only three years in power for deploring that action as a grave mistake. Stefan remembered his happiness on that occasion. There were public meetings out of doors and even those Romanians not communists at heart relished the excitement and relative freedom the 'maverick' political climate created. Today it is as if the same communist leadership, as suspicious of Russian intentions as ever, but wary of its own survival, has cast an immobilizing and dispiriting spell over its 22 million inhabitants with tighter security, a Maoist-inspired contempt for intellectuals and, above all, economic decline.

It was a woman, Ana, who wanted to explain the wretchedness of Romanian Maoism to me, the product of a visit Ceausescu made to China in 1971. She felt sorry for her children, facing the miseries of restricted courses and opportunities, particularly in the arts and media-related subjects, and no travelling. (Her family reflections took me back briefly to the young man in the museum. Life was treating him relatively well, I realized.) Ana's job was to write an agony column dealing with the official moral problems of Romanians under communism. What bothered her, professionally and personally, was the moral atmosphere engendered by the economic decline. Wasn't it grotesque to be feasting and wasting so much food at a time like this? And wasn't it a sign of regression for a rational society that the churches were packed?

Ana's concerns were sociological. The men I met were much more fierce and personal in their criticism of the dynasty. One could not bear to meet me in the restaurant of my hotel. 'It's full of shop managers on a spree. They're the only people who can do well for themselves these days,' he cried bitterly.

I watched Stefan, very lean and good-looking in his early sixties, back away from the forward waitress, though neither of us could escape the deafening music. 'No thinking person would come here,' he added, making me feel I had done wrong to invite him. He was a curious man, who had worked most of his life to enhance Romania's official image abroad and spent some of his own writing and teaching career abroad in positions of trust. A friend told me that not until retirement had he suffered political disillusion. (Remembering what Zoltan said in Budapest, though, this fate would seem to threaten sexagenarians in all the East Bloc countries. Communism lasts only as long as the working life.) He must have shown it, because he was evicted from his luxury flat and now his wife was ill and he had lost his faith in the value of writing. He looked around at the putative shop-managers, carefree, boisterous, unfastidious men and women, short of vision, locked in the present. 'What use is poetry to them?' he said bitterly. We talked about the purpose of my visit. 'Anything you write will be very superficial,' he declared, though without hostility. Anna, the anti-Maoist, had also doubted the ability of a stranger to understand Romania. But Stefan's words reflected more of an authorial crisis of faith. He was addressing me as a young writer from anywhere. 'What's the point of writing everything down? What you forget isn't worth remembering anyway.'

There were some Russians staying in my hotel. They come now as imperialist tourists, waving thick bundles of roubles and expecting everyone to understand their language, which almost no one here does. Their women leaders quickly got into a dispute with the young Romanian woman who changed the money and gave out tourist information. The Russian women were shouting. Queueing behind and finding myself caught up in a one-sided yelling match I offered to translate, so then they began to shout at me. 'It's not that she can't change our money. She doesn't want to!'

The caged Soviet psyche is programmed to react to bureaucratic difficulties like this, having been artificially fattened on a diet of petty powermongering. I feel rather sympathetic.

'You could go to the bank. It's not far.'

'And who'll pay for the taxi?'

The elegant trilingual Romanian moneychanger (she spoke everything except Russian) averted her gaze. The Russians continued to object on principle to any change of plan. What of the thirty Soviet tourists wandering about Bucharest without money? *Nu chto?* But there was no way out. Finally, with childishly lowered eyes and humbly grunted thanks, the Russian women decided to take what Romanian currency there was and change the rest the next day. Poor Russians, I thought, genuinely, and well played the Romanian mademoiselle.

I was browsing in a supermarket when I came across one of the greatest insults a government could deliver to its people, a box of export-reject produce. That day it was honey which had crystallized. All that was left of its export quality was the colourful, shiny label printed in Western languages and a pretentious octagonal jar, now lying dusty and face down in a box of straw. Ana Blandiana, a prominent contemporary poet, wrote some celebrated verses a few years ago about such offensive and pathetic objects signifying the state of life under the present regime. The poem brought her and the magazine that published her a great deal of trouble. Among the tokens of suffering it listed were overcrowded trams, trams that never came, export-reject apples, and Kent cigarettes. Most effectively the poem included not a single verb, a sure way of conveying Romania's impotence to do anything about its fate.

Will no one protest? It is a truism of East Bloc political observation that Romania has had only two political dissidents, the novelist Paul Goma, who was vocal in the 1970s and eloquent afterwards in French exile, and the poet Darin Theodoran, now also abroad. Ordinarily, Romanian political consciousness could not be further removed from the habits and experience of the Czechs, or the Poles, or the Hungarians, or the East Germans, for there is no tradition of political emancipation. A feeling that nothing can be done, that it is not worth banging one's head against a brick wall, that in fact Ceausescu is doing his best, knowing Moscow and knowing his 'people', is quite pervasive, or has been until very recently. *In extremis* the Romanian sin becomes collaboration.

Read Céline if you want to understand us, one writer said. I did, and the deep loss of faith in a humane society in Céline's work makes nonsense of the search for values underlying my travelling. The message of the anti-war novel *Voyage au bout de la Nuit* (1932) is justified cynicism in the face of a hellishly malignant human nature. In order to survive a man must lose all self-respect and allow himself to be led by fear. Céline was considered a collaborator during the war, though he disdained to take sides. He followed members of the Vichy government into flight in Germany, where he became medical adviser to the Vichy leader, Marshal Pétain. After being imprisoned in Denmark he returned to France in 1951, where he continued writing and died in 1961. He stood for the defeat of anything ideal, dispassionate and compassionate about human nature, at the opposite end of the scale from those who believe that the twentieth century, for all its carnage and corruption, can still attract moral commitment and religious faith. A brave and compassionate Romanian Jew was suggesting to me that Romania played a Célinesque role in Europe today.

We talked openly but nervously, in a very smoky coffee bar Mircea had forgotten existed, and where he doubted there would be coffee. There was quite good ready-sugared *cappuccino*, nothing else, and no cake. I wanted to show him a passage in a Western book about Romania. 'Put it away, please. I'm afraid.' Romanians dive beneath the surface to avoid collision, the proverbial wisdom goes, and that seems understandable when they have something real to fear. We turned to the pleasures of writing and reading and agreed that the present state of Romania was most conducive to quiet reading. He apologized for not being able to invite me home. It would be too dangerous. The law forbade entertaining foreigners. I found the openly avowed fear of a wise and experienced man like Mircea quite shocking.

In 1986 Romanians could not remember such a terror since Stalin. They were haunted by a Kafkaesque fear of the unpredictability of a party which had subordinated ideology to power and yet seemed to be powerless before the demands of Moscow. My score of educated, politically aware but hardly dangerous acquaintances braved difficult-ies they could not specify to give me hospitality. The repercussions they might face after I left clouded an otherwise joyful week. A young novelist, Tudor, struck an apt image when he said that although Romanians did not go to prison nowadays for their political views, few of them being active, every man in his silence received a bit of that jail into himself. Romania was inwardly in a state of war, like the Poles under martial law, although the Polish business seemed like an open conflict compared with the continuing unvoiced Romanian plight. The Poles take flight in nostalgia and rebellion as well as in apathy. But the Romanians shut down. Stefan and Mircea and Victor, sensitive but quietistic souls, put me in mind of my own occasional withdrawals from life. I am a train steaming along. Occasionally when I see where the rails lead I cannot bear to continue into the station. I don't want the passengers to confront me. I prefer to linger in the siding. The philosophy of my Romanian friends was superior: one of pale, fastidious, existential retirement and kindness to strangers. The pleasures they took were subtle and cerebral. Stefan was pleased he had once been able to express himself in a novel, which, though it apparently described the fate of communist partisans during the

Second World War, was concerned universally with what it felt like to be 'the enemy'.

Tudor's strength and self-confidence were being tried by mounting suspicion of persecution. He said he was becoming a 'dissident', because publication of his latest book was delayed. Someone was gunning for him. Did he know who the censor in question was? I asked. No, one never knows, but they are colleagues, usually untalented colleagues, 'men and women who can't write'. Communist Britain would produce the same responses in its literary men and women. But other Romanian dilemmas are almost unimaginable.

Radu, for instance, was in despair, having been professionally and personally maligned from abroad by a friend who had defected, and to whom he could not reply. How had he offended the friend? Was it to do with the fact that the friend was homosexual? Whatever the truth was, Radu had a personal score to settle and some emotional confusion to untangle, so he began writing letters, one to the President of the United States and one to the Senate, to inform them he was an upstanding man, the father of a family and a man who abided by his conscience and did not tell lies. He too might become a 'dissident', he threatened. His letters reminded me of the lunatic fringe of Soviet dissent ten years earlier. An insane state gives individual dysfunction a new choice of roles to play.

But I most often thought over the conversation with Stefan in which he had declared poetry to be of no further use. Mircea had commended to me the poet Paul Celan as another way of empathizing with Romania's pain, and Stefan's state of mind seemed to me raw with the same perpetual negation and paradox as Celan's. I do not mean thereby to elevate his bitterness.

The work of Celan, a dispossessed Romanian writing in German, from Paris, is so indirect in its approach to human loss and brutality that it can barely be read except as a thematic sequence. Permeated by the terror of the Holocaust it is a series of images offered by a tormented consciousness trying to distil beauty from deep disorder. The disorder is both within Celan and in the world. Celan was Jewish, born in the Bukovina, that part of northeastern Romania ceded to Russia at the beginning of the war. He lost his parents in the Holocaust, fled to Western Europe, studied German literature and taught

German at the Sorbonne. The inwardness and plastic intensity of his poetry recalls Rilke, but Celan did not have Rilke's faith to endure. He was a man on the path of non-survival in a Célinesque world, given to dying rather than lying. He committed suicide before he was fifty.

There was gossip of a suicide in high places in Bucharest. A highly-placed and powerful, collaborating intellectual had lost his son. This young man had suffered a nervous breakdown after his wife defected to Israel. Family pressure to minimize the political scandal drove him to kill himself soon after. The father was distraught and only his academic position and his political power sustained him. Colleagues said he had of late become all the more arbitrary and unapproachable, sitting for long hours in his plush office with cheap furniture and a photograph of Ceausescu on the wall. I met him once, briefly. His appearance was immaculately Western, a fastidious, trim figure in late middle age, with billowing, well-cut white hair, a good shetland pull-over, fine shirt, tie, discreet grey suit, sheepskin-lined leather boots. He must have wondered as much as I did where he could find satisfaction. The system he served and which rewarded him had proved insupportable to his son. The defection and suicide it provoked had destroyed a family and now threatened through the destruction of the father's reputation to claim another victim. What a life there was here crying out to be put on the tragic stage! When future playwrights are looking for an epoch marked by distorted idealism and muffled terror they will find it in extreme, so-called Stalinist communism.

I went out to supper that evening, preoccupied by forms of despair. My host, Mrs Gheorghiu, told me she had often considered throwing up her teaching job and her party membership, because of the necessary mouthing and instruction of absurd values. But I could see she wouldn't have harmed herself. She didn't want to lose her place in society. As she admitted, what she most feared at forty-five, a glamorous and non-bohemian woman, was *la misère*.

We dined on mullet caviare fetched from friends living on the Black Sea, and meat and vegetables, and fruit and cheese and gâteau, excellent wine and strong coffee. 'Now see if Romanians have nothing to eat!' declared Mrs Gheorghiu's only male guest, a suave, smartly-suited man who taught computer science. 'Today is not every day,' Mrs Gheorghiu said, 'but it's true, it's not so bad. We can find what we need. It's a case of knowing people, that's all.'

'Anna is such a good cook,' the cyberneticist's wife unctuously added. The only other person present at the table was Mr Gheorghiu, my host's elderly husband. I liked him for not speaking, though it turned out he couldn't to me, except in Romanian and a few words of German.

It was a rather muddled evening in which I was tempted to drink too much to escape the misery of fatuously comparing Romanian prices and wages with British and discussing the relative material wealth of the rest of the East Bloc. Everyone pretended to be very impressed with everyone else's French, except for poor Mr Gheorghiu, whose name I never learnt. Occasionally we plunged into German for the sake of politeness. The muddling factor was material generosity, for there lurked suspicions in everyone's mind as to what was really happening when an unknown English woman was invited to share an intimate dinner between two couples.

But in fact the conversation went very well. The two men, though Mrs Gheorghiu's husband was much older and more tired than his guest, were both keen to talk about world affairs. They explained the pleasure they found in listening to the BBC and following foreign news. Mr Gheorghiu admired the World Service coverage of the Falklands War as a model of impartial newscasting. The other man admired Margaret Thatcher for her forthright management of another country once threatened with economic decline. The subject arose of the new Russian leader, Mikhail Gorbachev. It was early days so far as his reform programme was concerned and everyone was wary. After the Geneva summit with President Reagan white doves had appeared as a new backcloth to Romanian television news, the cyberneticist observed scathingly. 'Gorbachev is a man who thinks like all the others but has the skill to appear not to,' he said.

Mention of the doves diverted everyone into denouncing Romanian television. It was broadcasting just a few hours every evening, and then only news and foreign films, some of them untitled, so that the broadcasting authority could avoid paying copyright fees. With an unpredictable, bargain basement mixture on offer, Laurel and Hardy one evening, Richard Burton as Wagner the next, people were buying aerials to receive Bulgarian television, and that rankled, because it signified a reversal of the old Balkan cultural pecking order.

We were straying into shallower, more gossipy waters now. The women talked with me about the arts, but mostly about clothes and our figures. 'I thought you were a student, from your clothes,' said Mrs Gheorghiu, for once openly critical, and I remembered her looking me up and down in my oilskins on first meeting. As I say, this is a sophisticated country. But the general tone of the evening remained smooth and mutually flattering. Mrs. G. had marvellous long strawberry blonde hair and a lustrous green robe, though I was pleased I was slimmer.

The museum devoted to the composer George Enescu was closed. 'Do you want to go? I can talk to someone, I can fix it.' This was the barter system in operation to provide services, I guessed, somewhat *à la russe*. (We used to get pictures framed in exchange for several bottles of export-quality vodka.)

Then the conversation took a sudden swing back to Gorbachev and play-acting. Was not the whole of Romanian society based on dissembling? said the cyberneticist's wife, a sharp-eyed, sharp-minded, petite brunette. 'Of course! Of course! But what do we do? I'd like to be brave,' said Mrs Gheorghiu, 'but I have to feel safe. I have to know there's money and I have to have a comfortable place to live. It's appalling what we have to say and do, but we need our jobs.' I offered a little summing up. 'No one believes what he says and no one is what he appears. Is that it?' They all smiled and the other woman faked dimness for my benefit. 'I once met an American diplomat and he was so sincere,' she said.

Still, I couldn't beat them, so eventually I decided to be disingenuous too. 'Have I met any Party members yet, Mrs. G?' I said on the way home. 'But, darling, we're all Party members, everyone is, well, with the exception of a few workers.' The statistics were about as true as the evening.

It's difficult living amid constant lying. I remember the pain of my friend in Poland and some of my own bursts of rage at reading or being given deliberately misleading information. But in various ways my Romanian friends have learned to adapt. Victor explained to me how deeply ingrained self-censorship had become in his case. It was a painful fact to recognize about himself and he felt undermined as a writer. After a decade of holding back he no longer knew what he wanted to say, nor how to say it. Stefan felt the same constraints but spoke of the liberating effect of writing in a foreign language. He explained that a literary critic might become an expert in a foreign literature in order generally to 'say more' about life and art than a specialist in Romanian. A poet too might try to write in a language other than his native tongue as a matter of spiritual survival. This was something Mircea had tried, and while making no claims for the quality of the poetry, he marvelled at the emotional release the experience brought him. Another charming elderly writer spoke of the advantages of being the translator of a great foreign novelist. He could ask Henry James or Graham Greene quietly: what would you have thought of a situation like this?

I'm very happy this week being reminded of the consolations of literature; and being amid people who not only accept but almost welcome the fact that times of political oppression are times for reading. But I regard those times more circumspectly nowadays, knowing *my* periods of withdrawal are only temporary, and a matter of choice.

Midweek, and I needed time to myself after days of talking. Deciding to travel, with great difficulty and after a queue three times as long as the one to go from Prague to Brno, I bought a ticket and set off for Braşov. The train rattled north from Bucharest into the mountains, past the former royal resorts of Sinaia and Predeal. It was a glorious day for winter sports and the train was full of young people with skis. It was also, 8 January, Elena Ceausescu's birthday and the party newspaper *Scînteia* had devoted nearly three of its six pages to her and her husband.

Romania has always been dominated, though under royal rule its suffering was not as great as now and it had considerably more *élan*. After Ottoman suzerainty ended, German royalty was brought in to sit on the Romanian throne. The last king to reign, Carol II, went into exile in 1944. Taking his place, the Ceausescus, the second generation of communist rulers since 1945, are obscure despots.

Braşov is one of the seven 'Burgs' of Transylvania or, as it is called in German, of the Siebenbürgen. The solid town is built around the vast, 'black' Protestant church and lies in a bowl beneath the mountains. There's a New Year's children's fair in bright toytown colours, now blanketed in snow, and an aeroplane fairground ride in the main square. Away from the centre are several small Lutheran churches, each with its own picturesque square. In the graveyards most of the names are German and many of the occupants from the 1940s died in Russia, somewhere unknown or unnamed. The inscriptions remind me what a vast difference it has made to my life that my friend Klaus from Timişoara, whose past I was searching for last time I was in Romania, was not killed in the fighting.

Rows of small, individual houses rose up the hillside and broad paths circled the wooded mountain. The main path gave a low aerial view of the town. Along it I passed a café and a bar. The day had apparently brought the first good snow of the year and the children were tobogganing continuously down the less busy streets. There was no time to go to a restaurant for lunch, so I bought some hard dry biscuits, one of the few items for which there was no queue, and a small bottle of local *ţuica*, which I enjoyed, though it reeked as if of manure. I walked for several hours and it was good to be alone, not talking, just feeling the air and the pleasure of being in motion. I went on, far up into the trees, then as the light faded I came down from the mountain into the German bookshop, with its yellow light and brown floor wet and slippery with melted snow. The day, with its sudden burst of physical exercise, and colour, and its Germanic atmosphere, had blossomed.

The idea of the Braşov trip had been to get out into the country, which I had done. Exhausted, I slumped back. To get a snack at the chaotic railway station had been a challenge, which brought back memories of the bizarre system in Russian cafés and shops. One had to name what one wanted first, pay for it, then go back and collect it.

The difficulty was finding out what the cake was called. The compartment was hot and crowded. One woman was crocheting mink-coloured berets with great speed and dexterity. She was the real Romanian economy; everyone admired her and had a question. But then a thin, quiet woman in her late twenties, sitting in the corner, had a peculiar turn. The woman alongside me began to rub the younger woman's limbs and she was ushered out to the window and ordered to take deep breaths. One of the men dashed off to the buffet to buy a sweet drink. The other man made soothing comments, leaving me the only person unable to show concern. Perhaps she was pregnant? I gestured, waking up and seeking an easy overture. He smiled and shook his head. She sat again, clutching her bottled drink, still pale. Now she had become the focus of everyone's attention she could tell her tale. It was to do with her small daughter living in Bucharest and the child's father, who was black. She was travelling up from Braşov to settle some problem urgently. 'Go to the Embassy,' one man cried. 'No,' said the crochet expert, 'go to the police.' The contradictory advice rallied back and forth until everyone tired of giving it. One supposed the father was trying to take the little girl away from the mother, and possibly out of the country.

Once the interest in being sympathetic died the young woman's tragedy became a source of entertainment. Everyone had a funny story of mixed coupling to relate. We rocked along on a sea of racist gossip, just as I had done with Dr Becker on the way to Lenauheim. 'Buna sera, doamni!' I said as I left, which raised smiles and fears that I had understood all they had been saying; but I shook my head, and said no, I was not even Hungarian.

I lost my way between the station and the centre of the city, after curfew time. 'Is this where the Number 8 goes from?' a Romanian voice asked. The overture established that I was a foreigner and I found myself walking with a stranger through the back streets instead of taking the bus. It turned out he didn't know Bucharest well, but he knew many languages. Who was this stranger who could speak to me in English, or French, or German, not to mention being fluent in Spanish? I didn't care. Petre I'll call him. I wasn't sure the name he gave me anyway was really his. We laughed, exchanging some vulgar suspicions about Bulgaria. They train Nicaraguan terrorists there, he said. They live in a luxury hotel outside Sofia.

About Romania? He shrugged. What could he say, except that it was so poor, and security so tight that we had to make this circuitous walk in the night instead of going for coffee. The poverty was all the Russians' fault for taking so much money and goods by way of reparations after the war. As he talked he seemed to be reliving his father's or perhaps a collective family experience, because like Vesko in Yugoslavia, remembering the famine in Montenegro, he was too young for the memory to have been his own. The Russian troops when they came wanted wristwatches. Petre knew the words they used: *'Davaite chasy!'*. ('Give us your watches!').

Arguments still rage over the precise order and political colour of events in 1944, when Romania, which fought with the Nazis, went over to the approaching Russians in the vain hope of staving off invasion. The then nascent Communist Party claims some of the credit for the turn though it seems to have been a clear case of switching sides for thoroughly pragmatic reasons.

We were within a few hundred yards of my hotel.

'I will ring you. I won't say who I am or where we shall meet, but I'll be there. We'll go to a concert at the Athenaum. Perhaps we can have dinner afterwards.'

'Yes, I'd like that. I'll look forward to it,' I said, shaking his hand.

'You know they're building a metro in Bucharest, mademoiselle? And do you know what's good about that? They've moved the Russian soldier into a field.' Tudor laughed from his belly. After the war a monumental column topped with a Soviet soldier was erected in Bucharest's Victory Square in memory of the Soviet 'liberation'. It rankled to have a foreign soldier in the one site in the city named after Romania's final independence from the Turks, but now he's away.

'You've heard the joke? If we had meat it would be like the war.'

'And the other one? A Soviet general was asked how long it would take to subdue the Romanians. Two days, or a week if they came out in the streets to welcome us.'

Romania doesn't believe in itself. It has the opposite of national pride.

I had an appointment with an academic in a political job, whose brief it was to further knowledge of Romanian culture abroad, and keep tabs on Romanian émigrés. His aides said the audience was an unusual privilege, so I shouldn't ask provocative questions. So we began grandly to discuss the history of ideas. *'Ah, mais c'est mon sujet aussi,'* he said, another one anxious to reveal his excellent French. Our meeting turned into a learned monologue on the Romanian Orthodox faith as distinct from the Greek and the Russian churches. 'You see the Romanian church is a homely, apolitical institution, mademoiselle. It's growing in popularity, and tolerated by our government, despite official atheism.' The chief propagandist was trying to sell me religion as a way to my possible eventual acceptance of official Romania, I reflected, giving me the harmless line dressed up as the bold one, the political cause dressed up as the culturo-historical. What a waste of valuable time.

Yet it was a strange encounter. I came away only with the impression of this high-placed man's fear of a foreigner. He wouldn't talk to me about anything real. I should have asked him why but I couldn't bring myself to cause a row.

'This is Mr Petrascu who not only edits a newspaper but is also a distinguished poet. Last year he was awarded a state prize.'

Petrascu bows, smiles and extends a large, plump, brown-suited arm. 'May I introduce my colleagues. Without this highly efficient team I would be, be . . .'

Everyone laughs and looks grateful to be part of the excellent team for another day. I remember something Stefan told me, that people can only afford to be out for themselves nowadays, and that there is no possibility of involvement in community life; that there *is* no community under this system and this regime.

I was visiting the offices of Petrascu's newspaper. A young man who looked and behaved like the Soviet chess champion Anatoly

Karpov spoke of his fondness for reading Gerard Manley Hopkins. He wanted to interview me for the paper about my positive impressions of Romania. He and his slick, jumpy colleagues feared me and feared each other. The communist era has encouraged artful dodgers, sacrificed pride and personal compromise. Men and women in the street look apprehensive and quickly confess to it, in the manner of Céline's Bardamu. It's extraordinary but the idea that under mature communism the state will wither away since every citizen will embody its ways is close to being realized in Romania.

Petre rang. The music was fully booked, so we had dinner in one of the most expensive hotels in town. A cat settled between our two sets of feet under the corner table where we were shown. Where was the listening device, in the plastic flowers or the cat's collar? Petre, whose manners were very soft, gave me a wry smile. 'It doesn't matter anyway, does it? Do you like to drink wine?'

The food came, some warm, soft, fried fish, warm chips softened by a spicy sauce and a salad of sweet and sour preserves. The wine was red and the plates were warm. We had a bevy of waiters to serve us. There were hardly any other diners. 'That's because it's too expensive,' said Petre. 'I mean it's a place for special occasions.' The food wasn't up to much and we hardly knew each other so we gave a good part of our attention to the room. A barely-made-up plain young woman with a plump figure, wearing a pale knitted top and slacks, was sitting alone at the head of the next table, staring out towards the distant, empty dance floor. Only one waiter brought her food. 'Mostly it's foreigners who eat here,' said my friend, 'Girls like her come and wait for them. They do well under our system. With an Arab it's 150 dollars a time.'

It was my idea to go on to the Intercontinental for coffee. The late coffee bar was on floor twenty-three. We took the lift but as we padded along the thickly-carpeted corridor Petre looked uncomfortable.

'Go on,' I whispered. 'They won't know you're not foreign. We'll only speak English. Leave it to me.'

'What? With me dressed like this? I *look* like a Romanian.' He plucked gently at his sheepskin coat.

In the event 10 p.m. was too late even for the late bar. We could have tried the *Bier* bar but our spirits were crumbling. 'No,' said Petre, 'I've got a plan. Trust me. You go to your hotel. Tell me the room number. I'll find you.'

When we did meet later it seemed like a miracle.

'Surely the corner room is bugged,' I said. 'I always seem to be lodged in corners.'

'Yes, but it doesn't matter. Let's finish the *ţuica*.'

Petre discovered some pieces of German wisdom in the far recesses of his head while I recounted some of the purposes of my travelling, some of the desire to sort out my priorities.

'You remember what Goethe said,' he began in German, ' "Where there's light there is also a lot of darkness." And why are you so interested in politics? I think that's a pity for a woman.'

We were sure we were being overheard, but the idea made us all the happier.

'Are you sure you won't get into trouble?'

We were like children. The prohibitions of the state had reduced us to a furtive whispering.

'No. Just be careful in the morning. Don't smile or say hello. A capitalist woman and a communist man mustn't be seen breakfasting together.'

Strange to meet Mrs Gheorghiu after this, but she's sensed something. She wants to know 'what it's like to be a Western woman'. She whispers in the stairwell, making a show of the risk involved in taking me home. 'I think it's different in the West,' she says. 'With some women here too. But I'm old-fashioned. I'm naive and I'm afraid of being exploited. I have lots of education but a peasant mentality. I want a man to look after me and be kind and generous and good, and I don't want to be left on my own.'

'That's too limiting, Mrs. G. I can't bring myself to want it. Don't you care about your freedom?'

'I'm afraid. I'm simply afraid. There's no use pretending. I met a millionaire once in France and he offered to take me all over the country and I was too afraid to go. I had other offers to stay abroad and I turned them down. When my first husband died I was in a panic who to choose next. I settled on the one I thought would be most kind and solid, though he was much older than me. And now look, it's just like the system. He lies to me. There are so many things we don't say to each other.'

An inner system of mutual disinformation to preserve external order and avoid direct conflict: the justification is security. The Party is a dishonest marriage, keeping hold of people by false rites of union, though some break away. A philosopher who often transgresses the bounds of what is acceptable to the Party, a political debauchee, tells me that when he is called in to account for himself it is as if by a hurt spouse talking excessively reasonably. She says: 'If you've been out meeting new people and enjoying yourself surely you want to share the experience with me. You must be bursting to tell me about it. Come home. You know where you belong.'

On the way back to the hotel at lunchtime I met Petre unexpectedly in the street. The meeting took my breath away. He asked me if I was having an enjoyable holiday in Bucharest and whether I had been to the art gallery yet. Then slowly, looking straight ahead of him, he walked on.

In the afternoon the opera started early because of the curfew. *La Traviata* was a splendid refuge and Violetta's extravagant glamour and dependence reminded me of Mrs Gheorghiu.

By the time I had walked back it was already mid-evening on my last night in Bucharest. Petre rang me, as we had arranged, pretending to be an anonymous student of English. He wanted to know what 'jeepers creepers' meant and 'over the moon' and by that means we said goodbye. The Party, having seized all the obvious means of communication, had turned us into stealthy adulterers and given us a bolstering brief romance.

8

A Lobotomized Country
East Germany 1986

What is freedom then? Everyone will answer me: it is to be allowed
to live according to one's own rules. One can call it scholastic,
bourgeois, reactionary and insipid, but it remains true and will
never be different, that to politicize the German concept of freedom
is immediately to distort it. Our religious and philosophical history
is at work in the least educated man, with the effect that forced by
this [Great] War to consider nationality, he can think and feel in
no other way. There is a symbol for the German separation of
intellect and politics, of radical theory and life, of pure and practical
thought: it is the two separate volumes of Kant's critical double
work which stand alongside each other ... I believe it to be the
plain and unshakeable truth that the German concept of freedom
will always be of an intellectual-spiritual nature: an individualism
which, in order to express itself politically, would necessarily have
to engender institutions other than the bald, abstractions of the
political West and of 'human rights'.

Thomas Mann *Confessions of an Unpolitical Man*

Germany at last! My first love affair, home of the sharpest and sweetest
erotic memories, of the keenest joy in reading. Goethe and Schiller,
Hölderlin and Nietzsche, Rilke and Mann: I had been saving myself
for communist Germany through the memory of the most beautiful
poetry, passionate, dignified and liberating, that I had ever
encountered.

I began my visit one cold March night in West Berlin. I wanted
two weeks' travelling and decided to cover as much ground as possible.
This seemed feasible, since for family reasons I wasn't bringing Eliz-

abeth on this journey. Moving on every day made me doubly lonely in the end, but the beginning was, as so often, teeming with impressions. West Berlin is that kind of high-living city instantly redeemed by its tumble-down neglected corners, the acute historical and political awareness its schoolchildren are taught, and forget, but which the city stores up for curious visitors, and its inevitable cosmopolitanism. It is a Western city, full of financial scandal, political gossip, commercialized sex and rampant, misdirected intelligence, but it is given a stronger character than most to resist blandness and indifference by its position on an island of free land in the middle of the GDR.

I stayed the night in West Berlin with a stranger, Berthold, a student of philosophy, the friend of a friend, who had a small, high-ceilinged apartment in a good inner city suburb. We drank *Sekt* – German champagne – with some friends of his, then when they had gone we stayed up to talk, sitting on the floor. One of my colleagues in Moscow turned out to be a friend of Berthold's father. I was half a generation older than my host, but it did not seem unnatural to have a long conversation about our ambitions. Berthold wanted to paint, and had a studio next door. He wasn't greatly taken with philosophy, but he loved Berlin, a deliberately chosen home. His manner was mild and interested and delicate. He didn't know much about the East Bloc. He lived on the doorstep of the GDR but had only been there once, very briefly, mostly in East Berlin. Instead of personal reminiscences he told me the story of a girl he knew. She had been having some problems with her boyfriend, on top of which came a bad day at work. She caught her train home to the suburb of Marienborn in a blur and fell asleep as the carriage rattled along. When she awoke she found herself by mistake in the East Berlin suburb of Mariendorf. Was it an innocent misreading of destinations? Or was it a Freudian mistake, induced by the desire to get away from her problems: who knows? The East German authorities put her under observation in hospital for a few days, then returned her home. I went to sleep pondering this story.

Next morning Berthold was up early and had laid out a stupendous German breakfast and a jogging route. His face seemed more assured at night, and looked softer and indecisive by day. He didn't drink coffee because it made him nervous. I ran along the canal tow path. I quickly met a Turkish medical student who was much more interested in the GDR than Berthold, more enthusiastic and a frequent visitor. 'People are much nicer to each other over there, you'll see. It's not all to do with money.' We did an extra circuit of the park together. Our breath was steaming in the sunshine.

Later, as Berthold and I second-breakfasted together, I enthused about Berlin and about being on the continent of Europe, that old feeling of excitement at being intimately caught up in a babble of nationalities and ideas. 'It's true,' he said. '*Das Anderswerden is leichter hier.*' ('It's easier to become someone, or something, else here.') I thought about his fleeing friend. More mundanely we talked about our daily routine: food, exercise, reading and sleep. Each recognized in the other a tinge of the monastic. Rather later in the day than I intended I set off for the Friedrichstrasse checkpoint.

Friedrichstrasse is where you cross into the German Democratic Republic by underground if you are not a Berliner. The warren of yellow tiles looks much the same on either side of the frontier, and every day without anyone obviously noticing or caring the trains screech and lurch their way through dark tunnels and past disused stations labelled in the old Sutterlin script, backwards and forwards from one Germany to the other, so it is hard to know when exactly you have become someone else, until you examine the weights and labels. On the communist side the chocolate is terribly expensive, the transport cheaper, the coins much lighter, and the rolling stock still nominally belongs to the Deutsche Reichsbahn. I was suddenly nervous about not being able to make the right distinctions – like Berthold's friend getting lost; afraid that I wouldn't be able to judge the quality of life around me.

From Friedrichstrasse I made my way to the Ostbahnhof and, finding I had more than an hour to wait for the train north, I took some soup in the comfortable, clean, warm buffet restaurant. The choice was between Gulaschsuppe, the Hungarian speciality which has become common property in Central Europe, or solyanka, a Russian style of sour soup which is far less well known, except in Russia and the GDR. Here the solyanka was made with pork and capers and a rich stock soured with lemon juice. It would have been hard to find better anywhere. I sat and ate it alone.

The train was crowded and didn't leave at the appointed time. In the end it was two *hours* late, without any official explanation reaching my ears, but no one complained. The young men in the carriage were shouting at each other over their bottles of beer. They played tapes of Bob Geldof's Live Aid concert and some old Beatles numbers from my early teens. The lack of individual style tempted me to think the entire West would seem camp to them, if the idea meant anything.

At the hotel in Neubrandenburg there were police forms to fill out and various bureaucratic regulations to comply with, all of which meant I wouldn't be able to realize my plan, conceived at a distance, of travelling overland the next day by bus. Vaguely I thought I ought to protest. It was absurd, but I would have accepted a commercial excuse more readily. It's because the State was involved I felt angry at being powerless.

Neubrandenburg was flattened in the war except for the four towers of the ancient city wall. It was rebuilt on the medieval cross within a circle pattern and early on Good Friday its deserted streets looked excessively neat. The only sign of life was some panting old coaches waiting to pick up their Russian loads outside The Four Towers hotel. I walked across the square outside the hotel to examine a statue where flowers had been laid. This Marx Engels Platz had nothing to do with German medieval town planning. It was vast and unsheltered, I suppose in communistspeak it might be called international. The statue was of Marx and had been adorned with chrysanthemums at some very early hour. Someone wanted to give the impression Neubrandenburg needed Marx's resurrection urgently, I decided, trying to amuse myself. Not out of scepticism, more out of ignorance I went close to read the inscription and verify I had put the right name to the familiar face. 'Marx?' said a young woman passing to the young man on her arm, both of them watching me. 'No idea,' he said. They walked on, tourists in their own country. I seemed to have given them a fleeting conscience about not being interested.

The rest of the town I took at a slow jog. I only had a few hours in which to see everything. Rows of very tidy closed shops and shuttered, flat-fronted little houses with brass plates spelling out the occurrence of this or that professional practitioner or craftsman stood quietly. Neubrandenburg seemed to have a proliferation of master shoemakers, *Schumachermeister*, who sounded all the more magical in their own language, like something out of Wagner or Grimm.

The real run began with the entrance beyond the town to the recently designated culture park. Suddenly I was beside the Tollensesee, one of the picturesque Mecklenburg lakes, almost in open countryside. The rain had stopped, the trees shone silver in an occasional burst of sunlight, and a slither of mist hung over the calm water. It was so clear I could see the bottom, and even the runnels in the sand. I stepped out along the tree trunk jetty. A dark strip of land jutted forth in the distance like a much larger jetty. A few people walked or cycled by, while the water birds made perfect landings in full view, inviting applause. In the summer the cafés would be open and people would hire boats.

I'm often overwhelmed by the solace of nature. If you include in nature the satisfaction of the body, let's say exercise and culinary and erotic pleasure, that's probably half of enough. But the other half is friendship. I would have to have friends if I lived here, people I could talk to like Berthold. I couldn't lead my whole life at the water's edge.

I thought of visiting the church, but it was locked, even on Good Friday. So I sat in the only café open, reading a play by the Expressionist Ernst Barlach, one that I had bought years ago, never read, then rediscovered when I knew I would be visiting his birthplace. Barlach was a writer, dramatist and sculptor, and a deeply religious man, who was moved and inspired by a trip he made to Russia at the beginning of the century. I think I can pick up the scent of Dostoevsky in this play's violent juxtaposition of spiritual inspiration and bluff everyday life, perhaps also Chekhov. It's called *The Poor Cousin*.

Northeast Germany from the train is a rural paradise. It doesn't seem to have been touched by the world at large. Of course from the Western political point of view it's a dangerously empty, ambivalent part of Europe, not a place for sightseeing, except by military personnel. For one thing there's a nuclear missile base near Neubrandenburg. But that doesn't destroy the natural beauty of these lakelands;

it even makes it more poignant. For me it's a part of the world immortalized in John le Carré's *The Looking-Glass War*, which appeared not long after the Berlin Wall went up in 1961. This poet of the Cold War created a story about British security using nostalgia to re-recruit a Central European agent who had settled in Britain after 1945. Headquarters lured him out of retirement because he couldn't resist leaving Western progress for this world unchanged since his childhood.

The lure is still there. You have to imagine a lost Europe almost, a world artificially sheltered from the economic and social progress of the post-war West, so old-fashioned and tranquil that the trains still travel slowly and stop at small halts and are late. The taps fall off the bath and the wine is Algerian. Ancient Hungarian buses with the unlikely name of Ikarus criss-cross the flat, sparsely populated countryside. I'm deeply taken with this old world.

So much so that when I emerge from the train in Güstrow in mid-afternoon my heart is racing. This town was not touched during the war and it represents, just as I had imagined it to be but never presumed to find intact, an old Germany, untouched by transatlantic fashion. It's given to solyanka not hamburgers, slowly simmered home-made table dishes, not ultra-fast, pre-packed snacks. And the town is laid out just as it was three hundred years ago, with the church in the centre, surrounded by the main square containing the only hotel and shops, and leading from the periphery, residential cobbled streets. There's a West German limo parked in one of the streets and it's so wide it almost blocks the way. But the streets themselves remain unselfconscious, with here and there a house falling down.

I take cakes in the little hotel, instead of lunch, and the room reminds me of my grandmother's parlour, padded everywhere with brocade and delimited by bad light filtered through net curtains.

Barlach, who lived here, concentrated his art on the humble life. The sculptures often figuratively represent men and women girded against the weather, at the mercy of nature but also an accepting part of it. The individuality and eloquence of the human form are submerged to reveal an intensified capacity for unembittered endurance. The plays are modern but emphatically Christian. They have on the one hand a strong flavour of Dostoevsky and Chekhov, on the other a medieval spirituality which would have appealed to Thomas Mann. *The Poor Cousin* takes place at Easter – I suppose anyone who travels for meaning must believe in coincidences – and concerns a man, Hans Iver, who wants to die to save the world from its suffering. His obsession obtrudes a disturbing religious consciousness into an oblivious society:

> Well, don't you sometimes have moments when you, the poor cousin, see the Lord on high go past in his glory? That is, you feel in yourself that something is coming close to you, something you realise you are related to. And your heart stops beating, you gasp for air and bellow like a cow in your misery. You, Mr Biscuit, don't you sometimes bellow over your misery?

There's no reason to imagine the setting for such an extraordinary event as the passing of Hans Iver would be much different today. They would be talking about it in Güstrow's special shop for spices and teas, and in the supermarket where they won't serve customers who don't take a basket, and in the post office. But there's a propaganda banner over the post office – OUR KNOWLEDGE AND SKILL FOR A STRONG SOCIALISM AND A MORE SECURE PEACE – which means something has changed.

Dinner in the hotel restaurant: with the Algerian red wine I ordered Wurstfleisch, chopped cooked meat in a piquant sauce with baked cheese on top, which seemed to be an East German provincial *Delik-atess*. The combination was quite edible, if unrefined. But the room was smoky and hot and because of my busy plans for the next day I decided to retire early. A drunken youth taking a break from the Easter weekend dance in the next room pressed against me as I collected my room key. He seemed delighted to be sworn at in English. 'That's just what he wants to do,' said his friend, laughing.

In Güstrow, just as from the first minutes across the frontier in Berlin, I wanted to be alert to all signs of coercion, to whatever seemed to be a misplaced, unwanted, unusually wordy, pseudo-philosophical super-ordering of daily life. At the same time, to counter it, I was looking out for signs of genuine devotion, genuine form, genuine thought. The magnified attraction of Barlach was his authenticity.

I checked how far it was out to the Barlach atelier, the largest permanent home of his work. Barlach lived there from 1910 till his death in 1938. About four miles on foot, they said, or there was an occasional bus. My train left at 11 a.m. The museum opened at 9 a.m. I decided to go on foot.

> The wind is rattling the tiles on the roof. Just listen. Just like fat Doctor World used to wheeze when he put his ear to a man's chest, and used to wheeze and listen and wheeze. He's dead, but he was like the world itself, wild and unable to make any sense of what was round about. But when I hear a wind like this, I always think it could be the doctor, the world doctor, who wants to listen . . .

As in the play, the wind blowing off the Baltic Sea was extraordinary. The four-mile walk would take me an hour, people had said in the hotel, probably more today, because of the wind, so I ran along the path, through a colony of holiday cottages and allotments, following the meandering water. The wind whirled through the man-sized reeds and bent the trees to breaking point. I arrived at the airy lakeside atelier a few minutes before the museum opened, an unexpected figure, I suppose, in my running shorts with a little bit of money tucked in my shoe.

A young attendant appeared and let me into a series of very light rooms. It was now Easter Sunday and a folio first edition of *The Poor Cousin* lay open amidst the sculptures and drawings. Printed explanations of Barlach's career and labelled exhibits said he hoped and desired mankind would get better.

I asked the attendant about the wind. Nothing special, he said, and I continued browsing through the postcards at the souvenir desk. We were rather shyly aware of each other. I decided to buy a largish reproduction of a Barlach sketch and began fishing in my shoe for a 20–mark note. 'How are you going to carry it?' he asked. True, I hadn't thought of that. 'I'll have to send it to you.' I smiled and scribbled down my address.

Wilhelm wanted to study sculpture. He preferred the elongated, weightless figures of Giacometti to Barlach – I think because he needed to get as far away from the spirit of socialism in art as he could – but he like his job well enough. He was something of a Giacometti figure himself – long and thin in jeans and a pale blue pullover, gentle-mannered and quiet. We were talking about our ambitions and disappointments. He urged me into a far room where we couldn't be overheard. I talked about plans to write this and that and leave my job, and what a shock life had been in Moscow, and in return he talked about himself. He wanted to study, but for political reasons it was out of the question. It involved too much compromise. Anyway he didn't want to commit himself to a particular way of life. He had no real plans but perhaps some day he would leave the GDR. Then he would travel to Italy. But it was hard to live like this, indecisively, surrounded by friends who were leaving, one after the other, in a country where people were leaving, thousand upon thousand – half a million since the Germanies divided in 1952. And an undecided life ruled out getting married and having children. He was experiencing the negative side of that openness to new experience and change which had hovered as an ideal over my talks with Berthold.

The conversation flowed as if we had both been starved of it for many years. I told Wilhelm about the life of a Russian nineteenth-century statesman who fascinated me, a man with a European education and a love of Goethe, who went back to Russia and became one of the most persecutory and anti-artistic figures of the century. I talked about the frustrations as I saw them of being a Western journalist in Eastern Europe. 'I'll send you books,' he said. 'There are lots of things you must read.' I had just read with enormous enthusiasm Christa Wolf's *A Model Childhood*, an autobiographical study of a child's experience of Nazi Germany and the author's attempt to come to terms with her memories. 'Yes, Christa Wolf, of course, but other things too, less well known.' Afterwards, outside the museum, I was so pleased to have made contact with a real person the ground felt like a trampoline.

In Schwerin Soviet soldiers loomed large at the railway station. I wondered what they thought of this country, and tried to eavesdrop on their conversation in the Mitropa buffet. Also I wanted to hear how good their German was, but nothing was audible. Later, after running into Soviet personnel and tourists all over the GDR, I concluded that this inaudibility must be deliberate, like the trick of not letting their eyes meet a stranger's. Such well-schooled people! From the station I walked down the hill to enjoy the view over the water. Young Soviet soldiers beside me who were brought up on tales of Nazi atrocities were inaudibly enjoying a cigarette. Locals find the presence of these foreign teenage conscripts and officers unremarkable and on the Soviet side the occupation must seem quite justified, even humanly necessary.

Schwerin, a once great Elbe trading city, is now a calm and picturesque northern town of mainly military importance. A broad, peaceful stretch of water reaches into the trading heart of it, giving the impression of an old-world and smaller version of Hamburg. The memory of Hamburg is comforting. It was a teenage acquaintance, a city which overwhelmed me with its style and luxury. In fact Schwerin is only faintly like it, given the vast difference in material prosperity, but its new shopping precincts behind the water fit as well as they can with the older, renamed narrow thoroughfares, like Pushkin Street. Potentially it has a similar elegance. At the foot of the town lies a massive, unassailed castle which was the home of the Dukes of Mecklenburg. Its design, in the midst of the water, betrays the Slav influence which has always been strong in this part of Germany. The State Museum nearby and a huge, open square called Alter Garten have the imposing dimensions of a chief city, though the pale green and cream façades of the old administrative buildings are peeling.

Two Russian women opposite me in the train were discussing dress material. They revelled in the discovery that a certain kind was better bought 'at home, *u nas*, in the Union', though their tone was mostly practical. Normally East Germany, because of its good economy, is a good place for anyone in the East Bloc to shop. One woman buys a dress, say in Leipzig, then all her friends 'back in the Union' borrow it to make a pattern. 'There's a Russian base near here, I suppose,' I said to a German woman after they had got out. She nodded without interest, but proceeded to chatter uninhibitedly. Her weekend in Schwerin had been pleasant and she wasn't looking forward to returning to the grime of Leipzig. At least our present train journey was peaceful. The ride up had been upset by football hooligans, who had been drunk and violent and slandered the state, she said, and eventually someone had called the police and one was arrested. This woman wouldn't have told me about football hooligans had she known I was a foreigner. I felt guilty not revealing my identity. We lapsed into silence.

In the dark I laughed to myself about Wilhelm. We had been so engrossed in our conversation in the far room that a queue had formed in the museum lobby of people wanting admission tickets. Then I thought how alien the style of this country must seem to its Russian visitors. Russia has always admired Germany for its powers of will and organization but never loved it. Goncharov wrote his famous novel *Oblomov* (1869) partly about the ambivalent relationship which has existed for centuries. He called the foil to Oblomov's aristocratic Russian character Stolz, the German word for pride, and showed that Stolz through his industry was not in the end any happier on earth than Oblomov though his dreaming and indolence.

It was raining heavily in Magdeburg and out of the huge plate glass windows of the hotel greyness extended everywhere in dull, massive, unrelieved, concrete shapes and wide open spaces. The hotel served the usual cult breakfast with all kinds of bread and meat and cheese and preserves, yoghurt too, and cake. It wasn't bad for early April but the apples were maggoty. April is the worst month for fruit and vegetables right across the East Bloc because of the lack of imports which bring colour and freshness to our markets between seasons; the cruellest month indeed. Then the waiter tried to cheat me. The hotel was a vast palace of luxury in a drab city, parts of which would never be rebuilt to heal the scars of the war. But for the tranquil, cloistered presence of the cathedral, the oldest Gothic church in either Germany, the beauty of earlier centuries had vanished. Winter, dried tubers, a fragmented Central European childhood, '*bin gar keine Russin, stamm' aus Litauen, echt deutsch*'. . . . A crushed place like this seems to signify loss.

I pushed open the door of the cathedral. I had tried church doors in Güstrow and Neubrandenburg and Schwerin without success, so I was doubly keen to glimpse the inside of an institution for which I had built up an image of praiseworthy outspokenness. The main body of the cathedral turned out to be 'under repair' and the three hundred or so worshippers were crowded into a side chapel. I sat doubting whether 'repair' was the only reason for closure, having seen so many 'repair' notices from Moscow to Bucharest and also knowing that what dissent there is in the GDR – and there is relatively little which is not swiftly crushed – finds shelter in the church.

The woman priest began to speak. She spoke of a light in our present darkness, and of 'love in this time of lovelessness and thought-lessness, and courage in this time of uncertainty and fear'. She spoke of having the courage to be christened and urged the congregation to absent themselves from work on Easter Monday to attend church, which was their legal right. Her words reminded me of Mann's insistence on the indestructible spirit of German inwardness as the key to the nation's well-being. She was saying the individual was superior to the state in matters of conduct and conscience; different; more alive.

Mann could not foresee German inwardness ever being forbidden or forced underground. It was an agility of soul which would become more necessary under modern political conditions of mass organizations, not less.

The economic situation which the [Great] War has produced will mean that after the War for decades to come everyone will have to work and earn virtually exclusively for the State. In that case ought not a man to be allowed at least intellectually and spiritually to belong to himself? Under the unheard-of conditions of social involvement and subordination, such as stand before us, won't the spiritual need for independence grow enormously? A culture full of love and a concern with the aristocratic and the individual, a great curiosity and sympathy for the unique individual soul and the eccentric values of the spirit, such things are essential counter-weights against the organised socialism in the state of the future: otherwise life will no longer be worth a brass farthing.

It's gratifying to read his *Confessions* between bouts of melancholy sightseeing.

In Russia this was how the leading religious thinkers – Semyon Frank, father of my elderly friend Viktor in Munich, and Nikolas Berdyaev – reacted to Bolshevism. They wanted to see 'spiritual aristocracy' preserved. They believed that there had to be an active inner principle, whether or not it derived from God, which would always work for the quality of a well-defined and conscientious and creative individual life against mass pressures, and all of them believed in art as an essential 'aristocratic' phenomenon, a saving grace.

From Magdeburg I took the slow train to a smaller, more manageable place, Quedlinburg, the town known as 'the gateway to the Harz forest'. It was a quiet, half-timbered historic spot where many holiday-makers would come in season. I checked into the self-consciously quaint inn in the centre. On the landing, on a crochet mat, was *Pravda*, albeit a few days old, and *Neues Deutschland*, the German equivalent. Downstairs the *Wirtin*, who had probably done the crocheting herself, was flirting with the postman. Not wishing to disturb her with questions about tomorrow's bus timetable I wandered off through the cobbled streets.

The town, more obviously a 'sight' than Güstrow, did not have the same modesty and authenticity, but much money and private effort had been put into making its rows of cottages with the family car outside look spick and span. A rather Italian-looking castle stood above the newer town, and near the castle was the house of the eighteenth-century poet Klopstock. I walked until dark, then took a rest. In my overheated room I left the window open and, lying in the plump feather bed, I could hear Russian voices in the medieval square below. Later on television I watched an East German soap opera, an episode in which the 'head' of what we would call a lower-middle class family was trying to better himself by giving up smoking and taking regular exercise. He had to get over the humiliation of being laughed at by his neighbours and workmates.

One looks around and it is abundantly clear: the social preoccupations, the clothes, even the forms of entertainment in the GDR are Western. The country wants, and to a large extent has, hygiene, civility, public order and a high standard of education; in short, material prosperity.

But it has all this without Western freedom and without acknowledging its German cultural and intellectual identity. It is a lobotomized country, a dystopia, the sort of perfectly-ordered world which was the subject of Zamyatin's *We*.

The little narrow-gauge Harz train from Wernigerode to Nordhausen chugged through the mountains, warm and swaying from side to side, belching smoke, and with a siren from a children's story book. I had never been in a country where the culture was such an improbable blend of quaintness and harshness. The little train reminded me of my first rail trip alone in Germany, down the Neckar valley from Mannheim to Heilbronn. Today I was reading le Carré, which endorsed the feeling of harshness, and watching the scenery, which had the opposite effect. The Harz was not spectacular by Swiss or Italian standards, but had its own drama and was commercially unspoilt. The way led through sandy pine forests and snow still lay on the upper slopes that April evening.

The quaintness and the harshness! Backwards and forwards one moves through the mentalities of before and after the war, from the vestiges of bourgeois institutions and continuing middle-class comforts to harsh pseudo-proletarian militance. It's an extraordinarily disconcerting reality.

You can see it in Quedlinburg where horses and carts shuffle past fierce posters denouncing President Reagan's Strategic Defence Initiative; and in Erfurt, an affluent, smart, modern city with a rich history, but where they deck their buildings like this:

THE INDESTRUCTIBLE FRATERNAL BOND WITH THE SOVIET
UNION IS THE FOUNDATION OF OUR ACHIEVEMENTS AND OF
OUR DEVELOPMENT TO COME.

And:

EMPLOYEES OF THE STATE AND THE SECURITY SERVICES!
GIVE US YOUR BEST SO WE CAN PROTECT THE ACHIEVEMENT
OF OUR WORKERS AND FARMERS MORE RELIABLY!

The savagery of the propaganda hits home because the style of the city, with its pizza take-aways, espresso bars, perfume and herb and spice emporia and richly stocked grocery stores, suggests something else. It's more vicious than anything similar in Poland or Czechoslovakia or Romania, because of having been purged of emotional and national elements. It is fiercely abstract and chiefly appeals for security and alertness in the GDR, which are the appropriate states of mind for a front-line Russian state. German communism cannot be national or patriotic in its appeals for loyalty, nor can it be collective, because of the Nazi past, so it aligns itself with Russia against Hitlerism and against Western imperialism.

The German communist authorities do not want to activate or analyse German guilt over the war, something which is at the centre of dissident awareness here. They need a dynamic, forward-looking nation and so they exploit the least reflective parts of the German character to encourage a militaristic ordering of reality.

A GOOD BALANCE OF PAYMENTS . . . LET'S HAVE YOUR
CONTRIBUTION!

EVERY DAY ON TOP FORM – THE BEST AS NORM!

OUR KNOWLEDGE AND ABILITY FOR STRONG SOCIALISM AND
SECURE PEACE.

Extraordinary it may be, but this country invites its citizens to practise communism in the same way they proverbially keep house, keep their books, and keep fit; that is, highly efficiently, with pride and craftsmanship. That is just the way Nazi Germany exploited the qualities of the nation Thomas Mann loved. It's extraordinary, but nothing fundamental has changed.

We think nothing has changed. But the GDR sees itself born, phoenix-like, out of the ashes of the Second World War, risen on the wings of a man called Ernst Thälmann, who died in the concentration camp at Buchenwald just outside Weimar in 1944. Thälmann was leader of the German Communist Party under the Weimar Republic and during Hitler's rise to power. Every East German town now has a street or a square named after him. I caught up with him in Weimar, a town which 'reads' like a government handout. This was the slogan opposite the railway station:

A Lobotomized Country: *East Germany 1986*

THE THOUGHT AND DEEDS OF ERNST THÄLMANN ARE ALIVE
TODAY. WHAT HE STROVE AND FOUGHT FOR HAS BECOME REALITY.

Thälmann's statue loomed, strewn with fresh flowers, on Lenin
Street as I walked towards the centre. The way led along Karl Marx
Street, Karl Liebknecht Street (Liebknecht was one of the founders
of the German Communist Party), and finally to Goetheplatz and
Schiller Street. It was as if I were passing through a book of allegories
and lessons, but in a distorted, anti-humanist world. Schiller, a great
classical moralist, had a precinct of Best Men and Women named
after him, which displayed photographs of good workers, but his
reputation was being pitfully parodied in order to instil the GDR with
meaning. Weimar! The disappointment was like seeing my friend
Klaus reduced to a mechanical costume doll in a Romanian museum.

In the early nineteenth century cultural pilgrims came to Weimar
from all over Europe and from Russia to pay homage to what Goethe
and Schiller represented: the cultivation of individuality, self-knowl-
edge and inner harmony as leading to beauty in art and moderation
and goodness in life. Liszt later came to live and work in Weimar,
and a fine musical culture grew which attracted Wagner and Richard
Strauss to the small Duchy where Johann Sebastian Bach was once
Kapellmeister. The Weimar Republic was itself a tribute to a rich
past. 'Hitlerism' knew what it was trampling underfoot and, equally,
the GDR, knowing what it stands on, knows what it has buried.

I peered into the bookshops. They displayed as many copies of
Russian and Soviet writers in translation as they did works of Goethe
and Schiller. Schiller's classical educational idealism rubbed spines
with Anatoly Makarenko's prescriptions for raising the new Soviet
man. Though I doubted this bilingual display truly reflected reading
habits in the GDR, it was a strange feeling to be in a country not
allowed to be itself, like being with an old friend who had suffered a
mental breakdown. It was a feeling of great loneliness.

The loneliness was compounded by catching sight in a central
square of a statue of Russia's 'national' poet, Alexander Pushkin,
erected in 1949. I happened to know Pushkin never visited Weimar
and took little interest in German literature. So I queued up in the
tourist office to hear the official explanation. The guide said Pushkin's

friend Zhukovsky once visited Goethe in Weimar. That was why there was a monument. But we both knew the real reason for Pushkin's token presence. After the war Russia did not want Germany to have a pre-eminent culture, past or present, anywhere.

I felt like a grey-haired professor of hermeneutics, limping round this disfigured Weimar with a stick, trying to tease out some reality, reading the few signs of the distorted past that remain, including my own reflection in shop windows. In Moscow I had the same feeling when *Pravda* adopted the tones of the eighteenth-century Enlightenment and wrote about Beauty, Truth and Goodness, and when I had to sit through *Tolstoy Our Contemporary*; and in Hungary when 1956 was ignored or dismissed as counter-revolution; here once again was the need to oppose the inscrutability of deep falsehood. Communism works that way, tightening its disfiguring grip on free culture by small, as it were specialist, steps, such as the Pushkin statue in Weimar. It will never quite be exposed in the daily press, 'serious' newspapers included, for the *intellectual* swindle it is, because one of its most dependable weapons is the subtle misrepresentation of facts and ideas which are difficult for ordinary people to check.

The Goethe and Schiller houses, to which I was bound to pay homage, were crammed with schoolchildren and roped off across their ultra-shiny floors. Bossy middle-aged women officiated at every corner and at the end there was another jam to buy postcards and souvenirs. I spent five minutes in the Goethe house, felt suicidal and went back to the spacious gilded landings of the Hotel Elephant, a distinguished resting-place for lady travellers from Madame de Stael to Charlotte Kestner. Charlotte was a lover of the young Goethe, a woman whom Thomas Mann imagined coming back to Weimar to visit her youth. (This complex, cerebral adventure is related in the novel *Lotte in Weimar*.) These associations belonged to the Elephant in a previous incarnation. I walked out to Goethe's summerhouse. I heard a concert at the Liszt Academy. But I couldn't bring anything to life.

Next morning the bus from the Goethe Platz to Buchenwald took fifteen minutes to drive up the long hill accommodating a Russian army barracks. I was on my way to one of the largest of the National Socialists' death camps, the first I had ever seen.

The camp stood high above the town in the midst of beech woods and looked out for miles over unspoilt farmland. On top of the ridge, with no buildings in sight, the silence, once the bus had pulled away, was broken only by bird song and the sound of a Soviet helicopter. It was a blue, sunny day, still cold, and the beech trees were not even in bud. Signs in Russian and German forbade transistor radios and picnics.

The entrance to the Buchenwald monument is a portico of blocks of rough, pale, unadorned stone, with four series of double columns. The so-called Street of Blood leads down to the two grass and bramble-covered craters which are mass graves. The name is reminiscent of the Field of Blood where Judas buried his silver. In the adjacent Street of Nations every country with Buchenwald victims has a memorial.

The descent, down broad stone steps, is marked by seven stone murals, about ten feet high, about twelve feet long, telling what happened to the prisoners, many amongst them, as if to mock the closeness to Weimar, artists and intellectuals. Some 56,000 perished before the camp finally liberated itself. The tablets, one for each year the camp existed between 1937 and 1945, are like stations of the cross. In the first three, men with bowed heads and bent backs are pulling a cart uphill, whipped by a guard; in the middle of the tableau two more men are being forced to erect a gallows post; on the far side a beech tree is being felled by a weary prisoner who had dropped his saw and is being kicked in the back by another guard. Behind them an inmate is hanging by his hands from another beech tree, while a compassionate soul passes him a cup from behind bars.

Buchenwald exudes a stately eeriness. It is a strange, affective experience, the more so for being out of doors and simple, and avoiding the creation of any suspicion of aesthetic contrivance. I and three off-duty Soviet officers were the only visitors that morning. They took snapshots of each other leaning on the parapet of the memorial bell tower.

The artistic achievement of the Buchenwald monument is outstanding. On the bell tower stands a sculpture of suffering men and women, grouped together and staring boldly out to the Türingian horizon. A poem is inscribed on the back of the murals by Johannes R. Becher, the GDR's most celebrated 'national' poet. I can only translate it approximately:

Here a death camp was built.
Barbed wire coiled remorseless.
Grey barracks stood and men suffered.
Searchlights blazed in the darkness.
A gallows towered up in a show of force.
Guilt! Think of those years of guilt!
This was the death camp Buchenwald!

Becher's poem reaches its height in these opening lines. It goes on less convincingly to mark the birth of the GDR in the resurrected spirit of Thälmann, who was himself a victim of Buchenwald:

Greetings to Ernst Thälmann, Germany's greatest son,
who stood before us bathed in light
while all around was celebration.
It was as if all peoples were in harmony
the International was sung –
this world must be ours, it must be –
and Thälmann raised the flag.

The idea is that a new age of humanism has begun. But there is no new age of humanism here. Look at Erfurt, look at little Weimar dressed up to look like a German Cheltenham but deeply sinister, and look now at Leipzig.

Everywhere I go I am troubled by the GDR's material prosperity, the grotesqueness of which is underlined by its soullessness. Tourism in all the East Bloc countries is a form of bribery, an exchange of comforts for tacit acceptance of the status quo, but here the comforts and the compromise are excessive.

From the panoramic window of my suite on the twenty-third floor of the best hotel in Leipzig I stared out over the city; it was grimy, but its size and the fog hanging visibly about the blueish white lights made it a little thrilling that night. I had warmth, a luxurious bathroom, a cocktail bar and a little medallion of chocolate on the pillow; the colour television set received West German and local programmes perfectly. From the GDR side they were showing a Soviet film about a beautiful, heroic girl windsurfer who fell in love with her suntanned, handsome, middle-aged trainer. Unlike the young self I caught up with in Lenauheim, this girl found the strength to resist Eros and channel all her energy into winning a gold medal for her country. That somehow also made her turn to a more suitable, younger man. It wasn't a sexy film, but the surfing finals were nicely done, with a nod to the Ride of the Valkyries in imitation of Francis Ford Coppola's *Apocalypse Now*. The TASS journalist typing out the result with one finger was a good example of even a cliché going out of date.

I switched off and wrote for half an hour about the guilt of the GDR, about Thomas Mann battling for German *Kultur* against French civilization, and about the possibility of calling the GDR an *Unland*, a metaphysical abomination, the very opposite of the old ideal of the nation-state.

Actually I don't want to stay in this hotel. It's not what I booked and either I pay less or they find me somewhere else. No freedom, no responsibility, I chanted – a distillation of a spontaneous longer sentence to the effect that if I wasn't free to choose my hotel then I wasn't going to accept being forcibly booked into one I couldn't afford and had emphatically turned down. The chief receptionist, a youngish woman, gave me a funny little look, just slightly raising her eyes. I had seen that look before, in Weimar. I saw it again in Dresden and it was the same look I got in the bank in Prague. All good communists learn it in school as a way of deflecting difficult questions by frowning on them as bad manners. But I won! I moved to a cheaper, nicer, much more central hotel, very near the Gewandhaus concert hall and the opera, one where the children making a noise in the corridor were Russian and breakfast reverted from being expensive pap to being reasonable, nourishing, honest fare. It was the victory I had been craving, a little show of resistance to say I wouldn't be crushed; but of course I would be, if I lived here.

In Leipzig I went to an art exhibition entitled 'Our Strength', including prints by Käthe Kollwitz; a play by the Swiss writer Friedrich Dürrenmatt; a concert of Bach motets. At the show everything paled beside

Kollwitz, who is a wonderful, rare portrayer of workers' sentiment, sensitive to passion and dignity but never sentimental, and who brings with her a whole tradition of Protestant sensibility; alongside her work some contemporary exhibits illustrating the death and resurrection of Ernst Thälmann were the most awful painful rubbish.

The Strindberg Play too was a kind of travesty. It had the aura of having been borrowed from another culture. It was housed in a cellar, after the manner of Western fringe theatre, with the now conventional trappings of an 'experiment'. But that wonderful happening, the modern theatre, despite modern acting techniques, was not taking place in Leipzig. To think Brecht was a GDR citizen by elective affinity! This play, because it was a satire on the bourgeois artistic treatment of bourgeois institutions, needed to be performed in a cultural atmosphere which was both knowing and artistically demanding. But here it was taking place in a world not at all interested in experiments in perception. I almost laughed when I saw the programme notes were by Friedrich Engels – about the hypocrisy of marriage and about the dual standards of civilized society based upon it. There was a quote too from the nineteenth-century socialist leader August Bebel linking the decay of bourgeois marriage to the gradual extinction of the bourgeoisie. The views of neither of these men were remotely relevant to the play, but their orthodox political appearance confirmed my worst fears: modern theatre is a chance for society to get outside itself, but that's an impossibility in a culture where all values are predetermined by the materialist dialectic.

Alas, Germany! That old, vast, middle-European community, bound by linguistic, cultural and religious traditions of extraordinary poetic richness, articulate inwardness and musicality, is utterly suppressed and perhaps even destroyed. Since the divide, sealed with the Berlin Wall in 1961, a *rapprochement* between the two Germanies at least in literature and the arts has been pursued by writers on both sides, but it is impossible to see this happening without a complete change of the political and social system. All one can hang on to are the shallowest coincidences of fashion and appearance and television, and little linguistic neologisms like *schönen Tag noch!* (Have a nice day!) which pitifully straddle the divide.

Dresden is stuffed with Russian tourists smoking those pungent native *papyrosy* which will make your nose twitch in recognition if you have ever been anywhere near Moscow. The tourist city consists of a half-mile long, 1960s-built, barren precinct. The old city is full of wide open spaces and emotive relics, a hymn to guilt, but not German guilt. A savage monument marking the Allied bombing of the city, amid ruins which have been left as a memory, warns of 'imperialist barbarism'. We're in the realm of the dead now.

But the churches are alive. They're packed everywhere I go and one can see why. In the face of official politics the church retains a Mann-like ambivalence and campaigns for causes which are not always approved causes, notably homosexual rights, environmental protection and nuclear disarmament. It counts both security policemen and atheist dissidents among its flock and its tradition is to look after the individual soul regardless. To understand the complexity of bonds between church and communist state in the GDR would probably give us outsiders the greatest available insight into the way this lobotomized country holds together today. The church, a patently popular and alternative institution, is tolerated as a useful safety valve for public expression. It is dangerous, but also the safest possible forum for political discontent, because its traditions lead away from politics.

I can't stand going out and about any more. I've read Len Deighton's *Berlin Game* in one hotel room and lapped up the sophistication and the slickness masking a deep knowledge of Germany. In another room I'm racing through le Carré's *Smiley's People*. The individualistic, quirky Western spy novel is partly a response to the façade of heroism, efficient bureaucracy and sincere public performance presented by the communist states, and the depressed East Bloc traveller reads it with pleasure and relief.

THE TASK OF THE RAILWAY WORKERS IS TO ACHIEVE MORE, TO LOAD THE PARTY CONFERENCE EXPRESS says a sign in the street. It's true, 'achievement', *Leistung*, has done it all. It's the concept at the heart of the classic sociological studies of Weber and Tawney on Protestantism and the rise of capitalism and it has ensured the GDR's brand of communism outstanding, if stupid, success. I leave the stupid loading the party conference express, knowing all too well that the same 'stupidity' allows me to buy my railway ticket by computer for the first time in the entire East Bloc.

How can the GDR come so close to repeating Hitler's regime and disgrace? And are there GDR citizens suffering new guilt because of their unwillingness to resist the Party? And will they ever break out of their silence in sufficient numbers? Television here brings home the existence of two continuous German cultures, but doesn't that make political submissiveness in the GDR all the more astonishing?

I spent my last morning back in East Berlin trying in vain to raise dissidents who had put their names to the latest dissident manifesto advertising a new human rights group and emphasizing their lack of freedom to travel even within the Soviet Bloc. I wanted to reassure myself they existed. They do, and in spirit there are thousands of them, and it was only a logistical problem that I wasn't able to get in touch. Yet however many dissidents exist they are not able, even the bravest of them, to tackle such a strong and ruthless state. I met one in West Berlin who had been forcibly deported, by being handcuffed to a train, because his activities had begun to be effective.

So I took coffee and cake among the pot plants and sumptuous furniture of an expensive coffeehouse on the Alexanderplatz, read my last communist newspaper of the trip, on a stick, and stared out of the square metres of plate glass at the undistinguished, almost Western-looking crowd. Anxious to reassure myself of the distinction, and that the right side of the mirror still existed, I couldn't cross the border soon enough.

9

Dionysus under Communism
Bulgaria 1986

Leaving for Bulgaria I had some odd facts in mind. It was the country making the most perfect strawberry jam and the most criminally perfect poison. With the poison it had shamelessly killed the outspoken émigré Bulgarian writer Georgi Markov in 1978 for what he had disclosed to the world about the incumbent regime. Shortly before my visit the Bulgarians accused in the papal assassination attempt were acquitted for lack of evidence, but suspicions remained of their involvement in the 1981 shooting in St Peter's Square. Other associations too, with arms and drug trafficking, and terrorist training, did not give Bulgaria a trustworthy reputation abroad. Petre and I had discussed this jokingly on our night walk through Bucharest. Bulgaria had the predominant reputation since the war of being the sixteenth Soviet republic and a mercenary state. The Bulgarians were perforce politically close to Russia, the system worked in the same way, the two countries acted in step. Markov said the system allowed ambitious men and women to rise without principles and without talent. Institutionalized unscrupulousness hovered like diabolic inspiration, offering Faustian possibilities. The metaphor reminds me now of *Temptation*, Vaclav Havel's play about survival and corruption in another communist country, Czechoslovakia. If all this was true, then Bulgaria with a political system encouraging the worst in human nature wasn't worth a jot.

We were staying – Elizabeth was with me again now – at a small resort on the Black Sea, not far from the Thracian, then Roman port of Odessos, now Varna. The Black Sea coast has only been exploited for international tourism since the war, after the visiting Soviet leader

Nikita Khrushchev suggested pressing this area of extraordinary natural beauty into the service of communism. The area north of Varna was wild, except for the former royal palace of Euxinograd and a few international sanatoria for tubercular children and tired workers. Poisonous snakes infested the shore, until overnight huge numbers of hedgehogs were brought in to eat them up.

Our resort centred on a natural hot water pool and we quickly established an easy routine of sitting there or standing in the water, enjoying the sun. Pop music, from when Elvis Presley was a GI in Germany, throbbed at high volume from an up-to-the-minute portable Japanese stereo outside the beach café. For snacks during the day we spent a sort of Monopoly money there, handed out in the hotels in lieu of food. The pool, though, was also the place where real money changed hands and where it was relatively easy to talk. I hoped to make up for my ignorance about Bulgaria, but what immediately overwhelmed me from the Bulgarian side was hunger for the most basic knowledge about the outside world. Bulgarians felt cut off. Before we were even out of the arrival lounge our Bulgarian guide had appealed for newspapers and magazines in any language on the pretext of wanting to pass them on to other Western tourists. 'Could we find work if we came to Britain?' 'Is it true that the Americans suppressed news of a great nuclear disaster? And that you have to pay for your schools in Britain?' 'Is Bulgaria safe?' This last question came in the wake of the Soviet nuclear disaster at Chernobyl, news of which had certainly been suppressed, and which drove home to people how ill their news media served them with the truth.

'So our newspapers lie?' I tried to explain the business about East Bloc newspapers, seen from the West, that they lied by distortions rather than untruths. On the risk of nuclear contamination I passed on what I had heard. British and UN authorities thought Bulgaria was safe. A man and his wife wanted to know how much people earned and what life cost elsewhere. Young men wanted to know if they could make a life in the West.

But not everyone was pursuing knowledge. Most of the young men, virile young princes and beautiful Balkan shepherds, the so-called herring gulls of the coast, kept a smile permanently ready for any dollar-rich damsel in distress. Their principal aim in life was to marry abroad.

In their presence, particularly on Saturdays and Sundays, the pool, despite its dense cluster of leathery, elderly foreigners abandoning themselves to sun-worship and gulping down the gushing hot spring water with cupped hands, seethed with erotic activity. Possibly these septuagenarian Germans, flirting with death, added to the charged atmosphere – a number ended their lives on the Black Sea every year. But it was the young men who ranged and disported themselves as if around the edges of a dance floor. 'If you haven't got a husband where are your father and mother?' said one curious bather. 'Mummy, everyone is looking at us,' remarked my eagle-eyed daughter, now rapidly growing up. When I said there was no work in the West none of the herring gulls, asking their questions in schoolboy Russian, would believe me. Surely all kingdoms under some other enchantment than communism had work to offer.

The pool was also a market place for anything valuable. In Druzhba there was a chic guesthouse for scientists and academics, the tallest building in the village. Did I want to have a meal there? asked one of its distinguished visitors, catching hold of my cheek as we stood in the water. Or would I like an introduction to 'influential journalists' in Sofia? A little way along the coast in the direction of Balcic there was a larger establishment for journalists. The writers had a palace in Varna. I could imagine similar offers being made all down the coastline. Evidently, as in all the communist countries – I thought of Mrs Gheorghui's offer to get me inside the closed Enescu museum – there was a rich trade in the commodity called permission. Here, adapted to conditions along Bulgaria's tourist coast, it bought women.

Our first evening was as usual confused. We wandered barefoot on the soft cold sand at sundown, finding the May evening and a fence keeping us out of some special Bulgarian establishment chilly. We passed hotels intended for East Bloc tourists and others for Westerners, carefully segregated. An old woman who purported to run a café down on the beach made me a plastic beaker of instant coffee with water from a kettle boiled an hour before. Perhaps she thought I was a *tovarishch* or perhaps it was my fault and I had strayed into the wrong pleasure sector. Elizabeth explored the swings and roundabouts while I eyed the huge brightly painted ornamental cubes ranged above her along the grass promenade. They were like stray objects from a giant's nursery, except that they were engraved with adult words:

INTEGRATION/UNITY/PROGRESS
UNITY/CREATIVITY/BEAUTY

They were words for which I would normally have some affection, but here, painted in the same colours as the solid wooden picnic furniture and the children's playground, and pretending to be as important as the soft sand, the sun umbrellas and the pedallos, they were absurd. I wondered if my final destination was to be not so much Bulgaria as self-parody.

Brigid Brophy wrote a funny, intellectual fantasy, *Palace without Chairs*, which would fit the unreality of Bulgaria. It is as Ruritanian an ex-kingdom now as ever it was when Bernard Shaw set *Arms and the Man* there. Never before in my communist wanderings have I been tempted to substitute for an account of my travels and thoughts a piece of placeless, ahistorical fantasy, and the temptation is a measure of how far away Bulgaria lies from any social and political reality I know. It is not entirely the consequence of communism. As the Bulgarian poet, Pencho Slaveikoff, put it in 1904, to pile up even a chronicle of *facts* about Bulgaria 'possibly would fail to impress an English reader with whom our history savours of fiction'. Essentially communism has not changed the nature of Bulgaria any more than it has changed any other country. A country once fabulous to the English mentality remains so. But the Cold War does make it at least seem like a new genre of fiction, or one novel, about people forced to live in a fairy tale.

'Tell me what's happening in the world,' said Sasha, who so adeptly homed in on my first impressions that I was tempted to believe he had been briefed beforehand. We talked about political reactions in the West to Chernobyl, and about the apparently widespread condemnation of the American retaliatory air raid on Tripoli, which had in fact revealed hidden sympathies in West Europe and overt support in Britain. This competent, smooth-mannered, very intelligent young man, of unprepossessing appearance, was in Varna to compete in a Russian-language Olympiad – a competition to find the best young Bulgarian speakers of Russian – and introduced himself on our first morning at breakfast. Before he came I had been parrying suggestions from the German breakfasters that I peel Elizabeth's cucumber chunks, and reading a newspaper in English for visitors, *Sofia News*, which reported it would soon be safe to eat lettuce again. Presumably the tourist authorities, in the present post-Chernobyl commotion, saw dollar signs disappearing before their eyes.

The oddest thing about Sasha was perhaps that he wasn't a herring gull, closely followed by the fact that he was very clued up. Normally, when he was not studying electronics, he looked after groups of Russians visiting Sofia. He was used to trying to persuade the Russians of Bulgarian competence and technological progress when they haughtily claimed only to be aware of exports of strawberry jam. In all but name his part-time job was public relations, information. 'You're a journalist, aren't you?' he asked.

We talked a little about Moscow. 'Well then you know Russia', he said. 'It's just like that here. They even bring the Russians in to catch the bank robbers. All the same, it's interesting.' I nodded and he asked when we were coming to Sofia. He would be happy to show us round. I did in fact have a plan to go the following day, but Sasha's origins worried me, so I made a very loose arrangement.

To judge by the warnings in pre-war guide books rail travel has always been difficult in this country. It has plagued all my East European trips, but this experience was the worst. The overnight train from Varna was crowded and there were no couchettes without prior reservation. After a terrible night of being jolted and woken up every ten minutes we arrived to look with sleepless eyes upon Sofia. On the border between East and West, of mainly European character, it much resembled Belgrade.

The multi-level modern railway station, labelled in French and Bulgarian, was linked to an underground shopping centre with shady open air cafés and fountains. From there it is just a few tram stops to the central square with its statue of Lenin. Stately, solid nineteenth-century buildings lined the broad central boulevards, small palaces and gardens were interspersed with villas or with shops and cafés in the narrower, shadier tree-lined streets.

Disaster struck almost immediately. We were refused a hotel room. By a quirk of interpretation the tourist authorities declared us illegal in Sofia.

Can one imagine being ordered to leave Paris? Without a reservation one might be forced to pay high prices. Freedom would depend on money but anyone could ensure against the pain of not being wanted by the big city either by saving up or not going.

It is our conviction that tourism is an exceptionally important factor in promoting mutual understanding and co-operation among nations. In our country tourism and recreation are not a privilege of a minority but a constitutional right of all citizens and an inseparable part of social policy.

This was President Zhivkov speaking at a meeting of the World Tourism Organization in Sofia just eight months before. But, *tovarishch*, Bulgarians are not free to travel abroad and Westerners who come to your country find it absurdly hard to move around. The few privileged Bulgarians who do travel because they are considered safe pay enormous amounts of money to do so. A couple from Stara Zagora I met in another train had spent a week in London. Each of them paid seven times the average monthly wage in order to go. It's the same old communism here then: humiliating, degrading, cruel, wasteful, all in the name of the protected economy.

In Sofia we heard some singing in St Nedelya church, where a dozen women had brought bread and dry cake to be blessed. Elizabeth crossed herself and kissed an icon, testing the feel of worship. This being an Orthodox church there were no chairs, and we were kneeling on the thinly carpeted stone floor to look up at the hemispherical roof in the candle-lit semi-darkness and listening to the singing. An elderly woman began telling us in her own language who the saints in the icons were. In moments like these I could see why all over East Europe people fell back on the quality of private life.

St Nedelya had been restored. It was blown to smithereens in 1925 by communist terrorists who had hoped to destroy many members of the right-wing government attending a political funeral inside. The attempt failed, but more than a hundred other people died in the explosion. Contemporary tourist guides don't hint at the event because since their initial admission of responsibility the communists have changed their minds about the advantages of owning up to violence. I found the details in a pre-war book.

The history of Bulgaria between the wars is a harrowing tale of violence, in which the communists were as much involved as any other party. Under the artful King Boris the military staged a coup in 1923 against the ruling peasant Agrarian party and murdered its leader. The historian Alan Palmer has estimated that in the ensuing conflicts, first with the Agrarians, then with the communists who tried to stage a counter-coup in the autumn, as many as 10,000 Bulgarians may have been killed. Thereafter the military-dominated government, its hands already awash with blood, struggled to contain murderous communists on the one hand and Macedonian terrorists on the other. The war, when it came, was relatively peaceful.

We walked slowly along the hot avenues of Sofia, stopping often to rest, and felt drained and sticky whenever we moved again. Suddenly we heard a brass band. Platoons of soldiers were lined up in The Ninth of September Square, opposite a straggly, reverent mass of around five hundred civilians. We went as close as we could. Half a dozen high-stepping infantrymen in white and crimson, with plumes and shining swords, were carrying a wreath to the mausoleum where the body of Georgi Dimitrov lay embalmed in the square marking the 1944 communist takeover. Dimitrov trained in Moscow as an international communist. (This is a good pedigree. Koestler gave it to Rubashov, hero of *Darkness at Noon*.) Dimitrov won fame when he conducted his own successful defence in Leipzig in the trial of the Reichstag fire; then in 1945 he arrived to become head of the Bulgarian Communist Party. Nowadays he is Bulgaria's most important national figurehead.

Was someone besides Dimitrov dead? Whatever the identity of the deceased he was important enough to have the local press photographers dashing across the square and up the steps of the sand-coloured, neo-classical National Art Gallery opposite to get a better angle. It looked like an important event. The women wore best dresses, always the least flattering feminine garments, and many had chosen Bulgarian national costume to please the Party as well as the menfolk. The men looked worse in their baggy blue suits, a variety of uncrisp shirts, and soft, pale, open-weave shoes. I didn't expect to know the name of the dead man, but who was he? A Sofia official? And these his family and his colleagues? The policeman keeping us few native and foreign spectators at a respectable distance from the solemn proceedings was relaxed enough and young enough to accept questions. It was no one. Or rather just the Agrarian Union, Bulgaria's other political party, a shadow of the pre-war peasant party, having a congress.

It was like an open-air dinner dance. The unstylish delegates and their wives strolled back to the Grand Hotel Sofia or went in fours to take the midday sun on benches in the park by the gallery. Today the Agrarian Union people are as closely aligned to the communists as makes no difference, except for the orange and gold wheatsheaf badges on their lapels, which was another reason for believing the occasion 100 per cent social.

It was an operatic spectacle. Inevitably it reminded me of recent opera productions in London – of Wagner and Tchaikovsky – which had attempted to borrow from totalitarian rituals. The trouble is that in their native setting totalitarian scenarios necessarily include disbelieving, coerced spectators and participants. Thus, like modern fiction, they readily undermine themselves, a message which cannot necessarily be found in the music of another age and culture. Communism may have given us a new concept of what is 'operatic', but it's not a simple one, and it will be fascinating to see if, one day, suitable music can be written to express its ironies and brutalities.

We kept the rendezvous with Sasha. I had doubts about his credentials, but I guessed now we were tired and stranded we had nothing to lose. So we drank Turkish coffee in a café and I paid. An old Bulgarian hand, as I once learnt to say, had warned me not to allow too much generosity. Sasha's student grant was too little to support himself, his wife and their child, and pay a private rent. His mother went out to work to help him. Then we set off to inspect a few sights and Sasha began to account for Bulgarian life.

The parliament building had been a theatre, pretty, with lanterns and a balustrade with staircases leading from either side – another operatic setting. The need for parliament came suddenly, after liberation from the Turks, and this was the only suitable existing building. Sasha told me that the name of this decorative, unserious-looking home of Bulgarian political life was Narodno Subranie, which reminded me of those silky, black Balkan cigarettes my mother used to smoke at Christmas.

The most serious monument in Sofia though – and there is a serious and credible national culture here – is the one marking the liberation from the Turks, achieved with substantial Russian military assistance in 1878, after centuries of domination. This is the most important event in Bulgarian history and smaller commemorative statues can be seen in every Bulgarian city. Some, such as the one in Stara Zagora, only a few years old, indicate that the event is still thought capable of yielding political capital. The Sofia liberation monument, inscribed to the Tsar of the day, Alexander II, has been re-dedicated: 'to our brothers'. A monument to the latterday brothers also stands nearby, commemorating their arrival in 1944, and the beginning of the communist era, also described as a liberation. The communists have this habit of making history look very neat. Meanwhile another great national monument, the Alexander Nevsky Cathedral, thanks Russia for 1878. Sasha patiently explained that this vast, neo-Byzantine edifice and favourite Sofia meeting place couldn't be called after Alexander II, because the Russian monarch had been still alive. So it stands today, the city's most famous landmark, bearing the name of a foreign chieftain from the twelfth century, and gleaming with a new coat of gold leaf – an unloved, but much admired building. Alexander Nevsky's son was the first ruler of the principality of Moscow.

Sasha was a skilled decoder, and I was grateful. I tried to switch off my fears about his identity. I admired a grey stone classical villa and its gardens. The police headquarters, he said. Before that the German school. We began to talk about German influence in Sofia, the result of imported expertise and trade links after the liberation from the Turks. Bulgaria chose as its first monarch Prince Alexander of Battenberg, a German, albeit a favourite nephew of the Tsar. Foreign policy, largely because of the German trade link, remained German-oriented as Bulgaria evolved into a monarchist dictatorship.

After three decades of domestic violence Bulgaria slid into the Second World War on the German side. Hitler exploited the weakness and the thwarted ambitions of a country which had been left diminished and friendless after the 1914–18 war. Europe cold-shouldered Bulgaria because it was a German ally and the country was without support locally for having betrayed the Balkans. Yet in the Second World War Bulgaria's role on the side of the Germans was mostly passive, as the object of Germany's manipulation and a pathway for Axis forces. Bulgaria said it would send no troops to fight against the Russians, and Soviet diplomats remained in Sofia, nominally an enemy capital. Sasha says Boris was a clever king so to arrange things. Whatever the reason, the facts look well today. The Russians were not resisted when they suddenly declared war on Bulgaria and arrived in August 1944.

Sasha has a view of his country which is particularly illuminated by his own connections with the German-speaking world. His grandfather was one of Bulgaria's greatest poets, the leading Symbolist and conduit for Western aesthetic ideas of the day. This man, Teodor Trayanoff, spent many years living and working in Vienna, though his bourgeois orientation means he barely scrapes an entry in histories of literature today. His son, Sasha's father, was walking along the street in Vienna one day after the war when he was kidnapped and brought back to Bulgaria. Sasha, who is about twenty-five, tells me this story willingly, in the faintly amused fashion of someone who has come to terms with life.

The Turkish occupation of Bulgaria lasted five hundred years. Every man and woman in the street knows this, and Bulgaria's best known novel, *Under the Yoke*, by Ivan Vazov, translated into English by Edmund Gosse in 1894, is an account of the exciting, bloody days in which it was finally overthrown. An educated couple in the train to Sofia insisted I read it, for being so enslaved meant that for Bulgaria there was no Renaissance, no Enlightenment, no written tradition. Turkish rule hit the Bulgarians harder than it did any other subjugated culture, with the exception of modern-day Albania. Christianity, which was tolerated, provided the only continuity with the enlightened medieval Bulgarian Empire.

Because of the liberation the bond of historical gratitude to the Russians in national political terms is genuine, though it did not stop Bulgaria fighting against the Russians only a few decades later in the First World War, and taking the opposite side in the Second.

Today most Bulgarians insist that the continuing bond is practical rather than mystical and does not imply any sympathy for the Soviet political system. They say so overtly if they can or decline to speak the Russian they learnt compulsorily at school, opting for the French or German they know less well. But Sasha is happy to speak Russian and reminds me of the shared bonds again: the Cyrillic alphabet, the Orthodox church. 'We're friends with the Russian people,' he says carefully.

We caught a few hours sleep in Sasha's empty, rather squalid, one-room apartment; or rather Elizabeth did. I was too nervous to close my eyes. Sasha left fresh bread and his ID card on the table, then went out to arrange our return journey and give us some privacy. I checked we weren't locked in. I wondered if I would see the money for the train tickets again. The round bespectacled face of a young man in a checked shirt, caught in an unflattering passport photo, stared up from the card. I guessed it was there to reassure me. His wife and baby were away, Sasha had said. I found it hard to imagine the presence of a wife in view of the filth, but perhaps she had been away some time. Then the door bell rang. A woman identified herself as Sasha's mother and didn't seem surprised to see me. She had just looked in to bring some shopping and that looked real enough, with fresh herbs, despite Chernobyl, spilling out of the top of the basket. Some time after she left Sasha came back with our tickets.

During the evening Russian friends looked in and Sasha's command of their language proved to be faultless. He must have been the champion of the Varna Olympiad. Other Bulgarians joined us. We sang Russian political ballads in the modern dissenting tradition of Visotsky and Galich, to the accompaniment of a guitar. Bulgarian beer was drunk, fetched from a cool spot next to torn-up Soviet newspapers, next to the lavatory. What a sight the place was though! Even with the baby away the apartment was impossibly cramped, lined with German technical manuals, hangovers from a study year in Leipzig. There was an odd typed poem of Sasha's stuck to the wall which he didn't want to talk about. But the atmosphere was relaxed and pleasant. We sat watching a Russian television film with Bulgarian actors, and then the news, which amplified on the Agrarian Union Congress and included a film report from Chernobyl. The television fell into the baby's cot, was recovered, and still the congress item was running, illustrated with slow and repetitive camera work. We had time to look for the sleeping delegates as well as the wide-awake ones who might be potential successors to Zhivkov.

At last the item changed. A government minister was announced as having arrived in Bonn. But we've just seen him at the congress. Everyone cried with laughter. This wasn't lying, just media unprofessionalism, official communist buffoonery, the sort of incident which gives everyone in a repressed country a boost of vitality. But this forced, fake official culture, of which I have sampled a good deal over recent years, makes me feel life is being wasted. I can see before me all the unglamourous, overdressed, uneasy men and women announcers I have caught sight of in this time, trying in vain to jolly their viewers along.

Sasha was kind and very professional. His solicitude ensured that we got a couchette under the roof of the train on the way back to Varna, and that when we climbed in at midnight we were equipped with a wrapped-up plate of hot sausage and cucumber. On a final professional note he called out from the platform: 'My best friend is travelling in the next compartment. You'll be all right.' Afterwards I sent him a John le Carré in gratitude.

In the train, as we readied ourselves for the night, our presence caused some embarrassment to an elderly man in the middle bunk. Sasha had used a false name to book us in, for no obvious reason, which led to a muddle over our sex. But in the end we all went to sleep. It wasn't worth the linguistic effort on anyone's part to try to rectify the error for the sake of propriety. In the morning we woke up stifling to find the man from the bottom row bursting to say he was missing his wife and child, who were like us. He wanted to show us Varna and to know if I believed in God.

Back at the pool I was reading C. S. Lewis's *The Lion, the Witch and the Wardrobe* aloud to Elizabeth late one afternoon and she was listening with her feet dangling in the warm water. An English-speaking Bulgarian joined us. The reading gave way to fitful conversation. The subject moved from Lewis to Tolkien and from there to various forms of spiritualism. This man, a university teacher, confessed a great interest in the paranormal. He knew all about the local dowsers, the sci-fi addicts and the black magicians and described a club for them which had flourished in Varna a few years before, when President Zhivkov's daughter Lyudmila was Minister of Culture. Then he suddenly became embarrassed. 'Of course I have to remain outside such matters for professional reasons,' he said, looking guilty.

The academic was embarrassed for himself as a scientist, but probably more so he was politically discomfited in front of a Westerner. A passion for the paranormal sits awkwardly alongside scientific socialism and atheism. But Bulgaria, like Russia, has a penchant for superstition and clairvoyancy. The late president Brezhnev became renowned in the mid-70s for consulting a Georgian soothsayer, and Bulgarians believe Zhivkov *père* and his entourage have similar tastes. An old woman called Vanga in the tourist village of Petrich, in the Rhodope mountains, became famous and rich in Zhivkova's day for telling fortunes.

Here possibly is the real Bulgaria of the people, a uniquely unmodern culture. The ancient history of Macedonia and Thrace and the continuity of ancient Greek legends in Bulgarian folk poetry have helped to ensure the pagan mystical imagination is still strong. Add to those factors a late, slight written literature and no Enlightenment, and a history of art which freely mingles Christian and pagan motifs, and the result is a popular tradition which has never been uprooted.

'Tell me more about Lyudmila Zhivkova,' I begged the teacher, but he went for a swim.

On 21 July 1981 Zhivkova died suddenly of a brain haemorrhage at the age of thirty-eight. Bulgaria was in the middle of celebrating 1,300 years of national existence, with rumblings of discontent amongst the extreme conservatives at home and in Moscow. Moscow was lukewarm over the national anniversary because it smacked of too much independence. Zhivkova's untimely death prompted an instant legend she had been disposed of. A theory that she had died in a rigged car crash even found its way into the serious Western press. In Bulgaria the myths accounting for her disappearance would not have been out of place in *I, Claudius*.

But the conspiracy theories seem largely empty today. What remains is only regret, for in her time as Minister of Culture, Education and Science she very effectively combined a revival of interest in traditional mysticism with a new enthusiasm for Bulgarian nationality and a revolutionary openness to the West. The arts enjoyed a brief freedom. Zhivkova might have brought Bulgaria out of the backwoods faster than is happening now, with the country seeming to hold fast to its isolation.

'What do you think of Zhivkova? And have you heard of this fortune teller Vanga?' I asked Manfred, a fellow Western tourist whom I met several lunchtimes later.

'Of course. My wife and I went to see Vanga.'

'What? You drove all the way from Berlin?'

'I didn't think about it at the time. We were coming to see my wife's family.'

'What did Vanga say?'

'Nothing much.'

'But you weren't disappointed?'

'No.'

'But did she predict your divorce?'

'No. But she asked my wife why she ever went to Germany.'

Manfred laughed at the memory of what probably now seemed an absurdity but must once have seemed a miracle. He had married a Bulgarian woman and set up house with her in Germany. After a few years, and annual holidays to her home, the relationship had foundered. In retrospect he claimed to have taught his Bulgarian wife to be reasonable about difficult, personal experiences, like falling out of love, for which tightly-knit Bulgarian family life had not prepared her, but it was she who had proved the better organized in her life, and the more rational. She was happy to stay in Berlin after they split up. And it was he, her former husband, a German Zen Buddhist, a rare Westerner straining eastwards, who came back to Bulgaria again and again, complained about the food, shunned the tourists, loved the countryside, and the peacefulness, and the chance they gave him to continue his Buddhist researches. He was in his fourth year studying the Japanese tea ceremony and had written a paper on it during his last holiday. He came because he felt misplaced and uncomfortable in Western society; misplaced because he did not have an analytical mind.

We were sitting in a cliff-top open air café in the evening eating omelettes with Iskra Bulgarian champagne (the same name as Lenin's newspaper), looking at the full moon over the sea. Elizabeth insisted she had seen the moon before and Manfred wouldn't drink. We were talking about Russia. Manfred, who was thin and very white-skinned, with a large forehead and a delicate mouth, began praising Russian women: their strength, their intensity, their passion. He praised 'strength' in Russian music and the playing of Andrei Gavrilov, Emil Gilels, Svatoslav Richter. I felt so sympathetic I kissed his cheek. The whole business of passion saddens me. We love what we're not, and love it with passion if we can find it embodied in an accessible person who will accept our love, otherwise our passions are Platonic, artistic, intellectual, or just hobbies; that is, the tiniest confessions of liking.

But he was the more attuned to sadness. He liked sitting in open-air cafés and watching the ants with children like Elizabeth, who happened along and reminded him that adult conversation was mostly a fatuous waste of energy.

'I learnt so late in life to assert myself, I was always being hurt. Now I've learnt to give up self-assertion too. All desire leads to suffering and the greater the desire the greater the suffering.'

He observed as the most momentous feature of daily Bulgarian life the sadness of its women. He was a furrier by trade, a job which ensured him some expertise in studying women's faces, and he would point them out to me in the street and in restaurants. A flicker of excitement before marriage would light up their lives for a year or so, he said, but ever after their brows were clouded, and gloomy, even when they appeared noisy and fashionable and laughing beneath their exaggerated Western-style make-up: cheek stripes and purple-painted eyes.

I don't think this is just a personal view, for the traditional folk culture of Bulgaria is characterized by an at once delicate and remorseless gloom about the end of love, and death.

So fled the years, the gay to the grave gave hand,
As they, foresooth, in the dawn of the world were planned.

It is thus, though in other words, that Manfred and *Sofia News* describe it even today.

Boris, the man from the train who wanted to show us Varna, turned out to be quite insistent, so we went with him about the green city, looking at the Roman baths and the port, and the zoo, and catching sight of a street named after Ernst Thälmann. It was an odd occasion, with much apparent pride on Boris's part, but not much to talk about. In the zoo a woman was squirting water at the monkeys and laughing, which made me feel a yawning cultural gap. Nor was there between Boris, who worked somewhere in an office for Bulgarian railways, and myself, much more understanding. We talked about the pleasure of eating vegetables and the private plot he tended a few kilometres outside the city. The government, as a result of recent legislation, was encouraging modest individual enterprise. Didn't that show how well it understood Bulgarian priorities and traditions on the land? What about decollectivizing altogether? I asked. Everyone says Bulgarian agriculture worked better before communism. But Boris ducked the question by talking about his wife, who was working as a doctor in Libya.

She had been in Libya, an outpost of the East Bloc Commonwealth, eight months and had written letters home about eating camel meat. More recently she had described the night the Americans bombed Tripoli. While she was away their son was being looked after by his grandparents and Boris looked after himself.

To hear the family story we went to a restaurant in the early evening where the service was reluctant and Boris helped himself to huge quantities of cognac, which made his eyes and his voice droop. The family matter became tangled in my own alcohol-suffused mind with his low-voiced account of the patrimony of Thrace and it didn't help that we were both speaking foreigners' Russian, laden with mistakes. The conversation dried up to the point where we were making polite enquiries about the number of each other's brothers and sisters. 'But you're not eating anything,' he said. Nervous and bored, I was suddenly afraid that Boris might turn into a psychopath. 'Don't you care about your personal freedom?' I said suddenly, surprising myself that to keep Boris at bay I was exploiting the political divide, knowing he was no defector even in spirit. He didn't reply, only observed once again that my plate was still laden.

On the way to the bus stop I recalled Varna briefly being called Stalin. This was Boris's home town and perhaps he put Stalin on the back of his envelopes when he was a child writing thank-you letters.

'Who told you that?' he said. Then he opened up a fraction, speaking with great political coyness. 'There was once a statue of the Soviet dictator in the park, which disappeared overnight.'

In Varna without Boris we visited the icon museum. The Bulgarian Orthodox icon developed only in the nineteenth century with the National Revival. It is an art form of conscious social record, painted in a deliberately primitive manner, and the style picks up from the Middle Ages, where the Bulgarian Second Empire left off. These icons set out to describe daily life in religious terms and to teach the patrimony of Kiril and Methodius, the monks who introduced the Christian written word to Bulgaria. In the museum pictures of the two monks holding Bibles and an alphabet were prominent. Some Vietnamese students were being shown round in the Bulgarian they must have learnt in order to study cheaply in fraternal Bulgaria. In one painting the Madonna – with those eyes the Cubists borrowed – had been given a huge Adam's apple.

24 May, Literacy Day, another landmark in the folk culture. It saw a bright parade through the town. The leafy central streets were packed with schoolchildren surging to and from hired buses. Babies and children in Pioneer uniform carried ice creams and waved flags: the

Bulgarian white green and red horizontal tricolor, various communist faces and depictions of the two priest-scribes. Some of the older schoolchildren were wearing diagonal paper sashes. Russian and Bulgarian have the same word for 'outstanding performer' – OTLICHNIK – and it was splashed across these children's best white shirts in big red letters. Photographs of the excellent pupils of the month were also on display in the music shop in the shopping precinct, near the sun umbrellas and the ice cream stalls, just like the dreadful Schiller precinct in Weimar.

The communist societies would reject the likes of Manfred, I reflected. Whether they are educated like the GDR or educating like Bulgaria, they burn with the need to label the conformists and the high achievers.

A song had stayed in my mind from early on our trip. 'Is Mr Don Quixote there?' A joky, high-pitched voice sang it from a tape as we sipped water from paper cups and handed out Wrigley's chewing gum to a family running a café on the side of the road. There's bland pop music everywhere and despite all this proud young nationality a very low level of Western culture threatens to take over if ever communism gives way.

Bulgaria was our last trip and we were more than half-way through it now. What happened next must have been overdue after half a dozen journeys in three years: Elizabeth protested. 'Whose life is it anyway?' she asked angrily, after I took her on a last excursion, to Plovdiv.

It was true the journey from Varna had taken many hours because the usual slow train went even slower and eventually broke down. We were hungry because there was no buffet car and when we arrived the hotel's facilities were closed. I had enjoyed the scenery across the Maritsa plain and into the hills but it wasn't much compensation for a child. Nor was the entrancing bagpiper who played during one of our overlong stops in a station. And it seemed to her I had been giving what little money we had – the key to our comfort – away. An amateur numismatist in the train had showed around a beautiful buff 1901 Russian rouble note, with a list of conditions for its use on the reverse side which included instant removal to Siberia for all attempts at counterfeit. I pointed this out and he looked uncomfortable, and said, yes, well such things happened many years ago, so in due course I gave him some German coins from my bag to ease the atmosphere. And then, like Dr Becker, the numismatist had begun re-planning our holiday – even the nicest men like to take over the organization of one's life, it seems. Possibly I too was beginning to tire of difficult situations, missed meals and endless political circumspection destroying conversations. Wouldn't the coin collector at least tell me about contemporary relations with Turkey? He'd been telling us about his travels there. But no. The question was too ticklish. Actually relations were very bad because Sofia was currently imposing a Bulgarization policy on ethnic Turks in Bulgaria.

Plovdiv, Bulgaria's second city, is famed for its picturesque Macedonian quarter of narrow cobbled streets and the Turkish casements which overhang them. The French romantic poet Lamartine had a house on that hill, one of three in the settlement called Philippopolis after Philip of Macedon and known to the Romans as Trimontium. The modern city of Plovdiv is a spacious, colourful and busy pedestrian centre at the foot of these now built-up hills, where one can buy good pottery, jewellery and ice-cream, eat pizza in a garden of sun umbrellas, visit the open-air theatre, or simply sit in the shade inhaling the natural perfume of acacia, robinia and lime. Our hotel, which swayed in the wind, supplied richly rose-scented soap reminiscent of the Valley of the Roses not far away, one of the world's greatest sources of precious rose attar.

Mid-morning I bought a necklace made in the Kiril and Methodius workshop, then we climbed up many flights of steps and along narrow streets to the white marble amphitheatre, which gleamed like a salt mine and where Elizabeth found the energy to dance on the stone stage. It was terribly hot. Elsewhere in the town the mosques were 'closed for improvement'; Maxim Gorki street ran through the middle of a setting from the Arabian Nights and Lamartine's house was closed. Georgi Dimitrov had taken over from Prince Alexander as the name attached to the main boulevard. There was a street named after Ernst Thälmann. My patience with these proud, meaninglessly homogenized signs of communist life, spread across half a continent in a false attempt to unify it and cut it off from the West, had vanished. I was no longer interested in the theory or the striving, just bothered by the barbarity of it.

I caught sight of my sweating face in a bad mirror. I looked at Elizabeth's beauty, untouched by any of my concern with that tired trio – beauty, truth and goodness – and I longed for a simpler life. 'We have to walk to the railway station now,' I said. This was when she turned upon me and rebelled. So instead we sat for a while outside the Lamartine house, picking wild flowers until it once more failed to open. Then we pressed them into my book, the Russian philosopher Nicholas Berdyaev's *The Fate of Man in the Modern World*, and slid stickily into another café.

She seemed to be asking me those questions which I now wanted to ask myself: 'Why always this relentless pursuit, always against the odds, always against the tide?' The questions surfaced because it was the end. The relentless pursuit, which had begun in Russia, the quest for an opposite way of life to anything I had known, was over. I had split myself in half and magnified my passions for austerity and philosophy and enlightening discomfort until they burst like overblown balloons. Though it was not for nothing. The world seemed a friendlier place, because I had proved to myself that despite the worst obstacles of political tyranny, bureaucratic obstructiveness, linguistic and cultural difference, life was accessible and individuals ached to make contact with each other.

Perhaps every system – including the unconscious system of personality – spawns its own antidote. Berdyaev, whose ideas blossomed when he developed personalism, a philosophy in defence of the individual spirit, began as a Marxist. Roland Barthes once speculated how pleasing it would be to look upon our world with the appreciative/critical foreign eyes we bring to the communist Bloc, to be a little divorced from ourselves in order to appreciate our 'exotic' qualities. For me it was as if I had developed the East Bloc side of my personality and now I wanted to make contact with the West again. Eventually I hoped the effect in myself would be to modify one world with the other:

His (admissible?) dream would be to transport into a socialist society some of the charms (I do not say: values) of the bourgeois art of living (there are, there used to be some); it is what he calls going against time. Opposed to this dream is the spectre of the totality, which wants to see the bourgeois phenomenon condemned *en bloc*, and the least appearance of significance punished as if it were a career from which a blot had to be removed. Would it not be possible to relish (deformed) bourgeois culture as something exotic?

Roland Barthes par Roland Barthes

Yes indeed. But even finer would be to see the two European cultures as complementary; as mirrors to each other; and to see their division as an essential stage in the direction of future united strength and survival.

. . . and now, I think, the sense of the way culture develops is no longer obscure to us. It must show us the struggle between Eros and Death, the life instinct and the destructive instinct, as it occurs amongst human beings. This struggle is the essential content of life, and that is why the development of culture can be called in short the life struggle of the human race.

Freud, *Civilization and its Discontents*

In Plovdiv we walked down from Lamartine's inaccessible house with its marvellous view of the city and the Maritsa plain beyond and the distant mountains, and into St Marina church, which was cool and bustling at three in the afternoon. A woman brought boiled sweets as we contemplated the beautiful dark blue interior. I stayed in the pews reading a pre-war French account of Plovdiv. As it got cooler we finally went to confirm our train tickets back. We walked along a street strung with banners bearing slogans exhorting work and productivity, anticipating a commemorative day on 8 June. 'Why are they there?' demanded Elizabeth, perking up. 'They're having another special day,' I said, to which she replied: 'But they've just had one. That's silly.'

The way to the restaurant where we spent a long, cool, lazy evening was very obscure, despite the doorman's detailed instructions. An Alice in Wonderland door in a side street was marked high up in tiny letters, 'entrance to garden'. Inside we were at the foot of a dark stone staircase which at the top opened on to a magnificent three-tiered garden restaurant recalling the amphitheatre.

The lights flashed on at dusk and models and male dancers began snaking down the staircase. The models feigned expressions from the insolent to the brutal in imitation of Western mannequins and their make-up was only a small cut above the jungle paint of the girls in the East European street. The clothes too were unremarkable. But the conception of the evening was grand. Every table decked with starched white linen was full. The end of the holiday was near and we had piles of the Monopoly money to use up. I ordered caviare, which made our neighbours stare down from the tier above. The snake-hipped men danced one routine in black T-shirts and dance trousers, then changed into suits to partner the women in gorgeous Flamenco skirts. The couples descended the stairs from both sides and whirled on to the floor. A solo woman singer with an enormous amplified voice took over the show, and the energetic band succeeded her.

Elizabeth was craning her neck over the ballroom floor below and staring bright-eyed and intent. Our neighbours had bought her a Coca Cola and asked her a question to which she could now reply: *kak ti zakazesh?* (What's your name?)

'Look Mummy we can go, you don't need a uniform any more.' This was her impression of those high-fashion costumes the models had worn. The evening had settled into free dancing and the band was playing the Beatles number *I'll Follow The Sun* as if it were a national anthem. I was sitting in the dark now with a book and a notebook I could no longer see, opposite a man who had settled himself down at our table and was looking at Elizabeth's books. I wanted to say I'm sorry, I can't talk any more. I'm exhausted. But we stayed in silence. Then suddenly she wanted to dance, and so did I.

'Come on then, let's go and dance.'

'No I can't. My brother won't let me.'

Oh, dear. She's never had a brother, nor mentioned the imaginary existence of one before. We got up and left.

'It was my brother who wouldn't let me dance. But we'll come back to Plovdiv, won't we? It's a good place.'

I toyed with a thought about hidden controls and threw it away.

Once again I was riding in a suffocating train, being asked if I believed in God. My questioner was a self-conscious teenage Adventist with a Bible on her bunk below mine and a breezy voice. Yes, I said, and meant no, meaning I didn't want her to take me for a *communist* atheist. She asked if there were any believers in England. Many, I said, exaggerating for the same reason, and adding, feeling she had cued me to ask: 'Is it difficult for you to be a believer?' She opened the window healthily wide and with a sheepish look on her bespectacled face let in the night air. She wasn't going to tell a stranger and a foreigner. Elizabeth fell asleep chanting: *kak ti zakazesh?*

Berdyaev calls for an economic communism which is not a social tyranny and which expressly exists to set the personality and the spirit free. I'm thinking of friends at home with tears in my eyes as we trundle along in this mobile hothouse. Manfed, you said desire was suffering, but I'm proud of my wanting, and you didn't mind whatever it was impelled me to kiss your cheek. Other desires too, and ideas felt as desires fill me to the brim from one day to the next. Nothing must ever deaden our capacity to aspire: to love, to knowledge, to understanding. (I think of Goethe's *Faust* here, not those modern allusions to Faust which show how communism has travestied human striving.) As desire, aspiration is what keeps us alive and feeds our personalities. I love difficult places. I love languages. Tonight I'll say all the different Slav words, an unusual variety, for train and for railway station. I'm collecting them now like counting sheep but I can't recollect them all and still I can't get to sleep, out of a mixture of excitement and exhaustion.

Back at the hotel Sasha had sent a letter which seemed to be written for a third person to read, outlining reasons why I shouldn't worry about the after-effects of Chernobyl in Bulgaria, and why we should keep in touch. At the pool a new batch of 'academics and specialists' had arrived for an international conference on 'biotechnology': a new series of waterside games and no doubt Havelian temptations was in place.

For me it was time to buy the souvenirs. But I went to the shop in my bikini and the pale, fiercely made-up shop assistant wouldn't serve me. I started to bellow with frustration, which brought an unexpected chorus of approval from fellow Britons in the little seaside department store and predictable consternation from the Bulgarian staff and wary glances from visiting East Bloc-ers.

A Bulgarian woman I liked later told me how unreasonable I had been. The shopgirl couldn't take anything out of the window for me because the displays could only be touched by arrangers and they only worked twice a month; she wouldn't serve me in a bikini because that was an unwritten rule; and she was cross because wages were low and hours were long; and because what I spent on a small vase was a quarter of her weekly wage.

Berdyaev had a better explanation:

> A new form of the enslavement of labour is arising in the modern authoritarian states, based upon a dictated world view. This is a suprising process. The social milieu becomes more unified, but in this very unification personality is more heavily oppressed than in a more differentiated society. Instead of the living personality of the worker, his welfare, the rights of labour, we see proclaimed as the supreme value the power and well-being of the state, the social collective. The means of production, instead of being given to the producers, as Marx demanded, are turned over to the fascist or communist state. The State is recognized as the subject, while man becomes the object. This is the extreme form of the objectivization of human existence: man is emptied of every inner value. The process of socializing economic life, a process not only just but necessary, now becomes a process of socializing integral humanity, that is, the subjection of man to society, in the most secret and intimate spheres of his being.
>
> ... This process is just the reverse of that needed to produce a true brotherhood of man, the communion of personalities, of 'me' and 'thee'. All men become the objects of organization.

Any human institution is damnable when it is so systematized that it excludes all possibility of the personal, individual and exceptional thing being said or taking place, day after day. That surely is the social legacy of communism.

In every East Bloc country, despite vastly differing national circumstances, totalitarianism has been able to take hold of millions of citizens and impose upon them uncivilizing privations. In every country it has demanded they give up personal integrity. Coming here one can see how life would be impossibly dull and formless without that integrity, without dignity, without the possibility of personal harmony and harmony between oneself and society; it would be like living in a world which only knew bad art, the world indeed of the distopia.

'I am a Turk,' Semeon whispered. 'My real name is Seban.' 'I don't understand. Once they told me I was Turkish. Now they say I must be Bulgarian. It's crazy. I have a cousin in Turkey I've never seen.' 'Some people have been killed over it.' We were sitting back in a beach basket. These facilities ranged around the pool were German imports designed to give shade from wind and sun, and they looked like wicker confession booths. We often used to whisper there, though it was not until my last evening, as we sat watching the seagulls plunder the refuse bins then fly high in the air with plastic bags, that the one friend I had made in Druzhba and whom I trusted began to talk more openly. 'Semeon,' he said, holding up a bit of himself for muster. 'Do you know what that is? It's the name of a medieval Bulgarian king.' Not that he really cared, his friends included Bulgarians and Turks, and he didn't mind what they called him. Perhaps originally his family had even been Bulgarian, he thought, conscripted into the Ottoman army, taken to Turkey. But now at home he was used to speaking Turkish and reading and writing Turkish. It wasn't fair of the authorities suddenly to make his family life illegal. 'It's bad, what they do in this country, isn't it? The most important thing is to be free.' I must have nodded. We were standing now, daring to exchange an intimate half-smile for the first time in two weeks, knowing there was no time or opportunity left. The sun had gone down and we were slightly shivering. No one was about except Elizabeth and the water was still.

One day, even in our lifetime, the East Bloc will be politically free. Then to all of us it may be not freedom but friendship, language, erotic attraction, nature, music, mirrors and the differences between things which will be allowed to matter most, though we shall always need unfreedom to appreciate them and to notice.

My travelling has been an attempt to place myself between the extremes of the bourgeois and the communist phenomena, and to discover how much the existence of one or other political system matters. The answer lies in the freedom I have had to undertake these journeys, inward and outward. All men and women should have the freedom to travel and enjoy and think and run into difficulties and express their thoughts publicly. They should not be forced to live alone in their heads, a wretchedness communism has inflicted on too many. Heaven knows, to overcome the constraints emanating only from within is sufficient task for one lifetime.